OTHER BOOKS BY EDIE RAMER

Contemporary
MUST WORSHIP CATS (a Miracle Interrupted novella)
MIRACLE LANE (a Miracle Interrupted novel)
YOU'VE GOT MURDER co-written with Karin Tabke

Paranormal
CATTITUDE
DEAD PEOPLE
DEAD PEOPLE IN LOVE (short story)
DRAGON BLUES
THE SEVENTH DIMENSION (short story)

Science Fiction Romance
GALAXY GIRLS
MIXING IT UP (a Galaxy Girls novella)

Short Stories and Essays
The Fat Cat in ENTANGLED, A PARANORMAL
ANTHOLOGY
(all proceeds go to Breast Cancer Research Foundation)
The Kiss in EVERY WITCH WAY BUT WICKED
(all proceeds go to Kids Need to Read)
Killing the Rat Bastard Disease in AUTHOR MOMENTS
Fighting Back in AUTHOR MOMENTS II
(all proceeds of the Author Moments books go to Cancer
Research UK)

For updates, go to http://edieramer.com

STARDUST MIRACLE

Copyright © 2012 by Edie Ramer

Cover design by Laura Morrigan

ISBN-10: 0985643706

ISBN-13: 978-0-9856437-0-6

Stardust Miracle

A Miracle Interrupted novel

Edie Ramer

Blue Walrus Books

ONE

A MIRACLE IS COMING

Becky Diedrich finally came across something that could silence the parishioners of the United Community Church of Miracle, Wisconsin, for more than two minutes.

It wasn't her husband's sermon.

Two hundred twenty-nine adults and sixty-five children stared at the rear windows of a complete line of parked cars. Some stared in shock, some in disgust, some with hope. Still others stared in sheer awe, as if they saw Jesus walking on water. And all because on the back of each rear window was a white letter. Each one perfect, as if done with a stencil. The prophesy started with the A on the rear window of Carly Mishler's Mini Coop that looked as shiny and cute as her, and ended with the G on Tim and Ardell Schauer's station wagon with the dented backseat door that didn't open.

Only the G on Tim's car was a little ragged, since he'd dragged his fingertip through it, licked it, then said – with all the surety of a man who'd put a lot of things in his mouth during his fifty-some years on earth – that it wasn't chalk or paint.

No one else offered to taste it. A few stragglers walked along the row of cars. The crowd stood back just far enough to leave a path for them. The lookers gawked and took photos with their cell phones. Seeing was believing, after all.

But Becky was having a hard time believing.

For a long time, she'd been having a hard time believing.

Murmurs began, the silence broken. Hushed sounds, like fairy whispers on the wind. But these whispers were all too human, and heads leaned toward their neighbors, all the better to hear.

Becky wasn't surprised. Even a Jesus sighting wouldn't keep this gang quiet for longer than a few minutes.

One clear voice rang out. "What's that, Mommy?" a boy asked.

Of course, Becky thought. The clearest questions came from children.

"Letters," a woman said.

Becky recognized Tina Genz's voice. At fourteen, Becky had babysat Tina. And now Tina had one child of her own and another on the way. Becky was twelve years older than Tina and had...no children.

Becky crossed her arms and hunched her shoulders.

"How come our car doesn't have a letter?" the boy asked.

"Because it's not in a word," one of the Schilling girls said. They all had voices like goats, as if they were going to 'baaa' any moment.

"That's silly," the boy said. "None of the cars are words."

"That shows what you don't know." The girl's raised voice sent a half dozen sparrows flying off of the church's roof, finished a year ahead of schedule because Becky's father had matched the donations.

"The letters on the car windows make words," Tina told her son, whose name Becky couldn't remember, though she tried hard. Remembering names was expected of the pastor's wife. During her fifteen years of marriage, she'd gotten good at faking it.

Faking other things, too.

"When the word stops," old Mrs. Jantze said, "there's a space. Your car is a space."

"I'd rather be a word," the boy said.

"Spaces are important," Mrs. Jantze said. "Otherwise the words would be running together without stopping."

I'm a space, Becky thought. *I'd rather be a word, too.*

The thought sat like a rock in her chest.

She shivered. She needed to get over this self-pity. She couldn't even blame it on sun deprivation. Not with the day so bright and shiny. The younger crowd had their jackets open. A few even took them off. It was the beginning of May in the Village of Miracle, Wisconsin. The grass was green. Lilac buds were unfurling. Spirits were rising.

And according to the letters on the car windows, a miracle was coming.

"There's Pastor Jim," someone said, and heads shifted, Becky's with them, her eyes catching Jim's still-golden hair. Not any grays showing.

Of course not. She'd tweezed a half dozen out for him yesterday.

"What's going on?" Jim looked at Becky's father, Carl Hoffman, for information. Carl stood in the middle of the group, about ten people away from Becky.

Carl gestured at the cars. "See for yourself."

"It says there's going to be a miracle," the Schilling girl bleated.

"Thank you, Mindy." Jim nodded his approval, and though Becky couldn't see Mindy's face, she knew the girl beamed. Almost everyone with two X chromosomes reacted that way to him...except Sarah, Becky's sister, who thought Jim was bossy and boring. But as their father would say, look at the loser Sarah married.

Men respected Jim, too. *Didn't that say everything?*

Another reason she needed to snap out of this funk. She was a lucky woman. Jim didn't even blame her for not being able to

3

get pregnant – though the way he looked at her when they found out the results of the fertility tests...

Her eyes burned, prickled by tears she held back.

I will not cry. I will not cry. I will not cry.

After all, she was a lucky woman, she reminded herself again. With no reason to feel as if strands of sadness were coiling around her. No reason to lie next to Jim in bed at night, every muscle in her body stiff as she listened to his snores while she held back screams of frustration.

The murmurs started again as Jim paced down the parking lot row, checking out the letters. Carl strode at his side now. If this were an old Western movie, the two men would be the rancher who owned all the land and the sheriff who made sure no one gave him any trouble. Instead, they were the rich cheesemaker who employed half the village and the minister who led half the village.

The crowd watched them like they were entertainment. Becky felt the shift in mood as they waited for Jim's pronouncement. Jim finally stood in front of Diane Lofy's car with the dents and the broken left brake light. Carl took his place in the front row of parishioners. As if Jim were going to give a sermon in the parking area.

Jim put his hands on his hips and grinned, shaking his head. "You don't really believe this, do you?"

Mumbles started. "'Course not," a man said, his voice half-hearted.

"I guess not." Sue Feucht hefted a sigh loud enough for Becky to hear, though two people stood between them.

Jim frowned, a look of disappointment on his face that was familiar to Becky. "You did believe it."

"Look at the uniformity of the letters," Mike Klink said, a waver in his old voice. "No one I know writes so perfect. Hell, teachers don't even make letters like that anymore." Someone started to say something, and Mike yelped. "Heck! I meant heck not hell."

A few people laughed and Mrs. Braun, who'd been Becky's third-grade teacher, said, "Mike's correct. The few of us who can still print like that were sitting in church while this was done."

"And I don't see any handprints on the cars," Amy Loosen said. The oldest of the six Loosen kids, Amy was taking college classes online and working part-time at Miracle Cheese Factory. "They're filthy. If someone wrote the letters, he would've had to put his other hand on the cars to keep his balance. There would've been handprints, and I don't see anything."

"Yeah," someone else said, this voice elderly and sharp — qualities that matched quite a few characters in the village. Of both genders. "'Sides, no one can do anything in Miracle without someone else knowing about it. We sure as heck don't need one of those Twitter things in Miracle. We're not used to something that slow."

That drew a few chuckles, the loudest from Jim. He stood with his legs slightly apart, letting people get a good look at him with his golden hair catching rays of the sun and the jacket of his gray suit jacket unbuttoned. The pose gave his figure — that had gained two waist sizes these last few years — the illusion of slimness.

Jim stopped chuckling and shook his head in the chiding way that he had. If there were one thing about Jim that irritated Becky, it would be the way he had to be right all the time.

Sometimes she just wanted to kick him.

"You can't tell me that we don't all have our secrets," he said. "I bet the prankster's friends know who it is and are laughing at us for falling for it."

A murmur rose again. Julie Lindemann on Becky's left leaned close to Becky's ear and said, "I won't let my kids to know how often I partook of your uncle's weed pile."

Becky smiled at her, though Julie's fondness for smoking pot wasn't much of a secret to anyone except her kids. "I know just what you mean," she lied. She bet her sister Sarah had partaken, though. Not that Sarah had been overly wild, but Becky had been the reliable one. By necessity, not choice. She had to take care of her mom and her two-year-old sister when she was only ten while her mom fought to stay alive.

When Becky was at school, a nurse took care of her mom, and her father paid extra for the nurse to watch Sarah. Carl couldn't help around the house. He had to be at the cheese factory all day and sometimes into the evening.

"And kids these days..." Jim waited for everyone's attention before continuing. "You know how inventive they are. They probably used a laser and didn't need to touch the car. I wouldn't be surprised if they programmed it to make the letters look perfect. They picked today for the weather and because of the church's car wash. They knew everyone would leave their cars dirty for today."

Becky nodded, and others nodded, too. The villagers of Miracle were known for their cheapness. If they gave the Girls for Christ three bucks, their cars would be washed, the money would go to the church's furnace fund – and a few cheapskates would even deduct it on their taxes. That always made them happy. Nothing like feeling virtuous, saving money, getting a clean car and sticking it to the government. A deal for three bucks.

The crowd split up, saying their good-byes and smiling. Women hugged women, and a few men were huggers, too. As Becky said good-bye to a few parishioners, she noticed the dullness in eyes that had glittered only moments before. Before their brief hope for a miracle had crumbled.

It was a silly hope. The most exciting thing that happened in the Village of Miracle recently had been a lost cat and the vicious death of another one. Only three weeks ago, everyone was watching out for coyotes.

The Kern's car slowly backed up, and Becky stepped to the side to give it room. On their car was the M for miracle.

As she watched it disappear, an odd thing happened. The M sparkled as if covered by fireflies. Hundreds of fireflies. Their little twinkling caught the sun and shone so brightly it hurt Becky to look at it.

But the body part that hurt most wasn't her eyes. It was her heart. As if a big hand reached inside her chest, grabbed her heart and squeezed too hard.

She sucked in her breath, stepped back and bumped against someone. "Sorry," Becky said, but didn't look behind her, too busy glancing at all the different cars and all the different letters that had one thing in common.

Now all the letters sparkled in the sunlight.

Yet, the talk and laughter around her didn't change. No one else stared. No one else seemed to notice. They exchanged last-minute gossip and said their good-byes. Some of them made plans to eat lunch together afterward. Then they got into their cars. Still ready to go to the car wash and wipe off the letters and the dirt and the oddity of what had just happened.

Lori Schwister, who always walked to church unless it was storming or snowing, stopped and looked at Becky. "Are you okay?"

"Do you see that?" Becky motioned at the letter on the back window of Ivy Cantrall's van.

"It's an A." Lori frowned at Becky, as if she wondered about Becky's mental stability.

Becky wondered the same thing. "Anything else?"

"It's dirty." Lori frowned. "Is this a sneaky test? What am I supposed to see?"

Though Becky knew the answer from Lori's lack of reaction, she asked, "Do you see any sparkles?"

Lori's frown lines deepened. "Sparkles?"

"Never mind." She gave Lori her 'everything is wonderful' smile. "The sun was in my eyes and one of the windows sparkled."

Lori's forehead cleared. "One of us needs our eyes checked. Most of the windows are so filthy, I'm surprised anything would reflect off them."

Becky laughed dutifully. Lori winked and strode on. When Becky glanced back, half the cars with letters were headed toward the back of the church where the Girls for Christ were ready with their hoses and their sponges. The remaining letter-free car windows looked like...windows. No sparkle, no shine.

Maybe there was something wrong with her eyes. Maybe seeing the tiny twinkling lights was like hearing a sigh no one else could hear. Just for an instant, and then gone.

She should check the Internet, type in her symptoms and see if she had a disease. Even though it didn't feel like a disease. Today's occurrence felt...magical.

"Miracles," a child's voice rang out. Making it a song. "We're gonna have a miracle, a miracle."

"Stop it." Tiredness dragged down Diane Lofy's voice. She'd worked at the cheese factory for the past ten years and in that time she'd had four kids. "You heard Pastor Jim. There is no miracle."

"I want one! I want one!"

"Me, too!" another small voice called.

Me, three. Becky crossed her hands over her baby-free belly and prayed that Jim was wrong.

TWO

At least the squabbling kept Becky awake.

This would be her last year on the village board, she promised herself. She'd made the same promise the last two years, but this time she meant it. It was almost as boring as being back in high school listening to Mrs. Petersen talk about algebra. A subject that Becky had worked her fanny off for a B- when she was sixteen – and had never used in the twenty years since.

Gloria was giving Earl the evil eye, the look that said 'I don't care how many years you've been village president. It's about time you had a pointy high-heeled shoe shoved up your ass.'

"Don't change anything," Earl Raasch said. The owner of Miracle Taxidermy and Reupholstering, Earl spoke slowly and loudly. With his grizzled beard and hair and thick body, he reminded Becky of a bear who'd recently come out of hibernation.

"Everything changes." Gloria Ehlke shot the words out like bullet points. "The trick is to take advantage of change."

"When you get to my age, you'll know more people complain about change than those that don't."

"Not everyone in this town is your age," Becky said. Besides, Earl had changed last year, too, when he gave into complaints grudgingly and repainted his shop sign so it no longer read: You Shoot 'em, We Stuff 'em.

"And not everyone wants to stagnate." Gloria gestured dramatically, as if the cold and bare room in the Miracle Village

Hall were her stage, they were her audience and she was about to break out into a passionate song. "The world is changing. Either we keep up or we disappear."

Earl scowled at her from across the table. "You're talking about your business. I'm talking about government. You change one little thing and someone will complain."

"They'll complain more if we don't fix the potholes." Gloria glared at him as if she wished he were one of his own stuffed animals to be mounted on a wall on one of the houses she sold. Though perhaps not. Earl's mounted body wouldn't be a selling point, and Gloria was all about the deal.

"She's right," Becky said. "Angie Newhart was complaining at church about the one on First Street being as big as a baby gorilla, and a dozen other people chimed in."

"Maybe fixing the pothole is the miracle that's coming." Gloria narrowed her eyes at Earl.

"They're going to like it less if we raise taxes next year." Earl turned to Derek Muench. "What do you think?"

Becky exchanged a glance with Gloria. It was like Earl to want Derek's opinion over theirs. Just because he and Derek had the same plumbing.

"Well..." Derek rubbed his chin, putting off the moment to give an opinion.

Becky crossed her legs. She suspected the only reason Derek had run for the village board was to get away from his mother for a few hours on a regular basis. Elaine was a sweet woman – though a tad controlling – who had muscular sclerosis, and he didn't like to leave her alone too long. He even managed to work from home, doing tech things that no one else in the area could do.

If someone needed a website, Derek was their go-to guy. Thin with glasses, he even looked like a geek. But he had a sweet smile and his shyness was kind of endearing. It made Becky want to cuddle him in the same way she wanted to cuddle kittens and small dogs.

She didn't know why some girl in her twenties didn't snap him up. As if reading her thoughts, Derek smiled at Becky then shuffled his papers.

"Don't keep us in suspense." Gloria leaned across the table. "The roads aren't going to fix themselves."

"Gloria's right about the roads." Derek turned to Earl. "We could go to the state for funds."

Earl's fist thudded on the table. "No damn way I'm asking the state for anything. We don't want the state poking around in our business."

Becky took a gulp from her bottle of water. She suspected Earl had let his licenses or permits for his taxidermy business lapse...if he ever had them. He probably didn't report his income. She set down her bottle and saw that the left side of Derek's mouth, the side away from Earl, was kicked up.

So, Derek had said that on purpose. Living with Elaine, he'd learned how to be sneaky. How to say one thing and think another. How to convince someone they wanted to do something when they originally wanted to do something else.

The unwritten job description of a minister's wife.

She blinked. Where did that thought come from?

"We could sell the old Chevy dump truck to Trey Nieman," Earl said.

Trey?

"What dump truck?" Becky asked, even as her brain cells woke up. The cells in the rest of her body brightened, too.

Trey had been the bad boy in high school in Tomahawk, two years ahead of Becky. He lived in Tomahawk, while she was bussed there. With his dark hair worn long, as if he flaunted his quarter-Ojibwe blood, he was the guy that every girl's father warned her to stay away from.

Not that Becky had wanted to go out with Trey. Everyone knew she and Jim were perfect for each other. Besides, Trey had made her nervous. Too much testosterone for her back then.

"The pile of rust behind the village garage," Gloria answered Becky's dump truck question.

Becky nodded. Trey did pretty much the same thing as her brother-in-law. The difference was she'd heard Trey made money at it.

"How much is he offering?" Gloria asked.

Becky's mind wandered. She'd been relieved when Trey left for California shortly after she started college. According to gossip, he'd only returned a couple months ago when he found out he had a seventeen-year-old son. Apparently the bad boy was turning out to be a good man.

Welcome back to small town Wisconsin, she thought. Where the beer flowed freely, the village board president didn't pay taxes and the biggest entertainment was each other's lives.

"Two thousand," Earl said.

That got Becky's attention. She sat up straight.

"Why the hell didn't you tell us?" Gloria demanded.

"I'm trying to get more."

"What's it worth?" Gloria asked.

Earl scowled at the fake wood table top, as if it had done something to offend him besides being ugly. "I looked 'em up. Depends on the condition."

"That thing's so rusted it doesn't have a condition."

"I got him up five hundred. I can get him up five hundred more. Some old '55 Chevy dump trucks sell for five figures."

"Does ours run?" Derek asked.

"Nope. But it could be fixed."

Gloria rolled her eyes. "When's the last time you took your car in for anything? It costs a bundle. And that's when there are parts available."

Earl transferred his glare from the table to her.

"Let *me* bargain." Gloria's eyes gleamed. "That's what I do best. I'll know when he's ready to walk away. I'll know when he's bluffing."

"What's he want it for?" Derek asked.

"He thinks someday he might use it for a movie," Earl said.

"*Someday*?" Now Gloria's face looked like a toddler's when he or she was about to spit out an 'icky' food. "That doesn't sound promising, but if anyone can do it, I can."

"I vote that Gloria handle it," Becky said. "And I vote we go ahead and fix the pothole. It won't break the village, and people are getting cranky about it."

Derek and Gloria quickly put in their ayes, then Earl said he was the president and he was the one who should say they were voting.

"Then vote to end the meeting," Gloria said. "My feet hurt and I'm going to soak 'em."

"None of us need to know about your feet or any of your body parts," Earl said, but he did announce the end of the meeting. Then he noted with surprise that they were done early and he should get back home to watch his favorite TV show.

Gloria asked what it was, and he was about to say when Becky reached for her brownie container to put the lid on. Earl slapped his arm forward to grab two of them, moving fast for a man of any age. Becky suspected he would have grabbed more but Gloria and even Derek reached in to take two each, then wrapped them in napkins.

Becky couldn't help but think she'd done something right.

Putting the cover on the container with its lone brownie, she scolded herself. What was wrong with her lately? Acting like she was walking around with a dark cloud over her head, when she was one of the luckiest woman in the village. Sure, her life wasn't perfect, but self-pity was like quicksand. Dip one toe in and it slowly sucked in the rest of you, until you were drowning in gloom.

As she walked out with the others, Gloria slapped Earl on his back. "Don't be so grouchy. Selling the old dump truck hardly counts as a change."

"That's what people say when they feel a tremor in their house. The next thing you know, it's a full-scale earthquake and the walls are falling down."

"You're confusing an earthquake with the big bad wolf," Becky said.

Gloria laughed. "If it were up to Earl, the village newsletter would announce a new motto for Miracle: Leave everything as it is. Do nothing. Because nothing is always better than something."

"You should've heard the other mottos," Earl said.

"What's that?" Becky asked, only because she could tell he wanted someone to ask. And she always did what someone wanted, even when she was thinking about eating the last lone brownie as soon as she was in the car. If she waited until she got home, Jim would pounce on it as if he were starving. As if he deserved it.

A sudden cold wind whipped at her as she and the others reached their cars. A reminder that spring might be here but if Mother Nature were so inclined, she could still drop a blizzard on them.

"We had a contest for a motto just after Vietnam," Earl said. "None of you were born yet."

"How come I never heard it?" Gloria looked at Becky and Derek. "Did you know about it?"

Becky and Derek shook their heads. Shrugged their shoulders. Another wind gust hit Becky.

Shivering, she sent a silent message to Earl to hurry. She wanted to go home. She wanted to turn on the heater. She wanted a few moments with her husband.

Once Jim found out the brownies were gone, he would probably go into his office. Maybe she wouldn't eat the brownie after all... Maybe if she didn't, he would sit and eat the brownie and listen while she told him about the meeting.

"You don't know about it," Earl said, "because Becky's grandpa refused to let us use any of the top choices. Said we'd be a laughing stock on all the comedy shows. That even the news shows would make fun of us."

Becky frowned, not surprised. She remembered her dad's father was always serious. Always ready to give his opinion. Whether it was wanted or not.

"C'mon, Earl," Gloria said, "spill. I've got a bottle of Merlot waiting for me at home."

"It's been a while, but the brain box is still ticking." Earl knocked his knuckles on his head two times. "Here it goes." Of course it didn't go immediately. He looked around, his lips pursed, making sure he had their attention. Only then did he nod. "'Don't give a damn.'"

Laughing, Becky put her hand over her mouth.

"'Under the radar.'" He winked at Becky. "If I remember right, that was from your Uncle Sam."

Still choking back laughter and with her hand covering her mouth, Becky nodded, though the motto would fit a few dozen villagers. Sam was her mother's stepbrother, but she and Sarah still considered him to be their uncle.

"Your mom liked that one," he added.

Becky's laughter stopped. Her hand slid down to her side.

"Is that it?" Derek asked, which was verbose for him, since he usually never spoke unless asked a question directly.

"Two more. 'We can always secede.'"

"Are you making these up?" Gloria asked.

"Nope. Ask around. I'm not the only one who remembers. You wanna hear the last one?"

Becky nodded, an odd feeling building in her chest. Her mother liked 'under the radar'? She mostly remembered her mother in the last few years. So sick and so needy. Always apologizing to Becky. Making Becky cry because she wanted to help her mom. *Wanted to.*

And at the same time she hated helping. She wanted to be like the other girls. With her mom healthy and taking care of her.

"What are you waiting for?" Gloria asked. "A drum roll?"

Earl grinned, his face pasty in the dusk, almost skeletal – though there was nothing skeletal about his belly. "'Screw the government. They're screwing us.'"

Derek and Gloria laughed, and Becky even chuckled. She could think about her mother later.

Or not.

"That one was from you, right?" she asked.

He nodded, and his grin turned sober. "Might be a good one for you to remember."

Then he opened the door and got in.

Becky looked at Gloria, who shrugged then mimed someone gulping down a beer and pointed at Earl's car as the motor of his old Ford revved up. Becky smiled. Earl liked his beer, though she'd never seen him drunk.

Derek's car door shut, then Gloria got into her car and Becky got into hers.

As she started home, she thought of Jim's surprise when she came home early from the board meeting. Probably the first time in two years.

She smiled slowly. Thinking of an even better surprise.

THREE

Becky stepped out of the garage and looked up at the stars that had popped out during the drive home, reminding her of last Sunday in the parking lot. Tonight it felt as if the stars were putting on a light show for her. A sign from heaven, telling her life was good and she needed to laugh more, dance more, love more.

Maybe that was the miracle – for her to enjoy life.

Even the wind had died down during the short drive home. A sure message from Mother Nature.

She laughed softly. She wasn't delusional. But tonight anything seemed possible. Even miracles.

She turned to the house, feeling as if a tiny star had slipped inside her chest. Blinking off and on. She felt hot. Hot all over but mostly down there.

Okay, she could think it. She could even say it. In her vagina.

"Vagina," she murmured low so no one else could hear. Not that there was anyone around, but it was amazing to her the things that people in Miracle knew about each other. She wouldn't put it past them to hear about what she'd said, somehow.

And tonight she felt like she might finally have something besides her thoughts to hide. Now even her skin was hot... Hard to believe that just seven minutes ago she'd been shivering in the village hall parking lot.

She shivered again. Maybe this was early perimenopause... Or it could be her hormones jumping, saying *this* would be the time for her to get pregnant.

The thought made her heart thump like a manic rabbit's.

Inside the house, the lights were on, but it felt silent. As if it were waiting for something.

The parsonage with the four bedrooms, three bathrooms and one office was too big for the two of them. Their cat had been devoured by a coyote three weeks ago, and since then it felt even emptier. Lucy the cat had tolerated Becky and adored Jim, but at least Lucy had been company for Becky when Jim was at church. Becky had wanted a dog but Jim said he was allergic to dogs.

Becky always nodded when he said that, not letting him know his mother let slip that the truth was Jim had been bitten by a Cocker Spaniel when he was five, and had never gotten over his fear of dogs.

She opened the office door but there was no light inside, just shimmers coming through the windows from the stars and the moon.

"Jim!" she called, walking through the house. She ran upstairs but there was no Jim anywhere. Finally she went downstairs again, to the kitchen, where she looked for a note.

Nothing on the counter. She dug her phone out of the purse she'd left on the table and checked her messages. Nothing from Jim. Just a voice mail from her father, saying he had a craving for meatloaf and the next time she made some for Jim, he'd appreciate it if she made an extra loaf for him and dropped it off at his place. She translated that to mean he wanted it tomorrow.

She'd planned on making a Mediterranean dish with leftover chicken from tonight, but she could make meatloaf. It wasn't her favorite meal, but that didn't matter. After all that her father had done for her and Jim, making him a meal every once in a while was no big deal.

She just wished her father would do as much for Sarah. With Sarah's son and another child on the way, and her husband not making much at his business, Sarah was the one who needed Carl's help.

A *picker*, her father liked to spit out, as if Marshall's occupation left a bad taste. Marsh bought old junk that he hoped to sell for more than he paid. He drove all over the state, and even neighboring states, hunting for bargains and steals. Sometimes leaving Sarah and Cody for days.

Becky liked Marsh, but she doubted he made enough to afford good health insurance for his family. She felt sorry for Sarah and ignored Jim's stricture not to mention her sister's name to their father. But as usual, Jim had turned out to be right. Trying to get her dad to help Sarah was harder than trying to lose ten pounds.

But tonight she felt…different. The extra padding she was usually so self-conscious about didn't feel so awful. Tonight she felt voluptuous. Sexy even.

The shimmers coming in from the window like dust motes danced around her. She spun around, dancing with them. They seemed to shine brighter for an instant. The next instant they vanished.

She stood still for a moment. "What are you?" she whispered. "And why me?"

No one answered her question. Her hands curled at her sides. Her silly questions. There was no message from God in the parsonage. No mischievous angel, no Disney character on the loose. Just a moonbeam, and now a cloud had drifted over its source of light.

She stepped out the back door and into the backyard. Jim's car was in the garage. Since he'd left no message, she could only think of one other place he would be.

He'd planned to work tonight on next week's sermon. He'd probably gone to his office at the church to look up something, and that led to something else he needed to look up, which usually led to another thing.

Sure enough, his office light was on. The shades were down, but light seeped around the edges. She took a step on the grass...and then stopped. An idea bubbled up inside her.

With a giggle, she hurried inside and up to their bedroom. Crouching in front of her dresser, she pulled out the bottom drawer closest to the wall. The one she only opened every month to change the sachet. And as she took out the top negligee, she smelled the lavender.

Lavender was supposed to be the smell that made men...well, horny.

She brought it to her nose and inhaled deeply. The shimmers still inside her danced wildly, as if something were waking up. As if something good were going to happen.

"Oh," she whispered. "Oh, oh, oh."

She set it on the bed and started to undress. Jim was going to be in for a surprise tonight.

***

Becky ran across the grass and laughed at her brashness. She wore her tan trench coat – her church coat – over her red negligee. Tonight she felt free. With a sexual appetite and playfulness she hadn't felt for a long time.

She couldn't swear that what she planned had never happened in the church, people being what they were. But it had never happened in the church before with her and Jim.

Laughter spilled out of her mouth, and she only stopped because she was breathless from an overload of excitement. The need to experience something more with her husband had been building inside her for a long time. Now it was finally boiling over – leaving her lightheaded and unlike her usual self.

She liked these feelings. Liked this side of her a lot.

When she'd stepped out of the car tonight and looked up at the stars, something happened. Something changed. For so long, she'd been carrying a dark weight around with her. Going through the days and nights trying to say and do all the right things, when inside something had felt all wrong.

She'd lost the joy in her life. Hadn't been fully living...just going through the motions. At only thirty-six, she'd felt old and dried up.

Now she felt young again. Free.

Jim wouldn't know what happened to his proper wife.

She reached the church's back door, using it instead of the front entrance because she didn't want anyone passing by to see her. Not that there was anything wrong with going to see her husband. But if anyone mentioned her late night visit, her face would probably turn the color of a ripe tomato and give away what they'd done.

She slipped the key into the lock but it turned easily. She stepped inside. Jim must've come in this way and forgotten to lock the door behind him. He was always preoccupied with his work and his parishioners.

She admired that. She did. But once in a while, she wanted his mind, plus a few body parts, to be on her.

And not just when her body temperature was right for conception.

She started toward Jim's office, and her heels clicked on the laminate floor that looked like wood. Laughing under her breath, she stopped and took them off. She wanted to give Jim a surprise he'd never forget. A good surprise. No. A *wonderful* surprise.

His door was closed. Habit, she supposed, since no one was here except him. She heard him speaking. Couldn't make out the words. Just his voice. Probably saying lines from the sermon he was preparing. Then his voice stopped, and she imagined him frowning at his computer screen while he wrote the next line.

She started to undo the buttons of her coat, then decided it would be sexier to do it inside with him watching. Kind of like a stripper.

Stifling a giggle, she turned the handle and flung open the door.

"Surprise!"

FOUR

Sitting on his couch, wearing only his white shirt, Jim stared at her as if she were his worst nightmare. So did Diana Kellman, who wore nothing, her brunette head lifting from his lap. Her fingers wrapped around his erect penis.

Becky put her hand over her mouth. She wanted to puke. She wanted to scream. She wanted to cry. But all she could do was stand there, a long, low moan ripping out of her throat. The sound of an animal in pain.

"Becky." Jim put his open hand on Diana's head and shoved her away from him. Diana fell on her butt on the gray and blue striped rug that Becky had found for Jim four years ago at an estate sale in Wausau. Diana squealed as Jim grabbed his pants and stood.

"It's not what it seems." Jim held his pants over his penis. As if Becky hadn't seen it before.

Becky welcomed a hot rush of whirling anger. No, not anger. *Fury.* She took a deep, shuddering breath. The excitement was gone. The moan gone. The feeling that she'd been stabbed in the heart... Gone.

"You mean you weren't getting a blow job?" she asked, and her voice only shook a little. She glanced at Diana, who was scrambling to her feet. Becky turned her head away and spotted Jim's cell phone on his walnut desk. Instead of running out of the office, she crossed to the desk.

"Please, Becky," Jim said. "We can talk."

She heard the clink of his belt and without even thinking, as if something from above guided her, she picked up the cell phone, clicked on the camera, and whipped around, holding the phone like a weapon.

"Becky, no!" Jim shouted, one foot raised to put inside his pants leg, his penis not erect anymore but not completely flaccid, hanging in a curve like a tired rubber hose.

Diana was bent over, reaching for her panties, her butt toward Becky, but at Jim's shout she glanced behind her.

Becky snapped the camera.

"No!" Jim put his leg out to chase after her. Becky clicked the camera again, catching the surprise on his face when he realized his foot was half in the pants and he was falling. Diana twisted around, her clothes clasped over her breasts. Her pants legs hung down, covering her hairless pubic area.

Too bad, Becky thought, snapping a photo of Diana. Her mind was oddly clear, as if this were an unpleasant dream instead of her life falling apart. She'd love to send the picture to the congregation newsletter list. Let everyone know that Diana had her pubic hair waxed off. Maybe last week while she was visiting her sister in Eau Claire.

But at least she'd gotten the ass shot of Diana.

Then Becky aimed down at Jim sprawled on the floor. As she pressed the camera button, his butt was coming up, so she had a good shot of the mole on his left cheek that was shaped like the state of Wisconsin.

Now she had two ass shots. His and hers.

When he raised his face, there was no more offered conciliation. Only fury. "You can't fucking do this to me."

One more click and then Becky ran. Ran like she hadn't since high school track. She left her shoes behind her. She had something much more important in her hands. The cell phone.

She ran across the churchyard to their backyard as if the devil chased her. And she knew any second that would be true – the devil in the shape of her husband.

Her mind was curiously empty. The rational part of her brain, the part that analyzed everything, told her she was still suffering from shock. It was too early to believe it really happened. As if she were in a dream state.

Or maybe she was too filled with emotion to dig into it. An emotional volcano inside her simmering and ready to erupt. Only instead of hot, burning lava, she was stuffed with hot, burning grief. Hot, burning horror. Hot, burning anger. Tons and tons of anger.

How dare they? How the hell dare they?

No, how dare *he*?

A stone dug into her left sole but she kept running, her breaths huffing. The churchyard was longer than she'd thought, or she was more out of shape than she'd thought, and her opinion of her shape was already pretty low. Right now, lower than ever.

A tear came to her eyes and she blinked it away. Still running. Never stopping.

Another tear tried to come, and fierceness roared through her. She would *not* cry over Jim now. Anger was better. Later she could cry. Much later.

She was amazed that Jim wasn't chasing after her yet. But unlike her, he was probably pulling on his shoes. Or maybe he was staying to shoo Diana out as quietly as he could. By now he was putting the pieces together in his mind, thinking of a dozen different ways to gull Becky into disbelieving what happened. To convince her that what she'd captured on the phone's camera wasn't what it seemed.

The house loomed up ahead. She was almost there. Good. Her energy was flagging. Her breaths came harsher. As if she were the big, bad wolf about to blow down a house.

Only her big, bad husband had already done that.

The church's back door opened and footsteps thumped in her direction. The sound carried in the silence of the evening. Not even the hum of an occasional car engine came from the highway three blocks away. As if this were a dead zone.

"Get that camera, Jim," Diana called. "If the pictures get out, I'll die."

The running steps and Diana's words spurred Becky on. She stepped on a branch and stumbled, feeling a deep pain in her foot. But she caught herself and kept running. Feeling the pain but not letting it stop her.

She reached her back door. One breath later, she was inside, locking the door behind her. She grabbed her purse, thankful she'd left it on the table. Her purse clutched to her side, she ran through the house. The keys were already in her purse. She could lock Jim out but he'd find a way in. And the first thing he'd do was wrestle his phone from her.

She needed the photos. The proof that she hadn't imagined or made up what she'd seen. Proof against his golden tongue.

She sped into the garage and jumped into the driver's seat of her car. With a click of her finger, she locked the car doors. Then she pressed a button to open the garage door, wincing at the loud squeal. A louder version of her squeal in the church.

Maybe the garage door needed someone to lubricate it, too. Maybe it needed that person to be faithful and not go around lubricating other garage doors.

The engine started and she laughed as she rammed it into reverse and then stomped on the gas. In the rear window, she saw Jim, waving wildly.

She pressed on the gas harder and watched him leap out of the way. She eased her foot, not wanting to swerve onto the lawn. Why should the lawn she'd spent sixteen years nurturing suffer because her husband was a cheat and a hypocrite?

She was looking over her shoulder when the knock came on her side window. She gasped and whipped her head around. The car swerved. In her peripheral, Jim's mouth was tight, grim.

"Stop the car, Becky," he shouted as she switched her gaze to the rear view mirror. The window blunted his voice but he was still as compelling as when he spoke to the congregation every Sunday. Still as confident.

"Don't be foolish. Don't ruin our lives over this. We can work it out. We can talk to therapists. Secular or non-secular. I'm willing to do whatever it takes to fix our marriage and make it better than ever."

She eased her foot from the gas pedal and the car slowed. A tiny doubt burrowed in her mind that maybe he was right. Maybe this would be a good thing. Not just for her marriage, but for her. For the dissatisfaction that had been mushrooming inside she. Maybe this would be the thing that would—

"Honey, listen to me," he continued. "We can't throw away fifteen years of marriage without trying."

The car was nearing the end of the driveway. She still backed up but her foot hardly pressed down on the pedal now. And even though she listened to him, she couldn't look at him. If she looked at his face—

"Just stop the car and give me my phone."

Her teeth set. Her arms tensed. *Damn him. Damn him to bloody hell.* That's what the plea was all about. He wanted her evidence.

She stomped her sore, bare foot on the gas pedal. She heard Jim shout as the car squealed into the street, and she could see he'd fallen on the grass. Good. He'd already fallen in her mind.

She shifted into drive. The car jerked forward then sped down the road. When she reached the corner, she realized she didn't know where to go. Wherever it was, Jim would be after her soon, demanding that she return his cell phone.

And next time she doubted he'd be so nice.

FIVE

She needed to go someplace safe. Her dad's was the obvious choice. Carl adored Jim. Always had. Jack, Jim's dad, had been Carl's best friend, a big charismatic man. A hunter, an athlete, a singer, a drinker and a womanizer.

Carl had taken Jack's early death in a plane crash hard. Becky sometimes thought harder than her mother's.

But she was his daughter. He would take her side. He would protect her.

Not that she needed physical protection. Jim had never hit her, but it dawned on her now that through their years together, he'd made her feel...insignificant. Not good enough. Constantly saying, in a sorrowful voice, 'I don't mind that you can't produce enough eggs so we can have a baby.'

As if she *could* – if only she prayed hard enough.

And, 'I know you want a child the natural way, but we can always adopt when there's no more hope. The doctors say there's hope yet.' And he'd look at her with a slight shake of his head, because they both knew that hope was dribbling out of her vagina, day by day, month by month, birthday by birthday, egg by egg.

She reached First Street and put her right blinker on...and in her left peripheral a light blinked. Then two lights. Then three. Her foot on the brake, she turned her head and saw a winding line of sparkles. Like a rope of stardust.

Without thought, not even questioning what she was seeing, she steered left, the sudden change making the tires squeal. She started to follow the tiny lights, and once on course they...

Evaporated.

She kept on going. And going. About four blocks across, to the last road before a dead end. Once again, she could go left or right, and sure enough, there were sparkles on her left. Providing her own GPS system. Saying, 'This way. Go this way.'

"I'm going," she whispered. She turned the opposite direction of her father's four thousand square foot house overlooking Lake Miracle, with four *en suite* bedrooms – three unused for over a decade – toward her sister's two-story house at the end of the road.

The only thing Sarah and Marsh's house overlooked was the field next to them, with three storage buildings where Marsh kept the old stuff he 'picked' in hopes of finding resale gold. Beyond that was farmland, including the weed Becky's Uncle Sam grew.

She was probably the only person under sixty in Miracle who'd never smoked any. But right now she could use something to calm her nerves. The events of the night were starting to kick in, and she was shaking as she pulled into her sister's driveway.

If a miracle were going to happen to someone in the Village of Miracle, it wasn't going to be her. Not tonight.

There'd be no making a baby tonight. When she slipped on the silken negligee, she'd hidden the secret wish in the back of her mind. So secret she hadn't dared whisper it to herself.

The lights were on in Sarah's house. Becky shivered again, though she wore the trench coat and it wasn't that cold. Her cold came from the inside. The inside of her bones. The inside of her chest, now hollowed out and empty. A cold, cold place. Too cold for her bruised heart. Even the inside of her soul was chilly, the edges frostbitten.

Instead of thinking about Sarah, Becky remembered Jim in his office. The shock widening his eyes when she burst in.

The numbness thinned and rage kindled inside her. She seesawed back and forth from burning grief to cold ferocious anger, not ready to let go of either yet. The vision of Diana with her face in Jim's—

Sickness welled up in her throat. She braked, put the car in park, jumped out and made it to the end of the front porch. When the door opened and Sarah called her name, Becky was barfing into the spiky bushes.

***

Becky's back hurt from sleeping on the sofa bed – the one she suspected had belonged to Marsh before he quit his second year of college eight years ago. And her heart? It felt numb, as if it had been injected with novocaine.

Good. She didn't want to feel. She heard voices and toilet flushes and water running. The guest room door opened and she closed her eyes, not uncurling from her fetal position.

Appropriate. She felt like a fetus today. Not ready to face the world.

Of all the doubts piling up in her mind, one thing she was sure of. Last night really had happened. Her husband was a cheat and a hypocrite.

No wonder she'd felt like a fake for so long. Walking through her days with a smile pasted on her face like a mannequin. Her whole life had been a fake. She just hadn't known it.

The door closed. A moment later, an outside door opened and more voices rose. A dog barked. A cat meowed. Puppies squeaked. The phone rang.

Sarah's family was noisier than hers had been. Fake families spoke in quiet voices. As if loud voices would rip through the façade.

A whimper made her open her eyes. She looked down at a small four-legged being covered with black fur. A puppy. It stared up at her with big brown trusting eyes. When she reached out to it, her hand landed on its head and its body wiggled.

Her heart beat hard and an ache came with it. The numbness was wearing off.

"Are you lost?" Becky whispered. "You shouldn't be here. You're too young to leave your mom."

It whimpered and stepped forward with its front legs stretched sideways. It tumbled backward onto its tail. She laughed, surprising herself, and rolled off the sofa bed and onto the floor. She was still wearing the red negligee from last night.

She picked up the puppy and held it while it licked her wrist and her elbow and its own nose. She had to pee, but bending to kiss its head, she didn't care. She just wanted to pet the puppy and not think about anything else. The world would be better place if every home had a cute puppy in it. And a part of her knew that as long as she was petting this little furball, nothing else mattered. Nothing at all.

"Hey." Sarah entered the room, her footsteps in her fuzzy socks as soft as her voice. She wore a sweatshirt and stretchy pants, her stomach pouched out. "I see you found a friend."

"He's a love."

Sarah bent down, her head tilted, studying the puppy. "That's our only black. He can't keep still. So far none of the others climbed out of the box. There's always one."

The dog wiggled to get away, and Becky uncurled her fingers and let it go. It skittered over to Sarah, who scooped it up, making a grunting sound. When she stood, she said, "I hope it doesn't pee on me. Looks like we'll need to put up a barrier in the puppy room. This one's an explorer, but the others will follow soon. I don't want all five wandering around the house."

"Not yet," Becky agreed.

Sarah pressed her lips together. "Not ever," she said firmly. "They're in pee-as-you-go mode."

Becky scrambled to her feet. "If I don't go to the bathroom now, it might be me leaving a puddle on your floor. Thanks for putting me up last night."

"Don't be silly," Sarah said as Becky hurried past her. "Stay as long as you need to. Dad called. Jim already called him and told him his side. Dad's on the way over. I'll run and find some clothes for you."

"Probably your maternity clothes." Becky hoped Sarah's maternity clothes would fit. Not that she cared about the extra pounds right now. In the midst of everything else, it was...

Oh, hell, she did care.

She wondered if the extra weight were a contributing factor to Jim's actions, but she quickly shut that gibberish off. *Jim* was the factor. Not even Diana mattered. If he cheated with Diana, he'd cheat with someone else. Maybe he already had.

The memory of all the nights he'd spent in his church office while she sat alone in their house reading books about other women's happy-ever-after stories slammed into her gut.

She shut off the scream inside her and hurried to the bathroom. Moments later, she heard the phone ring again. She was washing her hands when Sarah opened the door and stuck her head inside. "Jim wants to talk to you."

"Tell him to talk to someone who cares." She looked in the mirror. At least she hadn't put makeup on last night. No smeared black mascara streaks today. Good. Her dad would be here any minute. She wouldn't have time to clean up. Not even time for a shower. "Did you find any clothes for me?"

Sarah shook her head. "I'll tell Jim—"

"I'll tell him." A sudden blaze of anger changed Becky's mind about avoiding Jim. If he had any decency, *he* would avoid *her*. "You get the clothes, please."

"You're sure?"

Becky narrowed her eyes. "I'm not a wimp."

"You're used to..." Sarah's lips twisted. "Being treated well."

"He'll treat me well." Becky thought of the photos on his phone. "I think he'll treat me *very* well."

Before she reached Sarah's phone in the kitchen, she collected her purse with Jim's phone and sent the photos to her own phone and to her email – though Jim knew her password and she suspected he would delete them – and to Sarah's phone and Sarah's email. She almost sent them to Marsh, but decided it was enough to send them to Sarah.

Right now she didn't trust Marsh. Though he'd never had much in common with Jim, they were both men. She'd have to see. Her days of blind trust were behind her.

When she picked up the phone, Becky half expected that Jim had hung up, but he was still on the phone. "Becky! You're here."

His voice held as much surprise as if the president had answered. Did he, like Sarah, think she was a wimp? They both forgot she was the one who made Jim's life run smoothly. He was a gifted preacher and teacher but she was the one who handled the shepherding part of the job. Handled the mailing of bereavement, birth, special occasion cards. She took meals to the sick and baked cookies for shut-in visits. She coordinated the youth ministry and the youth ice cream social. She taught Sunday school and attended a ladies' bible study at night.

On top of that, she had to keep the house clean, and the parsonage looking nice inside and out.

It had felt like a continuation of what she'd done for her father and for Sarah when she was a teen. Taking care of them.

It was past time she took care of herself.

33

"We have to talk," he said.

"Do we? I don't think so. Don't call again. I don't want you pestering my sister and her family."

"Sweetheart, don't be like that."

"Good-bye, Jim."

"No! Please, Becky! This is important."

The phone was already away from her ear but she pulled it back up. Didn't say anything. Just waited. Her mouth settled in a grim line.

She knew what was coming next. Knew he wanted her to start talking. To do what she usually did. To say something that would make life easy for him.

Her days of making life easy for him were over.

"My cell phone... I need it back."

"I'll put it in Sarah's mailbox. Is that all? I have to go. Dad's coming."

"The pictures you took. You're not..."

"Keeping copies? You bet I am. I emailed them to myself and to Sarah."

"Dammit, Becky! You—"

She hung up and turned away. Didn't feel triumphant or happy that she had him worried. Her chest was too tight with unshed tears. Her eyes burned. But she would not cry; she would not cry. Her dad would be coming any moment and she would not cry.

Sarah's new kitten darted down the hall into the puppy room. Becky wished she could follow the kitten and spend time with it and the puppies. Instead, she hurried to the guest room to pull on a pair of Sarah's elastic-waisted pants and a long-sleeved T-shirt that Sarah swore weren't maternity. Sarah even had a bra that fit Becky, only because Sarah's breasts were fuller than usual now.

Becky suspected Sarah used the clothes for cleaning, but she was just glad she had something to wear besides her negligee.

And grateful to Sarah, though her father would stare. He wasn't used to seeing Becky dressed so...casually. As a pastor's wife, she always dressed as if she were about to teach a class of horny teens. She was the twenty-first-century version of June Cleaver.

She heard her father's arrival downstairs while she was tugging the top down, looking at her image in the full-length bathroom mirror. The top was a tiny bit tight on her and her boobs looked...well, good.

Provocative, she thought.

"You're missing out on this," she said, thinking of Jim.

Then she remembered Diana's tight, golden ass and her tight, golden thighs and tight, golden stomach. Becky walked downstairs, and her not-so-tight stomach twisted.

The only thing Jim was missing was his gullible no-longer wife.

She was now his gullible no-more wife.

Her dad was sitting on the couch when she stepped into Sarah's living room. "Hi, Daddy."

He shook his head, not getting to his feet. "You really messed up. I thought better of you."

SIX

She crossed her arms, ignoring a twist in her stomach. Hoping it wasn't the strain of flu that was currently ripping through Miracle. But she took her vitamins and usually remained healthy. Too bad vitamins couldn't stave off a cheating husband.

And now this. She'd been knocked down emotionally last night. And now she felt as if she were knocked down again.

"Really? *I* messed up?"

He stared at her for a long moment. She stared back and the hollow, hurting feeling in her chest grew more hollow and more painful.

"Baby, you overreacted."

"I caught Jim with another woman."

"I know, he told me. He didn't have to tell me, but he did and I admire him for it."

She stared at him. No longer hollow as other emotions swirled up.

"You admire him for cheating on me?"

"There you go, dramatizing everything. Just like a woman. I admire him for his honesty."

The swirling whirled faster and faster inside her. A tornado of emotions.

"I have the photos of him acting like a man." The words shot out of her mouth in a staccato rhythm, fast and furious. She uncrossed her arms and put her hands on her hips. "You want to see them?"

A spark lit in his eyes but he blinked it out and stood. "Calm down and forgive him. He's sorry. He wants to make up to you for what happened. He's not perfect. No man is."

"I didn't expect perfect. I expected faithful."

"Honey." He shook his head. Lines around his mouth and eyes creased downward in sorrow. As if she were a child and just didn't get it. He held his hands out. "He's a man."

"I know he's a man." Anger kicked up. Becky grew rigid. "And the person giving him a blow job was a woman."

"Becky!"

"What? It's okay for him to do it, but it's not okay for me to say it?"

"You're my little girl. I don't like you talking like this. You need a man to take care of you."

"Really?" She stepped toward him. In her peripheral, she saw Sarah standing in the threshold of the living room. "Was I a little girl when Mom was sick and I was taking care of her and your other little girl?"

His mouth opened, but she spoke before he could say anything, her voice low and hoarse. "I remember you calling me your big girl then. Telling everyone how mature I was. How I could handle it and that you wouldn't know what you'd do without me."

His eyebrows snapped together. "Don't talk to me like that."

"When you talk *to* me instead of talking *down* to me, maybe I won't."

"I'm your father."

"And she's your daughter, Dad." Sarah strode across to them. She stopped at Becky's side and faced their father. "And so am I. You didn't stand up for me, either."

His cheek muscles ticked but he kept his gaze on Becky. "Is that what this is about? She's been working on you since you came here? Turning you against me?"

37

"You don't get it." Becky felt a little crazed. As if she'd been walking around with blinders on and now she'd torn them off. And what she was looking at wasn't pretty. "The only one turning me against you is you. Sarah doesn't even talk about you. The only thing she said about you was that you called and you were coming over."

"You aren't important in my life," Sarah added. "I have nothing to say to you. My son has nothing to do with you." She put her hands on her stomach. "My daughter will have nothing to do with you."

He glared at her. "You brought this on yourself, marrying that...*garbage picker*. You disappointed me." He turned back to Becky. "And now you're disappointing me. Leaving a good man for something so little."

The whirling inside Becky speeded up, roiling up into her throat. She put her hand over her breast bone, her palm feeling the heat from her skin through the thin material. Now she understood so clearly.

"You cheated on Mom." The words slashed out her throat, her voice raw. "Didn't you?"

Sarah's hand gripped hers and they both stood in silence while their father continued to glare. Silence stretched until Becky *had* to speak again. The hurt lanced through her, and she needed to hurt him back right this second – more than she needed to breathe.

"While I was taking care of Becky and Mom, you were out fucking other women."

His hand came up and he stepped forward. As if in slow motion, she watched his hand swing out. She had time to avoid it but she couldn't move. Her mind rejected what was happening.

His hand connected to her cheek, the clap of flesh and muscle against flesh and bone, shocking and loud. Her head reeled to the side. A dog barked. She lurched back, her cheek stinging.

At the same time, Sarah let go of her hand and surged forward. Her arm straight out, she pointed at the door.

"Out!" she said. "Get out of my house!"

Goldie ran into the room, barking at their father.

Sarah grabbed Goldie's collar with her right arm, her left still pointed. "Get out or I'll let Goldie bite you."

Their father's still handsome but fleshy face was blotched with red. He stalked out. With every step, Becky expected him to stop, turn around. Apologize. Do the right thing.

But he kept going. Out the front door and onto the porch. Didn't look back.

The door closed behind him.

"Bastard," Sarah said, the sound rough.

Becky might've said something but she was running to the bathroom – her cheek burned, her hand pressed over her mouth – sick at heart and sick to her stomach.

SEVEN

A cool, slender hand brushed across Becky's forehead. She was hot. Feverishly hot. As if she'd been drawn down into hell. Hot and sick. Now only three fingertips drew across her forehead. It felt good. So good.

She tried to open her eyes and failed. Her upper and lower eyelashes were crusted together.

They popped apart, first her right and then her left. A woman with long white-blond hair knelt over Becky, her forehead creased with worry. Her eyes the same clear summer-sky blue as hers and Sarah's.

"Mama?" she whispered, her voice a hoarse thread.

She knew her mother was dead...for many years. But this woman looked like her mother would if she'd lived longer. And she kind of looked like Sarah.

Maybe this was the miracle? Not a baby but her mother returned to life.

A blinding happiness seized her. And she smiled, feeling... *Oh no. Oh no. Oh shit.*

"I'm going to—" She slapped her hand over her mouth and rolled to her stomach and stuck her head over the side of the bed.

Oh crap, her mother was brought back to life and she was going to throw up on her.

"Quick," Sarah's voice said. "Hold this." The woman who looked so much like her mother – who *could* be her mother –

held a bucket just in time for Becky to stick her head over it and heave.

"Are you sure she's all right?" the woman asked. "Two days of this is a long time."

"Joy across the street is a nurse at Sacred Heart." Sarah sounded worried. "She said there's a bad flu going around. Becky was watching seven- and eight-year-olds at church last Sunday. Joy said half of them are down with this flu and there's not much we can do but try to get liquids into her."

Becky's stomach stopped heaving. Nothing was coming out but bile anyway. She managed to roll onto her back, then looked up at her mother.

It wasn't her mother. "Elsa," she said, hardly recognizing the croaking sounds as her own voice. But now she recognized the Rev. Elsa Hahn, head of the *other* church in the village. The one that didn't believe in Jesus or even in God. Though the church members kept an open mind, they believed only in a 'higher power.'

Becky hardly knew Elsa. She'd moved here out of the blue about three years ago, and built her church. Didn't appear to know anyone in Miracle beforehand – at least not as far as Becky knew, or more importantly, Linda Wegner, Miracle's answer to TV gossip shows.

Elsa, a slender woman in her mid-fifties with a brilliant smile, had stopped by the parsonage and introduced herself once. Her intense stare, as if she were trying to see into Becky's soul, had made Becky feel uncomfortable.

Becky didn't want anyone to look into her soul now, including Elsa. It was too murky and dark.

"Sorry. I mistook you for my mother," she said, forcing herself to keep her eyes from drifting closed again, though it wasn't easy with her body craving sleep.

Once again, Elsa leaned down and brushed her fingertips over Becky's forehead. Becky closed her eyes to savor the sensation. When she opened them, Elsa was looking at her with a half smile.

"It's okay. Drink this," Sarah said, and a straw slid into Becky's mouth. "Come on, drink. I won't let you go to sleep until you drink."

Becky sipped, only because she wanted to sleep. She took about seven sips then turned her head away. Finished for now.

The bed gave. Sarah got to her feet, no longer forcing her to drink.

"Elsa brought chicken soup," Sarah said. "If you're good, you can eat it tomorrow."

"Thank you, Mom." Becky started to shake her head, but her stomach flip-flopped. "Elsa," she amended.

"I know what you meant." Now the cool fingertips touched Sarah's forehead and curved down the side of her face.

Becky's eyes closed again. She had more to say but didn't know what.

"I miss my mom," she said. The words didn't come from her brain, but from her heart. Her voice still sounded like a frog's but it felt important for her to say this. "I miss her every day of my life."

"I'm glad," Elsa said, and her voice was thick now. As if she held back tears.

Becky thought about opening her eyes, but it seemed too much trouble. *Why was Elsa here? Why?*

Though she wanted to know the answer, she felt sleep coming for her, washing over her. Swamping her.

Or maybe it wasn't sleep. Maybe it was death. Whatever it was, she breathed deeply with relief and let it take her.

EIGHT

"I'm going with you." Wearing jeans and a maternity top, Sarah stood in the guest bedroom with her feet braced apart and a stubborn expression on her face. At that moment, she reminded Becky of their dad – as if anyone who got in their way better move or they'd be sorry.

Becky pulled on a pair of Sarah's stretch pants as she considered practicing that look in the mirror.

Not now. Now she had something else to do.

She'd spent six days on Sarah's sofa bed with a bucket next to her bed – just in case. For another week, she'd slouched around Sarah's house like a recovering invalid. The bug still wasn't through with her, pulling her down at the edges. She felt like an old bag of leaves a bulldozer had smashed over.

Sarah told Becky she suspected it wasn't the flu that made her ill but fifteen years of being married to Jim. Or as Marsh referred to him: 'the asshole.'

"Jim won't be home." Becky looked down at her legs and thought her thighs looked almost thin. "At this time of day, Jim will be at his office at church. He takes off Mondays, and on Tuesdays he catches up with anything that came up after Sunday."

"Came *up* is a good description."

"You're going to make me throw up again." Becky shoved her feet into her shoes and headed toward the door less briskly than she wanted to.

"I'd throw up, too, thinking of Jim's penis."

A choked laugh came out of Becky's mouth. She preferred not to think of Jim's penis, too. If she wrote a song about it, she'd title it "The Places You've Been."

Her second song would be "I've Been a Fool."

Five minutes later they were driving to the house she'd never felt was hers. She didn't pick it out. It belonged to the church. And she already didn't miss it. Living in it was like wearing her grandmother's clothes when she wanted to pick out her own.

Sarah told her who'd called while she was sick. It was a pitifully small list of people who wanted her lists and instructions on what to do about church matters. Sarah had told them Becky was sick. If they wanted any information, they could ask their pastor. The one who was actually *paid* to guide their flock.

Right now Becky felt too crappy to care. The best thing about being sick was losing so much weight. One hundred eighty pounds in two weeks.

One hundred seventy-two of them had been Jim. She smiled, and when the car stopped in the parsonage driveway and they headed to the front door, her step was lighter.

They weren't inside the parsonage for more than ten minutes when the doorbell rang. "I'll get it." Becky had half a suitcase full, but out of habit left the packing to open the door. Besides, it was depressing packing the church clothes she wanted to leave. But she had to be practical. She might get a job in an office and would need the clothes she hated now.

She was still thinking about it when she opened the door and saw Jim's face.

He wasn't smiling, and that was the only reason she didn't slam the door in his face.

"I heard you were sick," he said.

"I heard you were at church. You're not supposed to be here." She put her foot behind the door so he couldn't push it open and walk in. She held onto the door, too, though her body began to shake. She felt like she'd rolled out of a garbage truck.

And before her stood the guy who'd tossed her in.

"Can I come in?" he asked. "I won't stay long."

"No." Sarah stepped next to Becky. Her voice strident, Sarah sounded more like a WW wrestler than a pregnant mom. "You caused her enough harm. Leave her alone to gather a few things."

"I know I was at fault," he said, looking at Becky, not Sarah. "I acted like my father. A womanizer. And I always said I wouldn't be like him."

She frowned. A month after the funeral for Jim's father, when his mother left town to live with a friend, his mother's expression had been alive, so different from the closed-up, unhappy woman Becky had been used to. As if her husband's death had set her free.

Now Becky was living with her sister. And she felt more alive – and more scared – than since she married Jim sixteen years ago. History was repeating itself, though her stay with Sarah's family would be temporary.

She stood back to allow Jim to enter, and Sarah groaned. Becky raised an eyebrow at Sarah. "I'm only letting him in because he asked. After all, he could've just walked in."

"He's smart enough to know you would walk right out if he did." Sarah glowered at him. "Plus, you've got the pictures." She glowered harder. "If that's why you came, you wasted your time. Becky has her cell phone well hidden. And I have the pictures on mine, too. And Becky opened up a new email account. One you'll never access."

Jim stepped inside. "I deserve your contempt." He turned to Becky, his brow creased. "And your anger."

"I'm not arguing with you." She still held onto the door. Sarah came over and put her arm around her shoulders. Knowing that Sarah had her back, Becky let go of the door.

"You mind leaving me with my wife for a few minutes?" Jim asked Sarah.

"Yes, I do mind."

Becky wanted to laugh but it would hurt her stomach. "Jim, you're wasting your time. I'm not coming back to you or this place. I'm not deleting the photos. I don't know what else there is to say to you."

"I screwed this up, didn't I?"

"Big time. Surely you don't expect me to disagree?"

"And don't expect her to change her mind," Sarah said.

"I already know that." He kept his gaze on Becky's face, his mouth pressed tight and radiating pain, as if he were hurting bad.

Another woman might've been flattered. Instead, Becky stared back, not impressed. She was too tired to care. Too numb. She just wanted him to leave. She just wanted to pack up so she could go back to Sarah's where she could eat some chocolate and figure out what she needed to do to get on with her life.

"I just wanted to say I was sorry. I tried to be a good husband and I failed. I failed you and I failed myself."

Out of nowhere, Becky's eyes prickled. She blinked hard. No tears. She would not cry in front of him.

"I've been thinking about our marriage," she said. In between running to the bathroom and sleeping and feeling like she never wanted to eat food again, she'd thought about a lot of depressing stuff. Most of it had to do with Jim and her dad.

"You should sit down," Sarah said to her.

Becky glanced at her. "I won't be long." She faced Jim again. "Our marriage wasn't good from the start. I realize now that I married you because it's what my father wanted. And you married me because it's what he wanted."

"Maybe that was part of it."

"A *big* part of it."

"Not all of it. I did love you." He paused and stared into her eyes.

46

She looked right back into his. Not saying anything. If he were waiting for her to say she loved him back, he'd be waiting for a long, long time.

Maybe she had loved him. She couldn't remember. But their marriage held only a tepid kind of love. Nothing like Sarah's marriage with Marsh. Their love was a Romeo and Juliet kind of love. Like a teapot steaming so hot it whistled. She and Jim, on the other hand, were like lukewarm water that never boiled.

Jim still didn't say anything. Just waited.

Sarah's hand on Becky's shoulder tightened, and Becky could feel her getting pissed.

"Not enough," Becky said quietly, only because if she didn't, Sarah might slug him. "You didn't love me enough."

"You're right." He sucked his lips in and then out, and bobbed his head. "Not enough."

"And you're still an asshole," Becky said.

He laughed, looking surprised. Then his laughter died and his forehead furrowed. "I was a jerk. I admit it. I already admitted all of it to the congregation."

"Of course you did," Sarah said. "Yet somehow you made them feel it was Becky's fault."

"I told them I was unfaithful and my wife left me. I didn't say anything more."

"They wanted to believe it was my fault." Becky glanced at Sarah. "He's their spiritual leader, after all. They *need* to continue to believe in him."

"I won't stand in your way," Jim said. "I'll split our finances."

"She should get more." Sarah let go of Becky and took a step closer to him. "You still live in this house rent free. She was working at the church since you were married. Not making any social security. Not making any wages. Not anything."

Jim eyebrows tipped down into a frown, and Becky could practically see his brain cells firing. "I already took half the money out and left half for you. My lawyer thought I was being generous. We've saved quite a bit. And it's not like we have kids."

Becky stiffened. *He already talked to a lawyer? Already took money out of their joint account?*

But none of it hurt like his last sentence, about not having kids.

She wanted to hurt him back. "Get out, Jim."

"Becky—"

"Out." She pointed to the door.

He gave her his 'you always make a big fuss about everything' look, then shrugged and left.

As the door closed behind him, Becky said, "Asshole."

"I want to hurt him," Sarah said.

"Me, too."

"When we get home, you're calling a lawyer. I know a good one."

Becky nodded, feeling sick again. "Let's pack and get out of here."

In the bedroom, Sarah told her to sit and she would pack.

"I can't let you do this," Becky said.

Sarah gave her a stern frown. "Hey, you were the one who raised me. This is just a small thing I'm doing in return."

"I'm living in your house."

"You changed my diapers."

"No, Mom did that. By the time she got too sick to watch you, you were out of diapers."

Sarah disappeared into the walk-in closet though her voice carried to Becky. "I think I still must've done a few disgusting things."

Becky laughed and lay on her bed. Her mind whirled and so did the ceiling. She hoped she didn't get sick...

The next thing she knew, Sarah woke her. "I think I've got all your personal stuff. It's in the car." She pointed a finger at

Becky's face, stabbing the air. "And don't say I should've waited for you. Is there anything else here?"

"Not that I can think of."

"I didn't take dishes or anything."

"I don't want them."

"He's keeping the furniture, too. Tell your lawyer Jim needs to reimburse you for your half of everything."

Becky laughed but it was harsh and joyless.

Sarah helped her off the bed, as if Becky were an invalid.

Fitting, because she felt old and decrepit, with no more energy than a zombie.

When they got outside, Becky stopped and looked back. "I won't miss that home or anything in it."

"Including the asshole."

"Most of all, the asshole." She turned to the car and hobbled toward it.

"Men drive women crazy," Sarah said. "They just do."

Becky laughed, and already felt better. Not happy yet, but as if she could see happiness ahead of her.

It wasn't the a-miracle-is-about-to-happen feeling, though. And she wondered if the sparkles at the church that Sunday before her life as she'd known it had fallen apart had meant...anything.

NINE

Four days later, Becky drove back to Sarah's from the big city of Wausau, feeling happy and sad, scared and brave. Her mood seesawed by the second. The sky was bright and shiny, and so was her future.

Maybe.

And on the passenger car seat were the papers and something else. Something that sent her heart thumping like a scared rabbit's.

Her father would be furious if he knew what she planned. She felt as if someone would arrest her any moment.

But of course, they wouldn't. It was *her* money. She could do whatever she wanted with it.

When she pulled into the driveway, Marsh was heading out. He stopped the van and stuck his head out of the window.

"How'd it go?" he asked.

"My lawyer is filing the papers." Becky heard the perkiness in her voice and winced. Her people-pleasing tendencies needed to stop. She really wasn't perky, and the person she wanted to please from now on was herself. She could even be a little snarky – at least in her thoughts.

Maybe she should put that on a resume. All she needed now was to find a job that required sarcasm and she was set.

"How long before you lose the loser?" Marsh asked.

She laughed too loudly but for once didn't stop herself. Maybe she was really the kind of person who laughed too loud. There were worse crimes than laughter. And what Marsh said deserved a super-loud laugh. He and Sarah were the only ones in town who would call Jim a loser.

"Four months, if Jim doesn't contest anything." And he wouldn't. She had the photos as insurance. But she felt free already. Freer than she'd felt for a long time. As if she'd been a bird in a cage and now the cage door was open.

And she was teetering on the edge, seesawing, a few strings still pulling on her, saying, 'Be careful or you're going to screw this up, too.'

"Great." Marsh nodded, a distracted look on his face, already thinking of someone, something or somewhere else. He was a man who'd settled everything in his mind and was ready to go on his way. Her father had that look, and so did Jim. If God were really a man, she'd bet He would have that look, too.

"Before you go," she said, "I've got something for you."

"Yeah?" He looked forward. Still mentally somewhere else.

She glanced in the rear view mirror but didn't see anything at the Webber's house across the street. The kids should be at school, Joy and Kevin at work. Sarah had driven to a gallery in Merrill to get appraisals of a few paintings Marsh had bought a couple days before. Becky had promised to be back when Cody got home from school, glad to do something for them.

No one else lived close enough to see what she was going to do.

Her hand slid into her overlarge purse that she'd used for church meetings and the deadly dull ministerial conventions she and Jim attended every year. She pulled out a manila envelope then held it out the window. "Here," she said in a low voice.

"Huh?" He looked at her, and his eyes focused. "What's this about?"

"About this." She waved the envelope at him. "Take it."

His eyebrows rose and he took it from her. She waited while he opened it and looked inside.

He lifted his head and stared at her. His face paled, and for the first time she noticed a spattering of orange freckles on his nose and across his cheekbones. He didn't speak. Just stared.

"Don't tell Sarah," she said. "Don't tell anyone. No one needs to know."

"Why?" His voice was harsh.

She stared back. Now she was speechless. Unable to say the words. *Because you were there for me. Because I should have done more for you long ago. Because I know your truck is falling apart and you can't afford another one. Not with the baby coming.*

Because I love all of you so much that I lie awake at night sometimes and when I think about you, it keeps me from going into the dark places.

"It's rent," she said.

"Well, fuck. Fuck, fuck, fuck." He pounded his steering wheel with each 'fuck,' grinning like he'd won the lottery. Like he'd been carrying a heavy load on his shoulders and it had just lightened up by a ton.

Then he put his mouth in a line. Looked down on his lap. Shook his head. Picked up the envelope and handed it back to her.

"I can't do it. I just can't do it."

"Come on." She wanted to hit him.

"Sarah wouldn't take it."

"I know. That's why I'm giving it to you." She wanted to hit him twice. "You need it. I got it. Our dad should've given Sarah and you money long ago."

"I never asked him for money."

"Neither did Jim or I. But he gave it to us."

His left eyebrow lifted in a skeptical arc. "Maybe you didn't, but I bet Jim hinted pretty broadly."

"Not around me."

"He didn't get blow jobs from other women around you, either. Besides, I don't base my behavior on his."

Tears welled up. She turned her head from him and faced the field, blinking away the tears. So tired of tears. She sniffed and looked back to him.

"Put the money in the bank. I gotta go." He grinned crookedly. "Hey, thanks for the thought. For half a moment, I was feeling pretty damn good."

"You can still change your mind."

He laughed. "You're a devil, you are." With a nod, he took off.

She'd just stepped into the house when her phone rang. She dropped the envelope on the table and dug into her purse, not as happy as before Marsh turned down her money. She *wanted* to help them.

There had to be another way. She would think of it.

The phone trilled again, and she looked at the Caller ID. *Derek Muench.*

She didn't want to talk to him now. The only person she wanted to talk to right now was a fairy godmother, and good luck with that. But unlike an imaginary fairy godmother, Derek was flesh and blood and wanted to talk to her, so she put the phone to her ear and pressed 'talk.'

"Hey, Derek. Thanks for calling while I was sick. I appreciate it."

"Mom says Pastor Jim doesn't deserve you. I agree one thousand percent."

"I filed for divorce today." The words dropped out of her mouth like rocks clunking onto a road.

She made a face. Why had she said that? Derek was a guy. They didn't want to hear this kind of thing.

"Oh." There was a pause. "Good. Would you, uh, like to go out to eat tonight?"

She frowned. "With you and Elaine?"

"No, not with Mom. Just me."

She looked down at her left hand. At her bare ring finger.

Was Derek asking her on a date? With romantic intentions?

"I'm not sure..." She stopped herself from saying more. She was being silly thinking he thought she was...well, datable. Or something more. Derek probably thought she was ancient. For a woman to be seven years older than a man was like a generation dividing them. Guys who were twenty-nine were dating twenty-year-olds, not thirty-six-year-olds.

Obviously he was inviting her to dinner as a friend. Payback for all the times she had him and his mother over for dinner. She was one of the few who asked Elaine to her home and smiled as the woman rambled on about all that she still did for Derek despite her physical problems.

"I know you like Italian," he said. "Paradiso in Tomahawk is one of my accounts. I just updated their website yesterday. Pete, the owner, said to come over anytime and bring a friend. How'd you like to be my first guest?"

Her shoulders relaxed. He just thought of her as a friend. They both liked Italian, and the meal was free. Nothing romantic about a free meal.

"Sounds wonderful. I'd love to be your first. Thanks for thinking of me."

"I've been thinking about you a lot," he said, and his voice changed. Deepened.

A small frisson went through her, like a tiny starburst shooting through her bloodstream.

They set up a time for him to pick her up. After she ended the call, she let Goldie outside then went to the guest bedroom to change into a sweatshirt and pants with an elastic waistband. Not that she needed elastic. She still hadn't regained her appetite, and instead of gaining weight, she'd lost another pound.

Three weeks ago, she would've been thrilled. Now she didn't care. Well...maybe a little. She went into the bathroom and looked at herself in the mirror. She could see herself from her hips up. But what she saw looked good.

"This is what you'll never have again," she said to her reflection, meaning the words for Jim, not herself.

Then she went to let Goldie back in to be with her puppies, and followed the dog into the puppy room. The black puppy tried to climb up her leg. No one wanted him yet. He looked too much like a black lab for perspective owners to pay the designer-dog price that Sarah and Marsh were asking.

She wanted to tell him she'd take him, but how could she? She had no idea where she'd be living. How much time she'd have.

Goldie barked, stopping her thoughts. The large dog got up on her feet and faced the front, barking louder. All the puppies squealed and the black puppy barked. Small, high barks that sounded cute now but she knew would soon be loud and irritating.

Becky climbed over the barrier that kept them from escaping – an old door in bad shape that looked like it should be firewood once the puppies were gone. Sarah had plans to spruce it up for resale.

In the living room, Becky peered out the large front window at a white truck, sized about halfway between a semi and a pickup. Squinting, she stuck her nose close to the glass to see a black and red emblem, with more lettering on the side. But all she could make out was one word: ANTIQUES.

The driver walked around the cab, and she breathed in – then couldn't seem to breathe out. The air stuck in her lungs.

Almost eighteen years had passed since she'd seen Trey Niemow, and she probably wouldn't have recognized him if Earl hadn't mentioned his name at the village board meeting. He'd filled out some. In a good way. His shoulders were broad under his blue long-sleeved shirt, and his hips and legs lean under his jeans. From this distance, she couldn't see too much of his face, but he wore his hair short now. He probably didn't feel he had to show the world he was a rebel anymore. Financial success did that to a person, she thought.

He headed toward the house, and she realized she was probably covered in dog hair. She had a frantic high school moment, wondering if she had time to do something to her face and hair, and knowing she didn't. She pushed her hands through her hair and then realized what she was doing, and stopped.

She didn't need to impress anyone. Certainly not any man. She was living in her sister's guest room, her brother-in-law's office, really. She wasn't ready for a puppy, much less a new man.

The doorbell rang. She headed toward the front entrance while Goldie barked madly and the golden puppies squeaked and the black one barked. Opening the front door, she put on a smile the way another woman would put on makeup – not as a decoration but as a weapon.

"Hello, Trey," she said. His face was wide, and so were his shoulders. On him both looked good. His nose was broad, too, his jaw square and his eyes wide. Everything fit nicely and with his olive complexion, he looked foreign, exotic. It was his quarter native Indian blood that gave him the always-tanned color, while she was the foreign one with the paleness she'd inherited from German ancestors on both sides of the family.

He didn't seem to mind her pale complexion as he looked her up and down.

Her body temperature went up a few degrees. One thing hadn't changed. He reeked of sex.

And one thing had. His appeal no longer scared the crap out of her.

He smiled with appreciation. "High school," he said, his eyes glowing with appreciation. "Becky Hoffman. It's been a while. I would've bet money you didn't marry a picker."

"You would've won that bet. The lucky woman who lives here is my younger sister, Sarah."

"That's right, you married the golden boy." He still smiled but the warmth in his eyes cooled. "The future preacher."

"He is a preacher and I married him, but we're..." Her tongue stumbled. It felt odd explaining anything. In Miracle, everyone knew already. Gossip sped faster than dandelion fluff. "We're not together now."

His eyes flashed to her bare ring finger then up to her eyes. "Recent?"

Her fingers twitched and she fought an urge to put her hands behind her back. She suddenly felt naked without the ring. Probably just nerves.

In all honesty, she was attracted to him, and the way he looked at her, his brown eyes warm and openly admiring, she sensed the feeling was mutual.

She couldn't remember the last time a man looked at her like she was his favorite ice cream sundae and he wanted to lick every inch.

"I saw my lawyer today."

"No kidding." He didn't say anything for a moment and she took the moment to study him. He didn't look like a bad boy anymore. Now he was just a big guy with a great body and eyes that were...kind.

As if he read her thoughts, his eyes gleamed. No longer kind but predatory. A hunter's eyes. And she was the prey.

Excitement sizzled through her body, even as she told it to calm down.

It didn't listen to her.

"Have you celebrated?" he asked.

TEN

Becky shook her head, and her heart thundered. This wasn't happening to her. This was like the opening scene of a porn movie. Or an erotic book.

Not that she watched any porn or read erotica. But if she did watch or read them, she knew a scene like this would be there – just before things *really* got hot.

He stepped back. "I have something in the truck that's just the thing for a celebration."

Wine? Champagne? Ribbed condoms?

No, her mind shouted as she watched him stride to the truck. But she remained silent.

She swallowed, wetting her throat so there would be no excuse for her not to decline with a firm 'no.' The kind of *Nooooo!* that three-year-old Keelie Woods screamed every Sunday when her mother left her at the church nursery.

"No," Becky whispered as she watched him leave. Heat and ice then more heat rushed through her.

She was pathetic. But after eighteen years of lukewarm sex, didn't she deserve at least one searing encounter?

"Yes," she said. "Yes."

He opened the passenger door of his cab and his head ducked inside. A moment later, he walked toward the house, holding a medium-sized paper bag.

Booze, she guessed. But as he neared the house, she saw it wasn't tall enough to be wine or champagne.

Candles? Thongs?

Her brain froze.

She wanted these ridiculous thoughts to stop.

She put her hand over her left breast. Beneath her palm, her heart thumped strong and healthy.

At least her thoughts weren't about Jim.

At least they weren't about what other people thought about her.

They were the same thoughts other women had every day.

It didn't mean she was going to act on them. It just meant that right now she was alive and there was nothing wrong with her body's heightened sexuality. Good to know it worked. Maybe all it needed was a new man.

She hurried to open the front door and saw Jan Brougham on the sidewalk. As Jan's gaze skittered to Sarah's house then to Trey's back, her white Chihuahua began to do his business on Sarah's lawn.

Putting on a big smile, Becky stepped onto the front porch and waved vigorously. "Hi, Jan! Great day, isn't it?"

Jan nodded, gave a smile that looked sick and tugged Clyde forward, though Clyde, not finished, barked his complaints in a voice that belonged to a bigger dog.

That's what I am, Becky thought. By smiling and waving at my detractors instead of shrinking and whimpering, I'm showing them I'm a bigger dog.

"Nosy neighbor?" Trey asked, nearing her. "Tell her I'm the big bad wolf and I'm about to blow the town down." Then he laughed.

Becky laughed, too, but hers was breathless. A Marilyn Monroe laugh.

The big bad wolf wasn't so far off from her own thoughts about Trey. But now she realized he was carrying a grocery bag.

"What are we celebrating with?" she asked.

"You like peanut butter fudge?"

She was suddenly ravenous. "Does Santa like cookies?"

"So I've heard. And chocolate. Do you like chocolate?"

"Do puppies pee?"

He chuckled, and dimples creased in his cheeks. How could she have forgotten them?

"You have puppies?" he asked.

"*We* have puppies." She claimed temporary ownership of the squirming, squeaking, peeing, pooping bunch. She felt happier on this one day in her sister's messy house that smelled like *eau de* puppy than she'd been for years in her own immaculate house.

Stepping back, she swept the door open. "Come in and meet them."

They went to the kitchen first, where she set down the bag on the table. Then on to the puppy room.

He stooped down with his hands out so the puppies could sniff and lick and nibble. When a golden puppy gnawed the toe of his right leather boot, he laughed and gently removed it, his hands big on the small body.

Petting the puppies, Trey didn't seem like the bad boy she'd remembered. Of course not. She should know better than to believe gossip. Especially since life as an adult in a small town was a lot like it was in high school.

Then he looked at her. Her body heated again and she told herself it was too warm in this room with the sun shining through the dining room's long rectangular window.

Goldie barked and Becky let her outside. Ignoring the puppies' whines, Becky and Trey went into the kitchen and ate peanut butter-chocolate fudge. "I can't think of a better way to celebrate my divorce," she said, and then thought of the dinner tonight. But whatever she had for dinner would have to be very good to beat the fudge...and spending a few minutes with Trey.

He gave her a crooked smile. "I can. But don't think it's what you want."

Her face flushed. "I was right about you."

"What's that?"

"You were the bad boy at school."

He leaned back in the chair and shouted with laughter; the two front chair legs lifted a couple of inches and his face glowed with life.

Deep inside her, something stirred.

This man, it said. *This man.*

He tipped the chair forward. "You know what I think?"

She shook her head, beyond thinking.

"I think Goldie wants to come in."

Flustered and hot. Embarrassed because he probably read her mind and knew just what she was feeling and thinking, she stood too fast. Her chair tumbled back, crashed into the stove, and the puppies in the dining room squealed and barked. While she righted the chair, her face flamed, and she heard his boot steps on the laminated floor.

"I'll get Goldie," he said.

She got water for Goldie and the pups, giving her heated cheeks time to cool. That taken care of, she stood in the hall between the kitchen and the dining room and watched him and Goldie head toward her.

Trey was having a strange effect on her, and she wasn't sure she liked it. She let Goldie into the room with the puppies, replaced the barrier then turned to him. "Why are you here? Do you need Marsh? I can give you his cell number."

"I heard he had some old Indian parts."

She frowned and he laughed. "The motorcycle," he said, and she recalled that Indian was an old Wisconsin motorcycle manufacturer.

"I'll call him." She went back into the kitchen for her cell. There were two pieces of fudge left and he offered one to her while she pressed the speed dial number she'd added yesterday evening. She shook her head and told him he was evil.

His face lit in a smile again, and sparkles deep within her did a little dance. *A dirty dance.*

By the time Marsh answered on the third ring, her skin was hot again. She wondered if it could be a lingering condition brought on by the flu. This had never happened to her with Jim.

She told Marsh about Trey and what he wanted, then handed the cell to Trey. In the other room, Goldie barked and the puppies started their squealing again. Who needed an alarm system with dogs?

She headed to the front window to see who was coming now, and spotted the back of Patty, the mail lady, hurrying across the street. She'd already delivered Sarah's mail.

Becky went to collect the mail and brought in a few sales flyers and bills. On the bottom was a sticky note on a Change of Address form, with a message from Patty telling her she needed to fill it out and either stop by the post office or leave it in the mailbox. If she left it in the mailbox, Patty would pick it up the next day.

On the bottom of the note, Patty had scrawled: I knew what Jim was doing.

ELEVEN

Becky leaned against the hallway wall, dizzy for a second. She closed her eyes. How many other people had known?

She felt like a fool. A stupid fool.

Fingers touched her shoulder and she jumped around to look straight into Trey's concerned eyes. "You okay?" he asked.

She nodded, not sure how her voice would sound.

His eyebrows contracted, not buying it. She tried a smile, but felt it wobble.

"I'm fine," she said, hearing the throatiness in her voice and hoping he'd think it was sexy. Wasn't sex what all men were supposed to think about? She'd read they thought about it once every seven waking seconds.

No wonder the world was in trouble.

He nodded at the mail. "Bad news?"

She looked down and saw that the yellow sticky note was crumpled in her fist, and the other mail clamped against her chest. "Nope, not a thing." She glanced up. "What did Marsh have to say?"

Trey handed her the cell. "He can tell you himself."

Marsh asked her to take Trey to the third storage building where he kept the motorcycle parts and call him back with any offers. By the time she clicked off, she was breathing evenly again.

So what if someone else knew that her husband was an asshole? Her soon-to-be ex-husband. After all, she'd behaved honorably. She had no reason to be ashamed. In fact, the note was Patty's odd way of being supportive, letting Becky know that someone else knew and believed in her.

It was good. From now on it was all good.

From now on, that was her new motto: It's all good.

She gave Trey a smile that made his eyebrows sweep up. "I'll be a moment. I need to change into my sneakers."

Five minutes later, Trey was happily looking through old rusty motorcycle parts while Becky wished she'd brought a book with her. At first, he told her what he wanted and then she called Marsh. But as the two men got into a heated back-and-forth price war, she finally gave Trey the cell, then stood back and watched his eyes burn bright. She guessed that Marsh's eyes were doing the same thing. Probably the same as an orchestra leader leading an orchestra or a shopper finding the perfect pair of shoes on sale.

When they agreed on a price that she thought was a lot for a rusty wheel, he handed the phone back to her. The phone-passing thing happened again and again, though she didn't know how an old license plate cost three hundred dollars. Or an old rear bike fender was worth two hundred. But Trey was smiling like it was a bargain. For all the attention he paid her, she could've been walking around naked, letting it all hang out – literally – and he wouldn't blink.

She told him to keep the phone while he continued to look around. There was an old car seat on the side, and she sat on it, her legs stretched out on the wooden floor. Closing her eyes, she dozed off, fuzzily aware that she trusted Trey and Marsh more than Jim or her father.

Of course, they could turn out to be rats, too. Maybe she just didn't know them well enough.

But she still let herself fall asleep.

An arm around her shoulder aroused her. Trey. She felt his bicep. Still drowsy, her eyes still closed, she recognized his scent.

She murmured and turned her face toward him, the sweatshirt material of his long-sleeved top soft under her cheek. Lethargy tugged at her. Thinking to lean into him a bit more, she raised her face.

He must've been leaning down because their lips met.

Instantly awake, she felt his arm stiffen and knew this kiss wasn't his plan, even though he'd sat beside her. He started to pull back, and inside her rose up a loud, clamoring *'No!'*

She reached up, curved her hands around his neck and drew him to her.

He resisted for one second, then he sighed. A sound of surrender. She kept her eyes closed, because right now she wanted to *feel*. Not look, not talk, not think. Just feel and smell and taste.

With an almost inaudible moan, he kissed her. His mouth opened, and hers parted under his. His hands on her back drew her against his chest.

The kiss went on and on. And it was good, so good. Their tongues met. And it was better and it was wonderful.

She drew closer to him, her breasts flattening against his chest, as if she wanted to meld with him. Small lightning streaks bolted through her, and she wanted more. Her body heated. Hotter and hotter...

Then he twisted away. His hands slid from her back and he gripped her upper arms.

Caught in a hot daze, she tried to lean forward, but his hands grasped her harder. Holding her away from him.

Her eyelids snapped up. His face looked changed. His color brighter. His eyes hotter. His breathing faster and harder.

Her breath huffed out even as he shook his head. "We can't do this."

"Why?" she asked in a breathy voice.

"For one thing, I don't have a condom on me."

She opened her mouth to tell him it didn't matter. That a barren woman probably wouldn't need it anyway.

That thought brought the old pain knifing back, cooling her faster than if someone threw ice water at her face.

Her body went limp, and for a second only his grip on her arms kept her from sagging. Then she sucked in her breath and drew strength with the long inhale. She gave a twist to her shoulders and his grip eased. Still looking into her eyes, he released her.

She smiled, even as she chided herself for being the same old people pleaser. But what was she supposed to do? Whip off her top and bra? Then say, "This is what you could've had, but you blew it."

Besides, she didn't need a man's help to take care of her sexual needs.

"I got a little carried away," she said.

"A *little* carried away?" He looked down at his lap then into her eyes. "Nothing little here."

She laughed and it caught in her throat that was not quite ready for laughter. She put her hand to her forehead and it was warm. "You were right to pull away."

"I won't take advantage of you."

"Don't talk like that." She shifted a few inches from him. How odd of him to phrase it that way. So old-fashioned. So…gallant. So *not* what she would've expected from him. "You weren't the only one in that clinch. There were two of us. I was kissing just as much as you."

He didn't reply, but his eyes darkened and his expression became hooded. She could've sworn she felt little testosterone pellets land on her face, her throat, stab her through her top. Slip into her partly open mouth, then slide smoothly down into her body that still simmered.

She leaned toward him again. Caught herself and jerked back. Her face heated even more.

66

Next time he came over, she needed to have a warning. She'd prepare ice shavings to slap on her face when needed.

He stood and stepped away. "You filed for divorce today. You're fragile right now." He smiled and she let out a breath she hadn't realized she was holding. "Back in high school, I noticed you."

"I know," she whispered. Of course she'd known, but she'd never admitted it. She'd noticed him back then, too. She'd never told anyone. She hadn't even written it in her diary.

Now she let herself remember the colliding glances that left her breath stuck in her throat as she looked away. The way she pretended they never happened.

She'd read about opposites attracting, and that's what those longing looks were.

Simple biology – her hormones on the hunt to find someone who didn't belong in her pack. Someone different, who didn't have a similar genetic make up. Someone who would give her a strong, healthy baby.

And today, eighteen years since he first left Wisconsin, his body was doing the same thing.

She guessed hers was having the same effect on him. She hoped it was.

"You and I were like the sun and the moon coming together," he said.

"I'm pretty sure that's not possible."

"That's what I'm saying."

She pushed her hair back from her face. "It's possible with us. Without any planetary explosions."

"I'll come back." His eyes glinted. "Next time I'll be prepared."

She looked him in his eyes, not grinning, not smiling – as serious as the divorce papers she'd left on the kitchen counter. "Don't take too long. I'm not waiting for any man anymore."

"I'll remember." He stared at her for a long moment, then he took out a piece of paper and pointed at the pile of stuff by the big doors at the front. "Here's the list and here's the bill. You can call Marsh to check it."

"I will," she said.

It took another twenty minutes to look at the pile of parts and signs and a few things she didn't even know the names of, but she trusted he wrote the right things down. She'd been let down big-time by Jim. But she had to keep trusting or she'd be angry and bitter for the rest of her life.

As she stood on the front porch and watched Trey drive away, his last words echoed in her ears and her mind and her heart.

'I'll be back for you, Becky,' he'd said. And then he gave her the slow smile that creased the dimples in his cheeks and slit his eyes and made her chest, plus a few other places, feel as though a match flared up inside her. "I'll be back."

Heading into the house, she remembered she was going out to eat with Derek tonight.

After this last hour with Trey, it was going to be hard to give Derek her full attention.

TWELVE

S itting across from Becky at the table for two, Derek looked spruced up and young. He glistened like one of the silver candlesticks in her father's house. His shiny purple shirt wouldn't look out of place on a hip-hop star, and Becky suspected he'd bought it for tonight. Probably he'd gone to Wausau to shop so no one from Miracle would see him. He was dressed better than she was in her black slacks and red top that was too loose since she'd lost weight.

She wished now she'd taken her skinny clothes to Sarah's house. She hadn't dreamed she might fit into them again.

Sarah had offered to let her wear one of her tops, but Becky had thanked her and said it wasn't necessary. She hadn't expected Derek to look so...*good.*

As she read the menu, she suspected her thinness wouldn't last long. Did Italians like everything with cream or cheese or both in it? Or were those the Americanized versions? Or just the menu items that caught her eye?

Why were the things that looked so good so bad for her?

That made her think of Trey. Not for long, though, because he wasn't here and the food was. She was ravenous. While looking at the menu she'd found her lost appetite and realized she hadn't exactly lost it. It had just gone on sick leave.

Now she was healthy again – and perhaps not so sad – and she wanted to order half the items on the menu. And all the desserts. In fact, she wanted to live here and never, ever leave.

The waiter came with their wine, a sweet Riesling for her and a Chardonnay for Derek. After the waiter left with their order, Derek leaned across the table toward her.

"I heard what you did today."

Her heartbeats thudded in her ears and she clutched the table edge. Lately, life felt like a carnival ride and she needed to hang on tight.

Did the whole town know she'd necked with Trey in the storage building? That she'd been ready to do more, but he backed off and gave her the 'you're not ready, and I don't want to take advantage of your fragile emotions' line? Not in those words, but that's what he'd meant.

As if Trey didn't know *she* wanted to take advantage of *him*.

"Heard about what?" she asked, her voice squeaking as she tried to think up excuses for being in the building with Trey for so long.

Derek reached across the table and held out his hand. She unclenched hers from the table edge. Feeling like she was having an out-of-body moment, she grabbed his hand as if it were her lifeline. As if without it, she'd fall into the deepest part of Lake Miracle and she needed to hang on or drown.

"That you filed for divorce."

"Oh..." Relief made her heartbeat slow and her muscles relax. She let go of his hand and gave him a grateful smile.

He smiled back. His eyes smiled, too. But on second look, she saw they weren't really smiling. They were...

Smoldering?

Her breath sucked in.

"Yes, I did." She grabbed her wine glass and realized she wasn't moping or devastated or even angry at Jim. Instead, it was as if she'd whipped through the seven stages of grief in the short time since she'd discovered him in his church office with Diana. As if she'd mourned the loss of him before it happened.

Her life with Jim seemed almost seemed like someone else's life.

Except she knew that was wishful thinking. Maybe today she was okay. But tomorrow she might be in the depths again. Nothing was this easy, especially not divorce.

"I hope he doesn't give you any trouble," Derek said.

She looked at his face straight on and a great affection for him rose up inside her. But not *that* kind of affection. Not as a lover. More like an affection for a good friend who was feeding her one of her favorite foods.

Her voice was an octave too high when she changed the subject to the restaurant and the food. His eyes changed to... Eyes. Just eyes. Whatever she'd seen or thought she'd seen was no longer there.

It must have been just her imagination – that impression that every man she was alone with for a few minutes was mad for her body.

She had to stop this. It wasn't as if she wanted or needed a man in her life. Right now the only male she considered living with had four feet, black fur and a tail.

The waiter came with their bread and soup. As soon as he left, she said, "Remember Goldie's black puppy?"

He nodded, a slight crease on his forehead. She recalled that the puppy had peed on the toe of his shoes when he picked her up to take her to the restaurant. But he'd laughed and used a paper towel to wipe it off.

"A friendly guy," he said. "Very sharing."

She laughed, loosening up. She hoped she was hiding her surprise at his play on words.

There was more to Derek than she'd thought.

"We've bonded these last couple of days," she said. "I'd love to keep him, but I can't see how that could work."

"He'd be a good watchdog for when you move into your own place. Friendly, but a barker."

"And a pee-er."

Cutting the bread, he laughed more than her comment deserved and his eyes crinkled into slits.

"I'd have to find a place that would accept pets," she added.

"I can't think of anyone in Miracle who allows pets for renters. And labs have a bad reputation for chewing."

"I probably won't stay in Miracle. I'll need a job and there aren't any in Miracle that I know of." She gave a smile that insisted on teetering. She grabbed the glass of water to hide her wobble. Another scary part of this new life... But other women had been through this, and they managed. She would, too.

"I do a lot of websites for businesses in the area," Derek said. "I could ask around. Check and see what's available."

A rush of gratitude clogged her throat. "Thanks for being a good friend." She heard the huskiness in her voice. As if tears weren't far behind.

Dipping his bread in the herbed olive oil, he hesitated then gazed at her. The look in his eyes was intent, as if he were trying to see what was in her mind. And his face... It shone. As if lit from within.

Her hand holding the spoonful of minestrone shook. Maybe it was because of the way he looked at her, so tenderly, but she was feeling...amorous.

Her spoon shook more, drops spilling. Good grief, this was ridiculous.

He dropped the crust, then reached up to steady her hand and guided it down to the cup. Her gaze followed the spoon. She couldn't look at his face anymore – it was too...unsettling. She wasn't ready for...whatever *this* was leading to.

"Look at me," he said, his voice low. And her gaze whipped up to his face. He didn't let go of her hand, and she released the spoon, her fingers nerveless, her heart fluttering wildly.

"I want to be more than a friend."

She opened her mouth but no words came out. It wasn't that her voice was stuck. It was her brain.

Are you crazy? Look at me. I'm seven years older than you. You could have a twenty-one year old if you put some effort into it.

Another part of her was picking out something sexy to wear to bed with him.

"Jim was a jerk to cheat on you," he went on, in the voice men used when they were on the edge of desperation. When they really wanted to convince the other person of something. A voice she never expected to hear from Derek. Or any man. She wasn't the kind of woman men said that to. She was too...unexciting. Too ordinary.

But she nodded for him to go on. That she was listening. Boy, was she listening. She felt oddly composed now, though her heart thundered inside her chest. As if she were watching a movie where the leading man said this to an older actress, and Becky was waiting for the actress to answer him...rooting for him. Wanting him to have his happy ever after.

"I know it's early," he continued, "but can you tell me if there's a chance you'll feel the same way about me?"

A moment went by while she stared at him. Waiting for the actress to answer him.

At the table behind them, someone laughed. A waitress threaded between tables, carrying two plates with pasta and some kind of meat that smelled like oregano and mozzarella. Two of her favorite smells.

"If it's 'no,'" he said, his voice so low she had to lean in to hear him, "then tell me. I'll still be your friend."

Damn it. She'd have to answer. She put her hand over her forehead and leaned in another inch. "It is too early." And then seeing the stillness in his face, the tension in his clenched jaws, she hurriedly said, "But, yes. There's a chance."

He sat back, smiling, his shoulders loosening, his back taller, the tension visibly rolling off him.

She smiled back and thought of all the reasons she should have declined. But all she'd said was that there was a chance. And so what if he were seven years younger? If their sexes were switched, no one would think twice about it. Diana was a good ten years younger than Jim.

Not that she wanted to be a man. Or to have her circumstances compared to Diana's and Jim's.

Today she quite liked being a woman.

"Good," he said. "Good."

She started eating her soup, her hand steady again. Eating was safe. Talking wasn't always safe. There wasn't anything to say right now anyway. By the time it was reasonable for her to be looking around, she'd know what she wanted.

Warmth settled inside her. Her friend Derek thought of her *that way*. He wanted to make love to her.

The idea astounded her, and at the same time thrilled her. She liked the idea. Liked it a lot.

For so many years she'd felt almost sexless. But now she felt desirable – and a bit wicked.

Derek asked what kind of job she was looking for, and her 'feeling-like-a-sex-symbol moment' deflated.

"I'm not qualified for anything." She glanced around the restaurant. "I could waitress." If anyone wanted her. "Or cook." She was a decent cook.

"You should get half the money. If Jim—"

"I do have half the joint bank account and any investments will be shared." She shrugged. She would've given Jim credit for that, but she put some of his compliance and generosity down to the photos of him and Diana. Plus, her father was still backing Jim. But if Jim treated her badly on the financial end, her father might change his mind.

"I have enough to get by for a while," she said. "If I'm frugal. But I have to think of the future. I don't have social security. I need to build up equity in myself."

"What do you want to do?"

Be a mom. The waiter came with her mushroom ravioli, and she managed to keep her smile on even though gnarled monster talons reached into her chest and squeezed her heart.

She went through the motions of eating – taking a bite and chewing – and the squeezing eased. The talons disappeared and slunk into hiding. Hypervigilant. Ready to spring out another day.

"I don't have any natural talents." She took another bite and this one she was able to enjoy. If she could only cook like this—

"You do have a talent," he said. "You make people feel comfortable."

She put down her fork. "That's called being a people pleaser."

"It's more than that. You have a talent for making people feel that you care. I've always felt that way around you."

She took a sip of wine before answering. "I always cared about you."

His mouth broke into another wide smile. As if she'd given him his greatest wish.

Her stomach clenched with a mix of dread and excitement.

What had she started now?

And what next?

THIRTEEN

They lingered at the table, long after the meal. Becky sipped an extra glass of wine, something she hadn't done since her wedding night. Finally only two other tables were occupied and they left. On the way out, Derek took her hand and she curled her fingers around his. She felt lighter than usual. It was partly the wine, but mostly she just felt happy.

"I'll remember this," he said.

"Me, too." She felt young tonight. On a date with a cute guy whose eyes shone every time he looked at her. Even on the street now, she could see the sappy expression on his face.

As she smiled at him, he bent forward as if he were going to kiss her. On a public street. With lights shining from every window and four street lamps on this side of the street.

Panic rose in her throat and chest, and she broke away from him. She hurried to his car parked in front of the laundromat two doors down.

Once inside the car, the panic diminished. "Sorry," she said. "I didn't mean anything. It's just that..." Just that she was stupidly embarrassed. She was even embarrassed to say she was embarrassed.

This dating thing was hard.

"Technically, you're still married," he said, the car starting. "I understand."

She thought he probably did. She leaned back and a lethargy swept over her. A happy lethargy. Her body relaxed. Feeling taken care of.

She remained wrapped in the glow as they drove out of the city. Stars blanketed the night sky and twinkled down on them like a magical scene out of a Disney movie. Cold Play was on Derek's car stereo and the waistband of her slacks was still comfortable.

She felt like a different woman. She *was* a different woman. No longer the quiet, responsible one who never smoked weed, who never dirty danced in public, who'd only made love to one man.

She still had never done any of that...but the last one might change sometime soon.

It occurred to her that she had a lot to make up for. She'd lived a tame life, and right now she wanted to get a little wild.

Too soon the headlights shone on the village sign that said there was a population of six hundred twenty-nine. Becky shivered. When they'd driven to Tomahawk tonight, she'd thought she was going to dinner with a friend. Odd to feel so different on the drive back home. As if she were in high school and wondering what was going to happen when they reached her house. As if she'd stepped into an alternate universe.

In a couple minutes they were at Sarah's house. The lights were out at the Webber's across the street. Derek pulled his car into the driveway and parked at the side of the house. A row of trees blocked his car from anyone else's view.

No one could see them.

The wind picked up, and it gusted down the street. Derek's breaths were harsh and fast. With an edge to them. Her heart thumped and inside the car the tension level elevated. Her skin heated and prickled.

If she stayed any longer, she would have to take her coat off. She would have to take all her clothes off.

Her gaze remained forward, her spine straight, but she could feel Derek's stare. She could feel her breasts tighten. She tightened all over.

"Remember when I asked you to the restaurant?" he asked, his voice thicker than normal. "You said, 'I'd love to be your first.'"

"Yes." She heard her voice. A whisper. Softer than the wind.

When he didn't reply right away, she looked at him. His forehead was furrowed, his shoulders stiff. He gave off vibrations of distress. Of pain. Emotional pain, not physical.

A sound came out of her mouth, and she leaned sideways, her hand on his forearm. His arm clenched, as if her touch caused him more pain. Instead of letting him go, she wrapped her fingers around his arm.

"What is it? What's wrong, Derek?"

"Did you mean it?" His voice croaked low with an emotion she couldn't name, and he stared into her eyes, as if he tried to read her mind in the darkness. "About being my first?"

"I came to the restaurant with you. So, yes... It was my pleas—"

He pulled his arm away from her, and she yanked her hand back to her side. In the dim light, she could see the withdrawal in his face. She'd said something wrong, but she didn't know what.

"Not my first for the restaurant." His voice was muffled and he looked ahead at the two-car garage.

And slowly, like watching simmering water turn to a boil, she *got* what he meant.

In his awkward, clumsy, nerdy way, he was asking her to...

A compulsion to laugh made her clamp her lips together and curl her hands tightly. She liked Derek too much to let loose. He wouldn't understand. But, oh God, her stomach hurt from holding back.

"I'm sorry," he whispered. "I shouldn't have said that. I'll walk you to the door."

She heard the click of the door opening and a silent cry rose up inside her head, killing the need to laugh, drowning it with a need to comfort. "No," she said aloud.

He started, turning to her. She reached out and grabbed his upper arm.

"I don't want to make you uncomfortable," he said. "I shouldn't have said anything."

Underneath his jacket, she felt the bunched muscle of his bicep. She had a stray thought that he was more ripped than she'd suspected.

"Yes," she said. And she didn't even know if this were the best thing for her to do. But she wanted to do it. She wanted it for him.

And maybe for herself, too.

"Yes, I want to be your first."

"Are you just feeling sorry for—"

"Shut up. Just shut up." She brought her knee up too quickly and it banged into the divider between their seats, sending a quick, sharp pain to her kneecap. A noise escaped her mouth.

Immediately he bent toward her, hands on her shoulder. "Are you all right?"

The pain lessened as she smiled at him. "I think we need to take this to the backseat."

He didn't reply, the silence loud. His face was only a couple of inches away from hers. In the dimness she couldn't read his emotions. But she *felt* his excitement. *Felt* his heat. *Felt* his tension.

And hers. She quivered with tension. Quivered with heat.

"Shouldn't we go to the hotel?" he asked.

"Artie Morgan works there."

"I wish I could take you to my house, but..."

She sat back, pulling out of his grip. She grabbed the door handle. "The backseat or the back door?"

"The backseat," he said, his voice low and intense.

They each went out their door, and she felt odd opening the back door. She felt odd getting in. A bit giddy, as if she'd stepped into a time machine that moved backward twenty years and she was once again a teenager with a cute boy.

His door closed before hers and he slid to her side. Then his arms slid around her, and they kissed. His lips were soft and she put her right arm around his back, her other arm caught between them.

If this were the first time he kissed a woman, he was a fast learner. She was getting warm with her jacket on. Her rising body heat and his had something to do with it, too.

At the same instant that she started to feel uncomfortable, her neck protesting the angle, he stopped the kiss and pulled away, breathing heavily.

"Do you have a condom?" she asked.

"Yes. I drove to Tomahawk this afternoon to buy it."

She laughed, and so did he. She reached up and cupped the left side of his face. "I've often wondered. How is it that no girl has snatched you up?"

"I'm no prize."

"Are you kidding? You're the grand prize."

"I'm a geek. I'm not what the girls around here want."

"Maybe you've been looking at the wrong girls."

He shook his head. "I'm not looking at a girl. I'm looking at a woman."

She stilled. Then she smiled. Of course he was looking at her. He *liked* her. And she liked him. Once he'd found out about her split with Jim, he probably thought she'd be a safe person to have a fling with and lose his virginity.

An ache pulsed through her. He was right. She'd be wonderful. Accepting. Non-judging. And grateful.

Maybe she should say no, but there was a sweetness about him that made her feel vibrant and voluptuous. Made her feel treasured.

"I won't regret this," she said.

They kissed again. This time she pulled away first. Though she'd had sex fairly regularly for the last twenty years, she was certainly no expert. But there was one thing she knew.

"This works better if we take our clothes off."

"Won't you be cold?"

"You'll warm me, won't you?"

They fumbled with their clothes. Zippers unzipping, buttons snapping open. Clothes swishing. His breaths were harsh. Hers made little puffing sounds.

He finished before her and she could smell him, his scent sharper now. She wondered if hers was, too. Her body was heated from the inside out. Her nerve endings ready for him.

She held back giggles. This was the most exciting and crazy thing she'd done in...forever. And with Derek of all people. Her friend.

Her bare feet flat on the car's floor, she lifted her tush to take off her panties, feeling his gaze on her. The first man to see her naked...other than Jim.

She turned to Derek. His arms reached out to draw her to him. She put her hands against his chest, stopping him. "I'm going to make this good for you." She resolved to give him a time he wouldn't forget. It was going to be so good that if he grew to an old age and kept his memories, he was going to think of her often and smile.

"I'm going to make it good for you, too," he said back, just as fiercely, and she had the quick impression that he'd thought about being naked with her before. Maybe thought about it often.

They kissed again, skin against skin. He touched her. Her back and her breasts. He held her too close for her to do more than clutch his back, though she felt his erection against her belly, heavy and full.

She pulled away. Her body felt full and heavy, too. And hot. So hot inside.

"We need to be a little apart, so I can touch you," she said.

"Just let me touch you." And he did. Gentle and sweet and reverent. Every place he touched came to life.

"This is supposed to be for *you*," she said. "I want you to know how it feels to be touched."

"I know how it feels to be touched. I touch myself all the time. I don't know what it's like to touch a woman." His fingers slid between her legs. "Like this."

His touch and the huskiness in his voice made her shiver. The air chilled her and she turned to him, but he didn't stop touching her. She leaned forward and bit his shoulder. Not hard but enough to make him moan.

She didn't know where that came from. She had a powerful need to touch him all over, but he was touching her all over, and there wasn't room in the backseat for them both to do it. She explained that to him, and he said the next time they'd find another place to do it.

There might not be a next time, she thought, and she clutched him tight as he told her how warm and silky she was.

"Juicy," she told him, and he laughed in her left ear and said he was getting juicy, too.

Then she told him they'd better do it before it was too late. She moved off him, and he picked up his slacks from the floor and pulled a packet out of his pocket. She helped him roll it on, and they laughed again, breathily and a bit nervously. Both of them were longer than the backseat, and they discussed positions, adding to the awkwardness.

Though she wasn't an expert, she could think of a couple ways to do it. After all, knees were made to bend. He was already sitting, and she ended the discussion by climbing on top of him, her legs spread. Then she rode him, up and down in an erratic tempo until he clasped his hands over her ribs and helped her find the rhythm for their backseat dance.

His breaths were harsh and fierce and hers were gasps. She'd started this with her heart feeling tender, but soon the tenderness traveled to her thighs that hadn't had a workout this intense since... Not ever.

It was going to be worse tomorrow, she thought, slowing and moving back a fraction of an inch. A delicious feeling shivered through her. She repeated the movement. And repeated. Another repeat and she clutched him. Her body shuddered, and she pressed her mouth against his shoulder to keep from crying out. Not caring if she left teeth prints on his shoulder.

His hands, curled around her upper arms, tightened and he jerked beneath her, calling out. A sound of triumph that made Goldie bark inside the house.

She sagged against him and his arms moved behind her back, holding her up, his breaths still harsh and ragged. She closed her eyes, her cheek against his shoulder, and wished she could fall asleep like this. Only that was impractical and silly.

The next instant he was sitting up straight, saying, "Holy shit. The back light is on."

FOURTEEN

S unlight streamed boldly into the kitchen, while Becky entered quietly, almost on tiptoes, though she'd come from the guest room, which she'd slept in by herself for the last six hours. But she still felt like a kid sneaking in, which was ridiculous. When she was a kid, she didn't have sex in the backseat of cars.

Marsh was gone at least. He'd left early this morning to drive to a small town in Minnesota, a four-and-a-half-hour drive. An antique collector he'd done business with in the past had died, and his kids called to say they wanted to clean up the place.

Not that they were giving it away. Sarah had scowled when she'd told Becky about it yesterday, saying amateurs were worse than pros. They looked up what the items went for at auction and expected the same amount.

Maybe Marsh hadn't told Sarah what happened last night. After all, it must have embarrassed him, too, catching her and Derek in the backseat of Derek's car, scrambling to put on their clothes.

Just thinking about it, Becky wanted to crawl into a dark space and hide. Standing by the counter, Sarah turned to her with a huge smile, the picture of a pregnant, glowing woman.

"You did it!" Sarah leapt at Becky and hugged her tight. Then she laughed, long and loud. Shaking her head. "I only wish Jim had seen it. Serves him right."

Becky winced. Plopping into a chair, she put her elbows on the table top and bent forward, her head down, her hands on top of her head. Her hair tumbled over her cheeks, hiding her face. Today she wished for an invisibility cloak.

She could've used one last night, too.

"I don't know what came over me last night," she said.

Sarah grinned. "I don't know what came over you, either, but I know what got into you."

"Bitch." Becky picked up a crumpled napkin and threw it at Sarah. It bounced off her chin and onto the floor.

Ignoring the napkin on the floor, Sarah sat on a chair and leaned in toward Becky. "So, how was he?"

"He was...very good." Becky raised her eyebrows at Sarah. Being desired so much had been the very good part. "Are you happy now?"

"I want details."

"You're not getting any." She wanted badly to tell Sarah that she'd been Derek's first. Sarah could keep her mouth shut, but of course she'd tell Marsh. Though Marsh was fairly discreet – as far as Becky knew – what if he had another go-to person to share with? And that person had one. And so on and so on. "I don't think I can face him again."

Sarah laughed but not unkindly. "Don't feel bad, you're just going through the hump and dump syndrome."

"The what?"

"You haven't heard of it?" Sarah shrugged. "I've known several women who went through the stage. I'm sure men do the same thing. Divorce is a form of rejection, so they tend to have quick, hot relationships to get back into control and feel desirable again."

Becky lifted her hands to cover her face again. "Oh God. That's me."

Sarah laughed again.

"Heartless bitch." Becky brought down her hands and made a face. "I'm not planning to dump Derek. I just feel...uncomfortable."

Sarah's laughter stopped, and she was making a 'yuck' face, like she did cleaning up after the animals. "You don't really want him."

"I don't know. Sure, he's younger—"

"It's nothing to do with the age difference."

"There's nothing else to dislike about him. He makes decent money. He's nice. He's cute." Her voice lowered, and so did her eyes as she gazed at a spot of ketchup still there from last night's dinner. "And he *wants* me."

"See. I told you. It's part of the syndrome. Feeling desirable again. None of what you said will make up for his mama."

"I like Elaine."

"So do I, but..." Sarah held up one finger in a 'wait' order, then got off the chair and swooped down to a cupboard. She came up with a long, narrow container that said CLING PLUS on the side. She set it on the counter and started pulling the cellophane out.

"She's a little clingy," Becky said. "I agree. But—"

"No buts. No talk, either. This is a dramatic demonstration."

Becky laughed nervously as Sarah efficiently tore off a two-foot long sheet. "You're scaring me."

"Don't worry. I won't hurt you." She raised her head and gave her a shark smile. "Much. Give me your arm."

Becky held out her arm. "You're bossy. What is this? Show and tell?"

"It's show and *learn.*" Sarah held the cellophane paper so it wouldn't curl up, then swooshed it under Becky's arm. "Your arm is Derek."

Becky put her lips together to hold back a giggle. Easy to see Sarah had been spending most of her days with a six-year-old.

A small frown of concentration appeared on Sarah's forehead as she wrapped the cellophane around Becky's lower arm four times. Tightly. Too tightly. Constricting Becky's arm.

Sarah smoothed the line so it wouldn't curl up, then sat back on her chair, her hands on her thighs. "The cellophane is his mama."

"A little overkill, isn't it?" Becky reached out with her left hand to pull it off. But the cellophane fought her. It felt icky on her arm, wouldn't allow the pores of her skin to breathe. "You wrapped it too tight."

"I told you, it's Derek's mama." Sarah crossed her arms, her chin stubborn. "That's how she rolls. Do you need a man that bad?"

Frowning, Becky grabbed an edge and started to peel off the paper. "I'll have to see him again. He's a sweet guy. If I don't, I'll feel like a slut."

"About time you got slutty and had some fun."

"But this was...special." Becky balled up the cling wrap. "You promise not to tell anyone?"

Inching forward to the edge of her seat, Sarah nodded.

"He was a virgin."

Sarah snorted a laugh, then held up her hand to show she was done laughing. "Good. When you tell him it's too soon to get involved with anyone, he'll still be grateful to you. At least he's not a virgin anymore."

"That's bad," Becky said. "That's really bad."

"Nope, that's life." Sarah got up from the chair. "I should leave. I'm taking the tables I repurposed out of old farm doors to a designer in Medford."

"Repurposed?"

"I take something old and make it new. Sometimes better than new. I scrape them down, saw them to size if needed, paint them, and sell them."

"No kidding. I knew you were doing something like that with the door in the puppy room once the puppies are gone. But I didn't realize how talented you were."

"You don't need talent to do it." Sarah laughed but her face turned pink. "Would you like to see them? I'll show them to you."

Becky left the ball of cellophane on the table, then followed Sarah as she grabbed her purse and keys. Becky slipped into the jacket she'd hung on a hook by the back door. Sarah put on her own jacket, leaving the front unbuttoned. It was too small for Sarah to pull over her baby bump and button up, and Becky thought that at least she could buy Sarah a coat before she left. But she knew Sarah would rather have clothes for Cody and the baby.

It made her angry for Sarah, that she didn't have enough money to do it all. But neither Sarah nor Marsh would take her money, and there wasn't anything she could do. So she kept her mouth shut during the walk to the van parked by the front curb. Sarah said Marsh had put the tables in the van before he left. Becky peered into the back and professed her admiration of the tables and Sarah's talents. Sarah's face turned pinker.

"What are your plans?" Sarah asked, closing the doors.

"I'll need to get a job."

"What kind of job?"

"Whatever I can get." Becky made a face. "I'm not trained in anything. I'll see what's available in the Tomahawk newspaper."

"Why Tomahawk?" Sarah asked.

"I was thinking of moving to a warmer place." Wine country in California had come to mind. After all, she drank wine. Or maybe the south. Someplace by the ocean. "But I want to be nearby when your baby is born."

"Near Derek?" Sarah's eyebrows raised and so did the corners her lips. "I hope my demonstration squashed that idea."

"I just filed for divorce yesterday. I'm not ready to hook up with anyone." As soon as her words were out of her mouth, the image of a man slipped into her mind. Not Derek. This one was taller, darker, badder.

She shivered and put her hands over her belly. "Could I learn to do what you're doing? Repurposing? Maybe I could find bargains at garage sales and do that, too."

"Oh, Becky." Sarah's mouth turned down. "I could kill Jim."

"Don't kill him. Just kick him in his balls."

Sarah smiled evilly. "I might just do that."

"I was just kidding." Becky shrugged. Sarah might not be bluffing. "Don't get yourself into trouble because of me. It's my fault for not going after a career."

"You *did* have a career. You were the perfect minister's wife."

"I've never claimed to be perfect, and it doesn't matter. Being someone's wife doesn't count as experience on a resume. I should've finished that last year of college."

"Again, you were helping Jim."

"No excuses. It's done. I don't want to look backward, just forward. I'll see what classes I need to take to earn my bachelor's degree. Then see what else I could do." She tapped her thumb nail against her lower left teeth. How pathetic to be thirty-six and not know what she wanted to be. "I can get my degree online."

Sarah reached out to hug her hard, her belly pushing into Becky's. When she released Becky, her eyes shimmered with tears. "I don't know how you can be so nice. If it were me, I would've sent the pictures of Jim and Diana to the entire church membership."

Becky laughed, hearing the shakiness. "I'll keep that in mind. I still have the newsletter list on my phone."

They hugged again. Then Sarah strode to the van to go on with her very full life. Becky stepped onto the sidewalk and noticed a weed growing between the cracks already. Standing on the sidewalk, she waited until Sarah drove away.

Only then did she trudge toward the house to look up employment opportunities and apartment rentals. She probably needed a book on how to write resumes, too.

Darkness settled over her... This was one of those moments people talked about years later that seem to be crappy but end up being the turning point of their lives.

Yeah, right.

But she remembered the Sunday before she caught Jim and his lover. The prophesy of a miracle on the car windows...and the tiny sparkling stars that no one else had seen. She yearned to see them again. To know they hadn't been a figment of her imagination.

The odd thing was that she'd never been an overly imaginative child. Maybe she was making up for her lost childhood now.

She stopped and looked at the sky. "Are you there, sparkles? Ready to come out and play?"

Still nothing. She sounded deranged. Maybe she was.

But that didn't she couldn't have miracles in her life. It just meant she might have to make her own.

FIFTEEN

Becky walked into Wegner's with her back straight and her chin up, her defenses firmly in place. It was early and there were only a half dozen customers. Five were church members. One was old Mrs. Jantz who said she'd missed Becky. Mrs. Jantz played the piano at church, and Becky immediately fought back tears. In less than a second she went from badass to needy wimp.

She managed a smile and a few words, then picked up the paper and a bag of dark chocolate. Dark chocolate was full of antioxidants. Although she'd recovered her strength after her bout of sickness, she needed powerful antioxidants to keep the germs at bay.

Two other church members were at the counter, Linda and Dean Wegner. Dean gave her a sympathetic smile. Becky suspected Linda wanted to snub her but wasn't about to alienate a potential source of gossip. Linda pushed Dean aside and stepped up to the register to check Becky out. Then she casually asked if she were really going to divorce Jim.

Becky smiled and changed the subject to the weather, while Dean looked at her with his sad eyes that made her want to shout at him to leave Linda. He'd be happier.

While Becky paid for her Tomahawk newspaper and the bag of chocolates, Angie Schuster from La Curl Salon (We Do Men Too) leaned in too close.

Sometimes it was a race to see who slung mud faster, Linda or Angie.

Neither woman got anything from Becky, but when she left, Rosa Fabrini from Fabrini's – Miracle's claim to fine dining and Italian food – followed Becky out to the sidewalk and told her she'd been meaning to call.

Becky thanked her. Rosa, her husband, and their kids went to the Catholic church in Tomahawk. Becky figured with all the problems the Catholics were having with their priests, the ones living in Miracle were probably giggling with glee at the news about Jim's downfall. The golden boy...not so golden after all. In fact, he was downright tarnished.

"Are you looking for a job?" Rosa asked.

Becky stared at her, her mind furiously searching for a way to...well, lie. "Umm..."

"It's okay." Rosa put her hand on Becky's arm, and Becky looked down. A lot of people were doing that to her lately. Their way of saying, 'I get it. I know how you feel.'

Maybe Rosa did. Becky had seen the way Rosa's husband Mike looked at the young waitresses. So far she hadn't heard that Mike had actually done anything with any of the waitresses. But no one had told her about Jim before she'd caught him and Diana in the church office, either.

"Would you come with me?" Rosa asked.

"To your restaurant?"

"We don't have any openings. I want to introduce you to a friend."

"Sounds mysterious."

"I'm a mysterious woman." Rosa seemed to glow in the sunlight, making Becky think Mike was crazy not to value her. Though their two oldest boys were in their twenties, Rosa was still a beauty with the kind of figure that men swiveled to watch as she walked by. "I feel like a matchmaker."

Alarm sizzled through Becky and she planted her sensible shoes on the sidewalk. "Not with a man. That's the last thing I need right now."

"No man. Come with me."

Becky looked at the understanding sadness in Rosa's brown eyes, and she nodded.

Rosa smiled then, her sadness lifted. She gestured Becky to her car, burgundy on the outside and buttery dark gray leather on the inside. Becky slid in and was so comfortable that she had an urge to close her eyes and sleep.

But she kept her eyes open as Rosa drove across the highway and toward the cheese factory, then past that, toward Becky's father's house. Becky tensed as they passed the house. When Rosa turned into the driveway at the end of the dead end street, Becky laughed.

The big electric sign on the edge of the sweeping lawn said 'Church of Radiance.' Elsa's church. Becky's father hated it and two years ago had tried to get the village board to say it was too large. But since there weren't any ordinances about large signs – and the Miracle Public School sign with grades 4K through 8th, was even bigger – they couldn't write one without pissing off too many people.

Her father hated the white modern architecture of the church, too. About half the size of the Community Church, the Church of Radiance was a basic rectangle shape with long windows and a soaring copper roof. Sleek and shining, it looked as if it belonged in Arizona or New Mexico, with mountains as its backdrop instead of Wisconsin's green grass and trees. And definitely not snow.

Becky had wanted to see the inside ever since it was built, but as the wife of the pastor of the other church – the one where Jesus's name was often invoked – she hadn't dared.

A smile grew inside her. Now she could dare any damn thing she wanted.

Rosa parked in the front. The only other car was Elsa's baby blue Mustang Convertible that was a few decades old. When Elsa moved to Miracle three years ago, looking like a movie star past her prime, no one could find the reason why she'd picked their quiet little village with not much going on. Becky suspected this mystery had kept Linda Wegner up for a few nights, scouring the Internet.

Once settled in her new home, Elsa had built her spiritualist church that apparently featured dancing, singing and talking – more about spiritual journeys than the bible.

Becky's father liked to say that if he wanted a journey, he'd consult a travel agency. A joke that always made Jim laughed heartily.

Rosa started to open the door, and Becky leaned sideways and put her hand on Rosa's arm. "You don't have to introduce me to Elsa. We know each other." Becky had a quick flash of Elsa leaning over her when she was sick with the flu, when for a heart-stopping moment, Becky had thought Elsa was her mother.

Becky brushed her hair back from her forehead with her fingers. As if brushing back the memory.

"Then I won't have to tell you how wonderful she is," Rosa said. "Come and have a chat with both of us."

Becky and Rosa crossed to the church. Becky was going forward in her life and didn't want revenge against either her father or Jim – though she wouldn't mind if Jim were to suffer from a sexual dysfunction. But she had a sudden wish that both men could see her walk inside.

"Aren't you Catholic?" Becky asked.

Rosa tipped her head but her mouth looked strained. As if she were holding back a scream. "Yes, but that doesn't mean I can't attend a friend's service once in a while." She stepped faster, heading into the church before Becky.

The first thing that struck Becky about the lobby of the church was the brilliant light that gave it a sense of peacefulness. The light oak-floored lobby invited her to grab an oversized cushion, sit cross-legged on it, and meditate...something Becky kept saying she should do but somehow never scheduled in. From the long windows she could see the green grass and the triple line of trees that separated the church from her father's four acres of land.

She turned to Rosa. "I still don't know why you brought me here."

"You'll find out in a minute. This way." Rosa smiled with her lips closed, as if she were hiding a wonderful surprise. Rosa led her to a hall that Becky hadn't noticed at first when she was too light-struck. "I think you two would make a good fit."

"A good fit for what?"

"You'll see." Rosa knocked on the door and a melodic voice invited them in.

From a chair in front of a long rectangular window, Elsa set a book on a small table then flowed to her feet with a smile. She radiated serenity. Her long hair was pulled back in a ponytail on the nape of her neck, and it seemed whiter and less blond than Becky remembered when she lay sick and stupid on her bed.

Though Elsa was Becky's height, her slenderness made her seem shorter. She wore blue. Nothing flowing, just jeans and a shirt. But an odd notion struck Becky that Elsa looked like a daughter of the sky.

This whole thing was odd, and she didn't know why she was paying so much attention to Elsa and the way she looked. But there was just something about her—

"I told you I'd bring her," Rosa said.

Elsa's cheeks tilted up with her smile, the skin around her eyes crinkling. "I appreciate it, but she's not ready yet."

"You don't know until you try."

"What are you two talking about?" Becky stepped back. This was getting a little freaky.

"Nothing sinister," Elsa said. "Radiance has been growing and I'm thinking of hiring a part-time assistant."

"It would be perfect." Rosa beamed and her brown eyes glowed as she poured her attention on Becky. "I know how much you did at the church. Since you left, I've heard rumbles about the youth group and the after-church refreshments and the music. I don't think anyone noticed how much you did. You made it seem as if everyone else was doing all the work."

Becky's jaw dropped and she stared at Rosa. Giving a shrug that lifted her breasts, Rosa said, "I do the same thing at the restaurant. I handle everyone. From chefs to busboys to the wait staff. But all everyone sees me do is seat customers and chat when I have time. Always smiling while the waiters and the cooks and my husband appear to do the *real* work."

Becky knew her mouth was gaping. She'd never thought about it, but even she had thought Rosa's chef husband was the reason behind the restaurant's success.

Rosa sniffed. "As if anyone could replace me. I do the food ordering, the scheduling, I help prep in the kitchen, I make the desserts...and so much more."

"You're Wonder Woman," Becky said.

Elsa and Rosa laughed. Rosa swept her arms to encompass the three of them. "We're all Wonder Women."

Becky didn't feel like Wonder Woman. She felt more like a woman in survival mode. A woman who might've made a huge mistake the night before.

Though at the time, it felt pretty wonderful...

She tore her attention back to Elsa. "I need a full-time job. And I'm not staying in Miracle. I can't. As soon as I find a job, I'm leaving."

"Of course you want to leave," Elsa said.

Despite Elsa's words, Becky had the feeling the other woman didn't think this discussion was over.

"Even if I stayed, I couldn't do this. It would be too much of a..." She hesitated. Jim didn't deserve her loyalty. And though the majority of the church members hadn't supported her, she couldn't do this to them. "A betrayal."

Elsa nodded. "I understand."

"But I'm happy to have gotten to know you better," Becky said, unable to stop staring at Elsa. She felt a pull toward the older woman. It almost felt as if they'd met before Elsa drove into town and decided to stay. But it was probably just that Elsa comforted her when she was sick.

"I'd better get back to the restaurant," Rosa said. "Sorry to have taken you on this wild goose chase. It wasn't Elsa's fault. She said you wouldn't do it. I should've listened to her." She shot Elsa a grin. "Elsa is always right."

Elsa's laugh was like silvery bells in an old Christmas movie. "No one is always right. Part of the pleasure of being a human being is trying new options." Smiling with her eyes as well as her mouth, Elsa radiated understanding. "And even if failure was pre-ordained, it's better to try than never try."

Becky murmured her agreement and started to turn away. At the last instant, she turned back.

She knew why Elsa seemed familiar. She remembered!

"This is really going to sound odd, but do I know you? Not recently. From a long time ago? Decades ago, when I was a child. You seem so familiar."

Elsa stilled. If Becky hadn't been staring at her with such intensity, she would have missed the widening of her eyes, the rounding of her mouth. It lasted only an instant. Then Elsa laughed softly and shook her head.

"If I knew you, it was in another life." She glided forward, almost as if she didn't use her feet. As if a low-hanging cloud carried her. She gave Becky a short but strong hug. Nothing ethereal about that.

"I'm so glad we had this talk." Elsa pulled back. "I'll see you again."

Becky nodded, walking backward, then turned and hurried out of the light-filled structure. Her heart beat so fast inside her chest that it felt like butterfly wings.

Another person had lied to her.

SIXTEEN

Puppies stink. Good thing they were cute, Becky thought as she cleaned up and changed the blanket, then tossed the smelly cover in the washing machine. If only her life could be cleaned as easily. She put Goldie out then headed into the puppy room and picked up the black puppy.

Of all the puppies, this was the one who came to her. Who wanted her to hold him.

A small, familiar ache throbbed inside her. But she couldn't listen to the ache.

"I can't keep you." She looked into his big brown eyes that stared brightly back at her. "I'll be working and not home for hours. I'd have to put you in doggy day care, and I don't know if I could afford that. And it wouldn't be fair to you."

Maybe it wouldn't be fair to children, either; perhaps it was just as well she didn't have any.

The thoughts made her stomach tighten and roil. Everything within her rejected them. If she had children, she would work it out. Just as millions of other women did.

The puppy licked Becky's chin and tried to reach her mouth. She tilted her head back, her chin up, taking her lips out of tongue range. The room felt gloomy, reflecting her emotions. During the drive back to Wegner's, the sky had darkened. The DJ on the radio had warned the station's listeners that a storm was heading their way.

Glancing outside the puppy room window, she couldn't blame all her emotions on the weather. She'd felt odd since she left the Church of Radiance.

A recollection had come to her inside the church. More dreamlike than real, but she remembered an odd half-memory of awakening when she was a child. Perhaps when she was seven or younger. A woman stood in her bedroom, haloed by light streaming in from the hallway. Something about that magical moment had imprinted itself in Becky's memory.

Now it came to Becky that when Elsa had been younger, she must have looked like the woman in her bedroom.

Becky had thought she was a tooth fairy, but she hadn't lost a tooth.

When she told her parents the next day, they said she must have dreamed it.

The woman had seemed so real. But Becky had put her out of her mind, thinking her parents wouldn't lie to her.

This was before her mother was sick and Becky learned that adults lied when they promised they'd get better. Trying to convince themselves as much as her. Becky had done it herself. Hoping that if they said it with enough certainty and passion, it would happen.

But if it had been Elsa, why didn't Elsa say so?

The phone rang, and Becky put down the puppy then climbed over the barrier. In the kitchen, she picked up the phone without looking at the display number. Derek, she thought. But it was Trey, his voice deep and husky.

Her heart pounded and her body tingled – and her body *never* tingled. Well, not unless she was about to eat a slice of Rosa's tiramisu cheesecake.

That made sense in a strange way. Trey definitely qualified as man candy.

Then she remembered Derek and last night, and she immediately felt guilty that she was interested in Trey. Stupid, because she hadn't made any promises to Derek. Nor had he asked for any. If he had, she would've said 'no.'

She could hear Sarah's voice in her mind, saying, 'Hump and dump.'

Darn Sarah. She was right. But after fifteen years of marriage to a man who'd never made her tingle, Becky wasn't going to grab onto the first guy who looked at her and expect him to be her happy-ever-after.

She would make her own happy-ever-after.

"I'll be in your neighborhood later today," Trey said, his words stopping the thoughts whirling through her brain. "Will you be there?"

"I should be." Her pounding heartbeat didn't slow. "Did you want to buy something else from Marsh?"

"Not unless he has something he wants me to check out. I'd like to take you to dinner."

She bit back the surprised words, 'You do!' She felt like a teenager with the cool guy asking her out.

It's just dinner, she told herself. Just dinner.

And then she thought of Derek again. He'd just taken her to dinner last night. And look what happened there.

She put her free hand on her forehead. Life was complicated.

"Sure," she said slowly. She remembered Elsa's words and decided part of her new life would be taking chances.

Trey asked if she liked Thai food. She said yes. Jim was a meat and potatoes kind of guy – like her dad and his dad were before he died.

But now she could eat anything she wanted, any time she wanted.

Trey said there was a Thai place in Tomahawk, and she recalled seeing it, not far from the restaurant where she'd eaten with Derek last night.

"No need to pick me up," she said. "I can drive down and meet you there."

"I'll pick you up." His voice was firm.

Though she'd made up her mind that no man was going to tell her what to do, her mouth curved in a silly smile.

A man picked a woman up when he was pretty sure he wanted more than a dinner companion.

"Is five-thirty good?" he asked.

"Yes." Her voice was husky, and she called herself an idiot as she said good-bye.

She hung up, keeping her hand on the phone. She was becoming a slut. And she didn't care. She was happy because he'd asked her out. As for Derek, she was happy she'd been with him last night, too.

Why shouldn't she have both? She could call it her own reality show: *Sex and the Village*.

She put her hands over her mouth, then her ears and then her eyes, as if she were the three monkeys bundled in one package. In her mind she again heard Sarah say, 'Hump and dump.'

Outside Goldie barked and rain started to pour down, pounding against the siding. She dropped her hands from her face and hurried to let Goldie in, her heart hammering, her step light.

She'd been good for so long – her whole life, it seemed. Maybe it was her turn to be a little...bad.

She reached the back door. As she opened it, thunder roared, the ground shook and lightning flashed across the sky.

SEVENTEEN

When the phone rang again, Becky's heart beat like an electric tambourine out of control. She wiped down Goldie with a towel by the back door but had an odd feeling that something was wrong. She let go of Goldie and dived for the phone on the counter.

Another boom thundered outside as she said, "Hello?" Goldie stopped a foot away from Becky, then shook her entire body, her skin and wet fur flapping. Water splattered Becky and she hunched sideways, leaning away from Goldie. The phone crackled as she wiped drops off her cheek and called, "Hello, hello!"

"I'm here," Sarah said. "Wow, it's coming down like bats and hogs."

Becky leaned against the counter, her pants too wet to sit on the chair, thanks to Goldie, who looked at her as if she deserved a treat for soaking her. After all, hadn't she saved Becky from taking another shower? "Idiot."

"Are you calling me an idiot?"

"Goldie. She just soaked me."

"Good on you. I have conversations with her all the time. Goldie's a great listener. Hey, I just called to say I'm on my way home."

"Drive carefully."

"I always drive carefully."

"You drive too fast."

"You drive too slow. I'm almost in town. I already shopped in Medford, but I forgot the evaporated milk for the puppy formula. I'll stop off at Wegner's. Want anything?"

"An Ouija board. Maybe it will give me a glimpse into the future."

"You don't need that. I can tell you. Now that you've gotten rid of Mr. Righteous, it will be good times ahead."

Another blast of thunder boomed and static came over the phone. Then nothing. "Sarah? Sarah?"

Sarah didn't answer. The phone was dead. Becky thought of trying to call Sarah back, but Sarah was driving and it was pouring out. Becky's mom used to say 'The sky is crying,' and Becky used to believe that the sky was sad.

Today's sky didn't sound sad. It sounded angry.

A whine came from Goldie. She stood outside the puppy room, the barrier blocking her from getting back to her puppies. Becky hurried over and let her in.

The puppies immediately surged forward, tripping over each other to get to Goldie. Each puppy rushed to be first.

Becky watched them for a few moments, with an ache in her chest. An ache because she still missed her mom; an ache because she might never be one. Finally she turned away and trudged to the table to look at the want ads.

She'd always had sympathy for any of the parishioners who were job hunting. But at least most of them had a career and experience. Maybe Rosa knew a restaurant owner in Tomahawk or Merrill and would call the owner for her. Ask them to give her a chance. Something to help with the everyday bills while she earned her degree.

Another blast of thunder and flash of lightning made her jump and gasp. Her heartbeat thundered along with the whimpers coming from the dining room. She looked at the rain lashing the kitchen window, then hurried to the office to unplug the old computer, not wanting it to be fried by a lightning surge.

Sarah should be home soon. At least Marsh wasn't driving in this. He was still in Minnesota where it was supposed to be sunny and warm today. When he got home, he'd probably tease them about his tropical vacation while they were stuck in a cold rain.

She grabbed a throw and hurried to the puppy room to clean up. She could look at the newspaper ads later.

Maybe before then, something else would come up.

***

Sometime during the next twenty minutes, the sky turned nearly black and sheets of rain gusted against the house. Becky started to think of biblical storms, and she worried about Sarah. Her nerves vibrated, on alert, and she listened for sirens. A couple of the puppies whimpered, but most slept snuggled close to Goldie.

She wished she could, too, but she kept thinking of the tornadoes that had ravaged two Wisconsin towns last year, killing a family that lived in a trailer park.

Finally the sky lightened and the gusts lessened. The thunder and the lightning moved to the east, not as loud or as frightening. Her nerves shot, Becky got up to fetch her go-to tranquilizer. Dark chocolate. Along the way to the bedroom, she checked Goldie and the puppies, and Goldie gave her a look that said she hadn't been scared.

"Ha!" Becky said. "I bet you were."

Goldie opened her mouth in a doggy grin, then her ears perked and her gaze fixed toward the road. She was up on her feet, barking happily before Becky had time to turn around.

"Mommy's home." Becky rushed to put her jacket on. "Everything's all right. I don't know why I was so worried."

Way too worried. As if something were about to go horribly wrong. Which was odd in so many ways. She'd never been a catastrophe junkie, but now it felt as if she were waiting for the next hammer to strike her on the head.

She reached the back door as Sarah hurried toward her, holding bags of groceries to her chest, raindrops coming down steadily on her blond hair.

"Any more?" Becky held the door open wide.

"Two more." Sarah barreled indoors.

By the time Becky made it back inside with the last two bags, the rain had lightened already. Yet the nervous feeling, like a bee buzzing along her nerve endings, wouldn't go away.

"I was worried about you," she said.

"I was a bit worried, too. That wind was wicked. The thunder sounded like explosions. I'm glad Marsh is safe in Minnesota."

"Yeah," Becky said, but she heard the uncertainty in her voice. The buzzing had transferred from her nerves to her chest, getting worse.

She put the grapes in the fridge and was picking up the half-gallon of milk when the phone rang. Feeling cold from the inside out, Becky turned to stare at it.

At the same instant, the front doorbell rang.

Sarah leaned toward the phone, looking at the Caller ID. "It's a 218 area code. I think that's Minnesota. Maybe it's Marsh. I hope nothing's wrong with his phone. He'd be lost without all his contacts."

A ball of tension gathered in Becky's chest as Sarah lifted the phone, saying, "Would you get the door?"

EIGHTEEN

"Hi, honey," Sarah said in the kitchen, her voice sounding far away as Becky looked at her father. Only a screen door and a few inches of air were between them, and she wondered if she should close the door on him.

Instead she just stared.

It all felt unreal. As if she were watching his face on a movie screen. As if she were hearing Sarah speak on her car stereo. As if the Village of Miracle and her life were figments in a crazy person's imagination.

That meant she was the crazy person. Because who else would imagine her non-exciting life?

Though last night had been pretty hot.

"Aren't you inviting me in?" Carl asked.

A bright comeback came to her mind, which proved she wasn't her normal self. She never thought of snappy comebacks unless it was at an inappropriate time. Like in church when Jim was giving his lesson.

Then she remembered she didn't have to be appropriate anymore.

The thought freed her. It whisked away the numbness and cleared the shadows hanging over her. At the same instant, the patters of rain stopped, the clouds broke up and sunlight streamed down.

"Well?" her father demanded. He held himself upright, giving off his I'm-the-man-in-charge vibe. Not yet aware that no man was in charge of her anymore.

"Why should I?" she asked.

"Because I'm your father." His eyes flickered. "It hurts me to be estranged from my daughters."

"We didn't turn our backs on you. You turned yours on us." As she said the words, she realized that she'd nurtured a tiny hope that he'd come here because he was sorry for the words he'd said the last time she'd seen him.

Sorry that he had been angry at her instead of Jim.

Sorry that he cheated on her mother.

And really sorry that he slapped her.

"I thought you'd listen to reason," he said.

"Your reason isn't reasonable to me." She remained standing inside the house, looking at him through the screen. Though he stood on the concrete stoop, about six inches lower than the entrance, she was still a couple of inches shorter than him. But for once it *felt* as if they were on equal terms. For once, she wasn't trying to please him.

"I was hoping you'd come to your senses and go back to Jim," he said.

"He was cheating on me, Dad." She heard the thickening of her voice. The throb of anger.

He frowned. "People make mistakes."

"I filed for divorce. I don't love Jim. I don't trust him. I don't even like him anymore." She reached for the wooden door behind her. Ready to step aside and slam it shut. "There's nothing you can do to change my mind."

"Go back to him and I'll give you a hundred thousand dollars."

"Really? You're trying to buy my obedience?" She stepped back, feeling a vein throb in her neck. "Good-bye, Dad."

"Wait!"

"Too late." She started to close the door, and he jerked the screen door open and stuck the toe of his leather shoe in the jamb to stop the door.

"I just want you to listen to me," he said.

Her hand gripped the round door handle. "How many times did I want you to listen to me and you didn't?"

"I'm listening now."

"It's too late."

"I don't believe that. It's never too late." The color in his face was elevated and she could hear the harshness of his breaths. She still wanted to close the door, but seeing him so shaken up disturbed her.

"Go on, but it had better be good."

"I know where you were this morning. I know you were at that place that calls itself a church."

Her eyebrows shot up. It was lousy luck that he'd seen her drive up with Rosa. But she wasn't going to discuss this with him.

"You were looking for a job, weren't you?" he demanded. "I know you bought the *Tomahawk Leader News.*"

She stared blankly at him but her mind was whirling. Linda Wegner must have called him the instant she stepped out of their store. Easy for Carl to guess she was looking for a job or an apartment in Tomahawk. Probably Linda had pressed her face to the window as she'd gotten into Rosa's car and watched them drive in the direction of her father's home.

"I don't want you to work there," he said.

"I don't care what you want." She heard footsteps behind her. Sarah.

"I'll offer you a better job."

She laughed, hearing the hollow sound. "Don't be ridiculous."

Anger flashed across his face. "I should've gotten rid of her long before this."

Sarah made a surprised sound and stepped to Becky's side. "Are you talking about me?"

Carl's ruddy complexion paled. "Of course not."

"It's Elsa." Becky half turned to Sarah. "Elsa Hahn. I talked to her about a job today."

Sarah stared at their father, her head slightly forward like a curious cat. She frowned and her lips parted, her tongue touching her upper lip...as if trying to make sense of what he'd said.

"Get rid of her? You mean kill her?"

"No!" He stepped back, removing his foot from the front entrance. "I'll get rid of her legally. That's not a real church. It's not affiliated with any religion. They don't even worship Jesus."

Becky's anger spiked again, along with a river of sorrow. "It's too bad she's not as virtuous as you." Even as she said it, she knew it was a waste of breath. He didn't realize how pompous he sounded.

"Dad," Sarah said, "you're a piece of work."

His face flushed. "Don't you—"

With a surge of disgust, Becky slammed the door shut.

"No!" he howled from the other side of the door.

Becky turned, her back to the door, adding another barrier in case he tried to break it down.

"I wish Marsh were home," Sarah said, and her strained expression reflected the horror and anger and longing that churned inside Becky.

"You got the good one with Marsh. All these years I thought I was the lucky one, but you were." Becky's voice cracked, and she stopped to get herself together.

"I can't imagine life without him." Sarah smiled but there was no joy in it.

Becky shuddered. There was no joy in her, either. Not after that talk with their father. She'd always known what he was like. She just hadn't wanted to acknowledge it.

The pounding began on the other side of the door. Becky flinched and Goldie barked. Becky heard small cries and at first thought they came from the puppies. But looking at Sarah's horrified face, she realized they came from her own throat.

Sarah held out her arms. "Oh, Becky."

Becky fell into them. They held each other tight as tears finally leaked from Becky's eyes. Not for the end of her marriage, or even because of all the years she'd let her father rule her life. She cried because this must've been how Sarah had felt when she married Marsh. Becky's eyes were now open to the manipulation. To their father's need to control. And Becky realized that when it happened to Sarah, she hadn't been there to comfort her sister.

"I'm sorry," she said, "I'm sorry."

"You did the best you could," Sarah said.

Becky didn't think they were talking about the same thing, but the tears stopped and so did the pounding. Her father had given up...for now.

But not, she knew, for forever.

NINETEEN

By the time Cody came home from school, Becky and Sarah had picked up the branches on the lawn that the wind gusts had blown off. Too bad the damage from the biggest wind gust – Becky's father – wasn't as easy to gather and burn.

But Cody's grin and happy wave went a big way toward shrinking the clump of unhappiness in Becky's chest. He hugged his mom then her. His thin arms wrapped around her waist for just one second, but Becky closed her eyes and imprinted it in her heart. Though she'd like to, she didn't cling to him. She wasn't going to be that kind of aunt. That kind of person.

Cody let go and darted to the fridge, eager to chug down a glass of milk before going to see the puppies. And he had another purpose. Between gulps, standing in front of the sink, he demanded for at least the hundredth time that Sarah keep the black one, because he wanted a dog of his own.

Sarah told him that the kitten slept with him and would be jealous of the puppy, but he said there was room in his bed for all three of them. Sarah laughed and told him three in a bed were too many.

Becky watched them, not really a part of it, but feeling residues of their closeness circling out to touch her. The ache started in her chest again. A good ache this time, because she knew she still could have and *would* have something like this. Somehow, some way, she would have this in her life.

Cody darted into the puppy room as Becky's cell trilled. She grabbed it from the counter and saw Derek's name. Her gaze went to the clock. Trey wasn't coming for another hour and a half. The phone trilled again.

"Trey?" Sarah asked.

"Derek."

"Ah." Sarah grinned.

Becky stuck her tongue out as she put the phone to her ear.

They talked about the weather and he told her that electrical storms affected Elaine physically. Elaine thought her increased pain had something to do with the atmosphere, but her doctor told her that she was imagining it and her pain must be mental.

"She needs a new doctor," Becky said.

"He's the only one around who specializes in this."

Becky didn't say anything, though a hundred thoughts came to her. This wasn't her road; she wasn't here to fix him and Elaine. Derek was a smart man. He knew he had alternatives. And just because she'd had hot sex with him didn't mean he'd become perfect.

The kitten that Sarah had adopted curled around Becky's ankles. Becky bent forward and scooped it up, then she sat and plopped the kitten gently on her lap. It immediately began to purr and knead with its sharp little claws.

Even kittens weren't perfect, though this one was close.

"I should research and find someplace that will help her." The words sounded as if they were dragged out of Derek by her silence. "Maybe the Mayo Clinic."

"Good idea."

"What are you doing tonight?" he asked.

She had an 'oh shit' moment. The kitten meowed a complaint, obviously responding to her tension. She reached to pet it, but it jumped off, leaving her lap empty. She sat up straight and crossed her legs tightly. She felt as if she were at an interview. "I'm going out to dinner."

"With Sarah's family?"

"No." She took a deep breath. Too many people had lied to her, and she wasn't going to do that to Derek. Even if she did, she'd probably get caught. Someone would see her driving out of town with Trey. "I'm going out with someone I knew from high school."

"Someone in Miracle?"

"He's from Tomahawk." The words came out, and it was as if flood banks crumbled and she vomited out more words. "You probably don't know him. He lived in California for a while, but now he's back. He's a picker like Marsh. He specializes in old motorcycles and cars."

"Oh."

There was a silence, and she clamped her lips together to keep her mouth from running again, like a computer that wouldn't shut down. As if her own brain fired up, she remembered Derek was at the board meeting when Earl talked about selling the old Chevy dump truck to Trey.

A hand landed on Becky's shoulder, and she jumped. Her clamped lips kept her from squeaking. She looked up at Sarah's sympathetic gaze.

Still Derek? Sarah mouthed.

Becky made a face and nodded, realizing her head was shrinking into her neck like a turtle trying to go into its shell.

Sarah patted her shoulder and mouthed *Good luck*.

"What about tomorrow?" he asked. "Would you like to go out for dinner tomorrow?"

"Um, I think I should stay home with Sarah tomorrow."

He didn't reply right away, and she bit her lower lip. She thought of things she could say about why Sarah needed her. A cleaning project. Helping to paint an old dresser. Even something to do with sewing, though everyone in the village probably knew she was the world's worst sewer and he'd know she was lying.

"I'll call you, then," he said.

She grimaced and said good-bye, then put the phone down and turned to Sarah. "That was awful."

"I'm so glad I'm not single. Dating sucks."

Becky wrinkled her nose. "Sometimes being married sucks worse."

"True. Even when you love 'em. C'mon, let's get you ready. A quick shower first. You're covered with bits of leaves and puppy hair." Sarah sniffed and made a face. "And you smell like puppy pee."

"Are you sure that's not an aphrodisiac?"

Sarah wagged her finger. "No joking. Dating is serious business."

Becky got off the chair and started toward the bathroom. "I thought it was supposed to be fun."

"Are you kidding?" Sarah surged past her, purpose in every step. "Dating is a form of war. You need all the artillery you can find."

"What if I'm just on reconnaissance?"

Sarah turned around. "You can't count on that. You never know when it will turn into the real thing and you'll need the heavy weapons."

Becky groaned and put her hand on her head, her fingertips rubbing her scalp, her hair flying over her hands. "Why do we do this?"

"Did you miss the biology class in high school? Now, go clean up. Change into something that doesn't smell like dog pee and make you look like you're about to teach Sunday school. You got curves, woman. Show them off!"

"You're scaring me."

"Because I'm normal. I know old ladies who dress sexier than you." Sarah shot her hands in the air. "Have fun for a change. Go a little wild. Have an affair with two men. After being the perfect minister's wife for so long, you deserve a couple flings."

"You're insane. I'm going for that shower now before you get worse."

She loped up the stairs, but distance didn't stop the 'couple of flings' from running through her mind. The word *fling* sounded like fun. As if she could fling off her inhibitions. Fling off her morals. Fling off her fear. Like a child with a ball. Just pick it up and throw.

But then she thought of Derek...and her heart warmed a little and she smiled. She hadn't done a bad thing last night. It had been good for her, and she knew it had been good for him, too.

And then she thought of Trey...and her body warmed hotter and she could've sworn her vagina smiled.

This...predicament... Could be her body saying this might be her last chance to have the thing she really wanted?

She put her hand over her stomach...over her empty womb.

A sudden stab of sorrow hit her and she bent forward. Her breaths rasped as she stared at the carpeted floor and tried to suck in deeper breaths. Tried to push the sorrow away, as if it were a physical thing.

Finally the sadness eased. She straightened, and her pounding heart slowed and her breaths returned to normal. She went on to the bathroom to take her shower. Because that's what people did – they adjusted and went on with their lives. Hoped for the best...

And feared the worst.

TWENTY

"Save leftovers for me," Marsh was saying as Becky went down the stairs to see if Sarah would give a nod of approval for a black top and pants. "I'm making good time. If I don't run into traffic problems, I'll be home after seven, so don't hold dinner for me. If I'm not home before Cody goes to bed, give him a hug and a kiss for me. Love ya, babe."

Coming around the corner into the kitchen, Becky heard Marsh repeat the message. Sarah was leaning over the counter, her back to Becky, listening to Marsh's voice on the answering machine.

At the kitchen entrance, Becky stopped in mid step and held her hands over her mouth as emotion swelled up inside her. Becky waited 'till the message stopped for the second time, then moved forward, clearing her throat. Her chest and throat felt tight. In that moment, witnessing the kind of love she'd always wanted, she was happy and at the same time sad.

Happy for Sarah. Sad for herself. She'd spent too many years pitying Sarah when she was the one whose veneer of happiness was so thin and so fake that she was surprised it took this long to crack into tiny pieces.

"Hey," she said, and Sarah snapped around.

"Hey, back at ya. You caught me being a dork." She made a face. "Marsh called while I was walking Cody across the street. You must've been in the shower. Cody's having a sleepover with Kenny tonight."

"Too bad Marsh won't be home for dinner. Maybe you'll get lucky when he gets home."

"I plan on getting very lucky." Sarah grinned, then her gaze raked Becky up and down. "Are you wearing that?"

Becky immediately felt defensive, and she sucked in her belly. Then let it out. Too late to fool Sarah on that. "I was." She could hear the doubt in her voice. "What do you think?"

"All black, huh?"

"I thought of draping a scarf around my neck, but that looks matronly on me."

"Never do that. You don't want to take attention away from your moneymaker."

"My *what*?"

"Come on, you know. You got the breasts." Sarah gestured at Becky's chest then slapped her own butt. "And I got the booty."

"My booty is perfectly rounded and perfectly fine."

"We all have our delusions." Sarah's eyes narrowed. "You need some color. Do you have any jewelry that isn't silver or gold?"

"Jim liked silver and gold. He thought they were classy." Becky's cheeks heated. How did she let Jim's tastes dictate the jewelry and clothes that she wore?

"Typical. He had a classy wife and a slutty mistress."

Becky smiled weakly. She wasn't quite at the stage where she could make jokes about Jim and Diana. In her mind, her jokes all tended to end in Jim getting run over by a truck or something out of a *Road Runner* cartoon.

She didn't *really* want him dead. But the animated image made her smile.

"Classy never worked for me anyway," she said.

"Classy is boring. Right now you look like a biker chick."

Becky looked down at herself. She wasn't wearing boots, but otherwise... "I could change. I have a yellow top—"

"Are you nuts? The biker chick look is hot."

"Right. It's on all the high fashion runways."

"Just the smart ones."

Becky laughed and Sarah stepped away from the counter. "I'll get the turquoise necklace Marsh gave me for our anniversary."

"I don't want to wear your anniversary present."

"Don't be silly. And with you and Cody out of the house tonight, Marsh is going to be putty in my hands." Heading out of the kitchen, she waggled her fingers above her head.

Becky put her hands over her eyes. "Don't leave me with that image."

Sarah cackled like the Wicked Witch of the West. "Worry about what you're going to put in your hands," she called, out of Becky's sight. Then her steps pounded up the stairs to her bedroom.

Becky checked the clock above the sink, and excitement built up inside her. It was a date, she told herself. *Just a date.*

And Trey was just a man.

A really hot one. She groaned and put her head in her hands. She was acting like a schoolgirl again. When was she going to get over this? It was all new and scary – and happening faster than she'd thought. Like traveling on a jet plane when she was used to driving thirty-five miles-per-hour in her Chevy Camaro.

Sarah rattled down the steps a few minutes later and pounded into the kitchen, as usual, living life at top speed and with a whole heart.

She wouldn't be afraid of being on a jet plane.

"Here's the..." Sarah stared at her, her forehead puckering. "What's the matter?"

"I was just wondering whether I was to blame for what happened." She gestured toward the direction of her former home.

"No."

"I can't blame it all on Jim. My nature is to be...reserved. I was like an—"

"You didn't have a chance." Sarah bit out the words, her tone severe. "You were Daddy's good little girl, and then you became Jim's good little wife. You were practically trained from birth to be someone's good little wife."

"But—"

"Don't agonize over this. Thinking you might be responsible for the carnage is one of the early stages of grief. The pain and guilt part. You should be over it."

"The stages aren't always in sequence," Becky said, feeling as if she were on automatic. She knew the stages of grief. When Jim wasn't available, parishioners had come to her with their problems. She'd counseled them and consoled them. "Sometimes we bounce around."

"Well, bounce out of it." Sarah put her hands on her hips and gave Becky the same fierce stare she aimed at Cody when he didn't want to go to bed on time. "Now, get over here and let me put on the necklace."

Becky trotted over to Sarah, feeling like the little sister instead of the big one. Once the necklace was on, she looked in the bathroom mirror and agreed that the turquoise necklace and matching earrings were the perfect touch.

The sound of a truck rolling to a stop came in through the open front windows. "It's either your guy or mine," Sarah said. "Since my guy's traveling from another state, I'm guessing it's yours."

"He's not mine."

"Not yet." Sarah grinned then hurried toward the front room before Becky could think of a comeback. Not that she could have even with more time. Her tongue seemed to have blown up, taking more room in her mouth than it should.

Oh God, she was dating...for the first time since she and Jim became a couple in high school. Derek didn't count because she hadn't thought it was a date. She'd told herself she was going to dinner with a friend. She'd even taken money along to pay for her half of the dinner, making sure she had extra one-dollar bills, in case it wasn't a free meal from Derek's website client.

Her hands grew sweaty. Following Sarah, she wiped her palms on the sides of the pants and hoped they didn't leave damp spots. At the front window, Sarah looked around at her with a big clown smile.

"It's your guy, big sister."

"Keep saying that and I'm going to hit you."

"Oooh, I'm so scared." Looking back at the street, she added, "His cab is only a two-seater."

"There're just the two of us." Becky stood next to Sarah. With a front window view, she watched Trey stride around the front of his truck to the sidewalk. He wore black jeans and a blue long-sleeved shirt tucked into his belted pants. He looked yummy in a dark chocolate way – sweet with a bite.

"You don't get what that means," Sarah said.

Becky was glad to transfer her attention back to Sarah. "Of course, I know what you mean. That we can't have sex in the backseat."

"Exactly. But you know what the storage part of the truck is?"

Becky shook her head.

Sarah's smile widened, and Becky's dread deepened. "A bed. They call it a bed."

"I thought that was just for pickups."

"Call it what you want, but I have the feeling you're in for an interesting evening."

Becky turned back to the window. Trey headed for the front door, striding up the sidewalk. Watching him, Becky felt her legs wobble and her heart beat faster. He glanced at the window and nodded at her and Sarah.

Her stomach twisted. She hadn't known he could see her, otherwise she would've been less obvious.

Sarah didn't turn from the window. "Looks like he's eager to see you."

Becky's hands grew suddenly cold. She had a weird feeling about this evening.

The bell rang. Goldie barked. The puppies whimpered. The kitten disappeared.

Sarah grinned at Becky. "Go get 'im, girl."

Becky crossed the three steps to the door, feeling cold on the outside and hot inside.

Life was moving fast for a woman who drove the speed limit.

She needed to learn to run faster. Starting tonight.

TWENTY-ONE

Becky felt oddly calm talking to Trey as they ate at the Thai restaurant in Tomahawk. There were no unexplained twinkles of lights. No weird feelings. If her laughter had a nervous edge, if she fluffed up her hair like a teenager and if her skin had goose bumps, it was probably the same thing that happened to Eve when she first met Adam.

A few times they made eye contact with each other. Once his foot brushed her ankle. She was talking and her voice faltered. He smiled as if he knew he'd affected her.

When she tried to finish her sentence, she couldn't remember what she'd been saying. All she could think of was the way his brown eyes warmed, as if there were a fire smoldering inside him.

Matching the blaze that was heating up inside her.

He picked up the conversation, and she remembered then that they'd been talking about favorite desserts. Usually a safe topic. But his husky voice wasn't safe. And the way he looked at her – as if she were a triple chocolate fudge cake and he was a chocoholic and couldn't wait to dig in – made her want to melt like butter in the hot sun.

She put her fork down. Not hungry for food anymore. Instead of picking up her tea, she took a slug of ice water. She needed cooling.

The waitress came and asked if they wanted dessert. Becky shook her head and asked the waitress to box her leftover seafood curry. As soon as she requested it, she wondered if that wasn't a cool thing to do on a date. Then she realized no one had ever thought she was cool, and it was too late to worry about that now.

While the waitress was wrapping her leftovers, she hurried to the bathroom. Inside the empty one-stall bathroom, she speed-dialed Sarah. "I feel like I have a fever," she said.

Sarah laughed. "I still get that fever with Marsh."

Becky looked at herself in the mirror. Her face glowed. She put her hand to her cheek and felt the heat of her skin. "I don't know what to do."

"Then Jim must've been a really bad lover."

"Or I was."

"Jim was a selfish one," Sarah said, her tone firm. "Him and his blow jobs."

Becky laughed and heard the nervousness in her voice. "I'd better go. This is not what I'm used to."

"Because it's not boring? Or predictable? Or safe?"

"I think Trey is safe."

"No man is safe when they're in heat."

"It's the female who goes into heat."

"Oh, sweetie." Sarah's voice was sympathetic. "If you don't know men go into heat, too, Jim really was a lousy lover."

The color in Becky's cheeks deepened, and she turned away from her reflection.

"I'm going."

"If you don't come home tonight, I'll understand," Sarah said.

"I'll be home." Becky made her tone positive. She was not going to have sex with a man, especially a different man, for the second night in a row. "I'm bringing back leftovers. You can have mine."

"Can you stop off and bring me milk? I tried to call Marsh, and he's not answering."

"Maybe he's in a dead zone." As Becky said it, a sudden chill ran down her spine. As if the air from the far north gusted over her. "I'll get the milk. See you soon."

When she returned to the table, she felt less flustered than when she left. She saw her bag of leftovers ready for her and money was already on a small black tray. On a white plate were two fortune cookies.

She avoided looking at the money, uncertain whether she should have offered to pay. Tonight, she was questioning everything. Dating was...odd. One minute it was exciting. The next...it was horrible. She couldn't remember that from her teenage years. Just a crushing shyness that she tried to hide with a smile.

"I talked to Sarah," she said. "Do you mind stopping off at the Quick Mart on the way home so I can buy milk?"

"No problem. She forget to ask Marsh?"

"Can't reach him. He's not home yet."

He took a slug of his Chinese beer from the bottle. "He probably miscalculated the time. Friday traffic's busier than normal. People get their paychecks. Grocery shop. Go out for fish fry."

"Stop off at the bar..." she added, eyeing the cookies.

"Have one." He gestured at the plate. "I was waiting for you to choose first."

Warmth bubbled up inside her. It was a small thing. But for a long time she'd missed the small things. She took one and he took the other. When she read her fortune, she groaned.

"It says 'You live only once, but if you do it right, once is enough.'" She lifted her head. "I'm not even sure what that means."

He laughed. "I bet it's a quote from someone famous and dead. They lift it, then they don't have to pay anyone when they use it. Mine is worse. 'The more you are given, the more you should repay.'"

"That is awful. I could make up better fortunes. How about 'You will be wealthy and happy beyond your wildest dreams'?"

"I'm already wealthy and happy beyond my wildest dreams."

"Do you tell that to all the women you're dating?"

One side of his mouth kicked up. "Maybe. But I wouldn't admit that to you."

"Here's another one," she said. "'A cute black puppy will soon be with you.'"

He laughed. "Not me. No buyers yet?"

"No, and he's a darling. If I didn't have to find my own place soon, I'd snap him up in a second."

He shook his head. "Puppies don't suit my lifestyle."

She nodded, even as she thought that neither did a wife. He seemed so...self-contained. A man who liked his job, liked himself, liked other people, liked life. But didn't need anyone special to share it with.

Not that she was a great judge of people. She'd proved that. Even her own father...

"Hey." He reached forward. Touched her hand.

Realizing she was frowning, she immediately put on a smile. From his corrugated forehead, he wasn't buying it.

"You'll find someone who wants the puppy," he said.

"I'm sure he'll find a good home." She wasn't sure of anything, but giving the impression she was moping about a puppy probably wasn't the best way to get asked out again. And she very much liked to go out with Trey again. And even do a few other things with him.

She'd had sex with two men in her life. Not that numbers counted, but her body that had been running hot all night was saying '*This man. I want this man.*'

This was crazy but she wasn't going to deny her feelings. She wasn't going to lie to herself.

She felt like Peter Pumpkin's wife, living in the pumpkin shell. Now she'd broken the shell and was out in a brand new and confusing world.

She didn't know how long she'd want Trey. If she'd want him later. Or tomorrow. Or next year.

Or if he'd want her.

For so long, she'd known every day what the next day would be. Now she knew nothing.

The thought was scary, and at the same time, exhilarating. Anything was possible.

He took a chug of the beer then set it down with a small thud of finality. "Ready to go?"

She stood. More than ready to leave.

He offered his hand and she took it.

TWENTY-TWO

They reached the city limits when a loud boom sounded. Becky sucked in her breath and Trey, who was talking about buying cars for a movie set in the 1950s, stopped in the middle of a word.

"I don't like that," he said.

"Could be fireworks," she said. "Kids goofing off." But her voice wobbled and she clutched her hands on her lap. As if all night she'd been expecting something bad to happen and now it was beginning.

"Nope. I know that sound. More like a bad accident. Not too far up the road."

Becky looked ahead. Traffic was still moving down the two-lane highway, so there wasn't a traffic jam. Tomahawk's population was under four thousand and their rush hour wasn't like a big city's.

A song came on the radio about a fun time tonight, a woman and a man sang. Kind of bluesy. It was perfect for their mood a moment ago.

But that mood had changed in a second. Becky felt tense now, her breaths shallow, though she told herself she was being silly. And Trey felt it, too. He turned down the radio and turned to the local station.

Even if there were an accident, it didn't have anything to do with her.

The speed limit changed, but instead of going faster as the sign indicated, the traffic ahead slowed. The brake lights of the cars in front of them glowed red in the dusky light.

To counter the heavy feeling inside Becky's gut, she told herself to calm down, that it was just fireworks, no matter what Trey had said. After all, the simplest explanations were usually the right ones.

The slowdown could be from a deputy giving someone a ticket. That always made drivers step on the brakes, so they could see if they knew the person being ticketed. Or at least slow down because they were scared they'd be next.

The loud whine of a siren came from town and Becky's breath stuck in her throat. Okay, not a speeding ticket. Someone could have hit a deer, but there had to be damage for an emergency vehicle to be on the way.

"Hope it's not serious," she said. Traffic still rolled forward slowly, though Becky knew whatever happened must be close.

She leaned forward as much as the seatbelt allowed. Trey's truck cab wasn't as high as a semi's, but high enough to see over the roofs of the cars in front of them. Ahead of them, less than a city block, Becky could see a gas station and a highway crossing.

"Looks like someone missed the stop sign," Trey said.

Becky nodded. A van's rear end was partially in the road, its front end was in a ditch. An SUV was stopped crookedly in the middle of the lane, as if it had plowed into the van.

A couple of cars had pulled over to the side. Becky spotted a man and a woman running toward the ditch.

Trey's truck inched along, moving closer. The sirens were louder, catching up to them. Becky knew a little CPR, but she thought the paramedics would make it there before they did.

They were six cars away from the highway crossing when the sheriff's car caught up to them. Trey pulled his truck close to the right of the road to let the sheriff's car pass them. Behind it was an ambulance. Sirens blared from both vehicles. Lights revolved and sent splashes of blue and red into the cab of Marsh's truck.

Becky's anxiety tripled. Someone was hurt. She could see the ditch more clearly, and in the light from the gas station, the streetlight and the headlights, she could see it wasn't a van but a truck.

A yellow truck.

With black writing on the side.

Mangled. The driver's side smashed. Crushed in.

Her breath shuddered.

Her heart stopped.

Marsh's truck was yellow with black writing.

The sirens blared now. Her heart thumped. She slowly turned to Trey. The dusky light sapped the color from his face and he looked like a still picture in black and white – the planes of his face sharp, a cord in his neck sticking out, his mouth a grim line.

He turned to her, and she saw in his ashen complexion and fixed gaze the same fear that twisted inside her.

"Marsh," she whispered. "It's Marsh."

She opened the door. Not thinking. Hardly aware of what she was doing. The horror taking over. Her mind screamed its abhorrence. *No! No! No! This can't be. Marsh is on his way home. Sarah is waiting for him. This isn't real. It can't be happening.*

She spilled out of the truck and stumbled two steps into the ditch before she caught her balance. Then she ran, not caring that she left the truck door hanging open. She just ran. A need driving her...to get to the wreck. To see Marsh. To do something to make him live.

"Wait!" Trey shouted, and she heard his door shut. But she kept running. Not waiting for him or for anyone.

Footsteps pounded on the ground behind her. She passed cars parked on the edge of the road, but they were a blur.

Trey caught up to her. She was aware of him at her side. Keeping pace with her. Not trying to stop her.

All her senses were jumped up. On alert. They passed the last car. Emergency people were already at Marsh's truck. Firefighters ran from a fire truck. Someone grabbed her arm and yelled, "Stop!"

She twisted out of his hold.

"It's her brother-in-law," Trey yelled.

Someone else stepped in front of her. Big and bulky. Wearing a firefighter coat. Arms out. She barreled into him. Tried to knock him out of the way with speed and force.

He staggered back, but his arms came around her and held her to his protective jacket, the shiny material cold and hard on her face. As cold and hard as the ball of fear in her chest.

"You can't go further," he said in a deep, reverberating voice that sounded like God. "You have to let us take care of it."

His arms were like bands around her back, and now that she'd stopped, her legs suddenly lost all strength. She kept herself upright by force of will. A hand splayed on the back of her shoulder, and she felt the warmth through her thin jacket.

Marsh, her mind said. *Marsh.*

"I'll take her," Trey said.

She turned her head to look at him. She wanted to say that no one was going to take her. She could take care of herself. But her horror stopped the words.

This was happening. This was real.

A scream started in her mind. Her scream. Silent and awful.

The firefighter released her and she turned into Trey's arms.

"We have to get out of the way," he said.

She let him half-drag her to the side of the road. Tense voices behind her called out short sentences. The smell of gasoline was thick in the air. Thick and deadly.

Hanging onto Trey, she looked up at him. "Marsh is dead."

"We don't know for sure," he said.

She turned her head toward the truck, her silent scream still there. Not loud but constant and chilling. The desperate need to reach the truck wasn't pulsing inside her anymore but she had to see if there was a chance—

Her breath sucked in.

Above the trucks and the people, a white form rose into the air.

Sparkles surrounded it. Just like she'd seen in the church parking lot. She'd half convinced herself it had been a trick of the sunlight. But there was no sunlight here. There was no trick.

A moan came out of her mouth and at the same time the scream inside her mind abruptly shut off.

The form looked her way. Over the voices of the firefighters and the deputies and the paramedics and the loud beating of Trey's heart under her ear, she heard Marsh's voice. As if he stood right in front of her instead of floating in the sky.

Take care of Sarah. And Cody and the baby. They'll need you.

"I will," she whispered, her voice thick with tears and wonder and sorrow. "I will."

"Will what?" Trey asked.

Marsh nodded and she felt his smile. Then he faded, the sparkles leaving with him. One by one.

She turned her gaze to Trey. "Marsh is dead. Let's go back to the truck."

Trey looked into her eyes, nodded, and they walked back in silence. His hand gripped hers, as if he were keeping her from breaking down. But the gesture wasn't necessary. She was numb. Going forward. One foot in front of the other.

Marsh was dead and she couldn't change that. It was done, and this is what people did after a horrible death. They moved forward.

And the sparkles...

She couldn't think about them now.

The passenger door of the truck still hung open, the truck at a forty-five degree angle, and Trey had to push her up into it, his hands on the seat of her pants. And she didn't care. Didn't worry about the size of her butt. Didn't feel anything sexual.

None of the he-she stuff that had been so important ten minutes ago was important anymore. The only thing that mattered was that Marsh was gone and she would have to tell Sarah.

One lane was closed and they waited about five minutes before they were waved through. Trey put the stereo on, and flute music flowed out. A crow cawed in the background. She slumped back in the seat, too numb to think.

"What's this?" she asked. "Not a radio station."

"A CD. Cherokee music."

She nodded. Of course. Cherokees had known deep grief, too. She could hear it in the music. Profound grief. Crushing grief. And voices from the dead telling them they must go on, even as they wondered why.

TWENTY-THREE

Lights blazed from the windows of Sarah's house. The front porch light, the kitchen, the living room, the downstairs master bath, the light outside the back door. When Becky walked into the kitchen with Trey behind her, Sarah was waiting. Red-eyed. Frantic. Scared. Crying soundlessly even though Cody was across the street on a sleepover. In a toneless voice, she said someone she knew from high school who lived in Tomahawk had driven by the accident site and called her.

Becky held her and let her cry on her shoulder in dry heaves. All the while, Trey stood near. Silent and still. In case they needed him.

"What's happening?" Sarah demanded, her voice croaking. She lifted her head, and her blue eyes were dark, the pupils dilated, the whites bloodshot, the skin around them puffy. "I need to know."

"Of course you do," Becky said. But she couldn't tell her what she knew. Couldn't tell her about Marsh's ghost. Couldn't tell her about what he said to her.

Not now. Sarah wasn't ready to let go of Marsh now.

Later she would tell Sarah. Later the knowledge would comfort her sister.

Sarah was still sobbing when Jerry Ackerman came ten minutes later, wearing his Constable uniform. His face emotionless, he told her about Marsh. That he had died upon impact.

And then his face crumpled and he cried with Sarah.

"Marsh was my friend," he said, his voice thick. "This isn't right. He shouldn't have gone."

Tears ran down Becky's cheeks. She glanced at Trey and saw moisture glisten in his eyes, too. Becky grabbed his hand, squeezed it, then let go and went to look for the tissues.

When she returned with the box, there was a knock on the door. She headed to the living room to answer it, Trey behind her. More tears spurted. Not in sorrow but because it was painfully wonderful to know that someone was there for her.

For years she'd been the support system whenever anyone had needed it. For tonight at least, Trey had appointed himself hers.

Her knight in shining armor.

In the front porch light, she saw Joy from across the street. Becky opened the screen door, feeling raw from the inside out.

"You heard," Becky said.

Joy's gaze flicked up at Becky and then at Trey. Her eyes widened, then her gaze shifted back to Becky and her forehead creased. "I can't believe it. It's horrible."

Becky nodded her agreement, not telling her they'd been at the scene of the accident. Not ready to talk about that.

"It must've been terrible for you to see it," Joy said, toppling Becky's belief that she could keep it a secret. That no one had seen her going a little crazy by the accident site. "I won't wake Cody. I'll send him home after breakfast tomorrow, unless Sarah wants me to keep him longer."

Becky nodded. "Thanks."

"Sarah won't want to talk to me now." Joy thrust out a sandwich-sized baggy. "I had to bring this over. Give it to her."

Becky took it, frowning. At first glance the baggy looked empty. Then she saw the pill in the corner.

"It's a sleeping pill," Joy said.

"Sarah doesn't take sleeping pills. Besides, she's pregnant."

"She does take them, but not often. We have the same GYN, and Dr. Johnson says Ambien doesn't cross the placenta. I borrowed her last one a few weeks ago. I don't know if she renewed the prescription, but I owe her one." Joy gave Becky her mom frown. "Just tell her I gave it to you and she should take it. She needs to sleep tonight. When she wakes up tomorrow, she'll be able to process this better."

Becky nodded. Satisfied, Joy nodded back. "This is really shitty," Joy said, her voice thick. With a sniff, she headed back to her house.

Becky turned to Trey. He stood there. Unmoving. Like a rock. *Her rock*. But also there for Sarah.

Gripping the baggy in her curled fingers, she put her arms around Trey's neck and leaned on him. Her ear against his solid chest picked up the steady thump of his heart. His arms slid around her, his hands splayed on her back with gentle pressure.

They stayed like that for a moment, then she sighed shakily and pulled back. She looked up at him. "Thank you."

He cupped his hand on the side of her head. Didn't say anything. But his brown eyes darkened. With a soft breath and a loosening of his lips, he slid his hand to her shoulder. Then he turned and together they walked into the kitchen where Jerry was telling Sarah if she needed anything, she should call him or his twin brother.

Sarah shook her head, walking backward from him. "I wouldn't bother Rob."

"He needs to be bothered. He's still alive."

"He's healing." More tears spurted from Sarah's reddened eyes, her voice hoarse with pain and sorrow and anger. "He shouldn't have been deployed to Afghanistan a fourth time."

"I'm with you there." Jerry nodded, his eyes sad. "I'm with you."

"It makes me so mad." Sarah's mouth trembled. Her nose was red now, and her eyes filled with tears again.

Becky stepped forward and hugged her. Behind her, Trey and Jerry muttered something, but she was murmuring something to Sarah, not realizing until the back door closed and Trey started to rub her back that she was singing *Angel* by Sarah McLachlan, a song she remembered from the American SPCA commercials. She didn't realize she knew the words until she heard herself.

With that, her voice stumbled into silence. She lifted her head and so did Sarah, tears in her eyes and mouthing *Thank you*.

Becky leaned forward, kissed her on her lips, then drew back. "Joy was at the front door. She's keeping Cody until after breakfast tomorrow morning."

Sarah nodded, silent tears seeping over her lower eyelids and down her cheeks.

"She brought a sleeping pill."

"I don't want—"

"She said it's the same pill she borrowed from you a few weeks ago and won't hurt the baby. Do you want me to call your doctor? I will."

Sarah's gaze flicked down to the pill in Becky's palm. "I see it's the same pill. Becky, I don't—"

"You're taking it."

"But—"

"You're taking it."

"You won't give up, will you?"

"Never."

"You always did think you knew better."

Becky remembered just a few weeks ago she'd been smug in her belief that she'd married the better man. "I'm wrong often. But not about this."

Sarah nodded and stepped back, but then she staggered and Becky jumped forward to steady her.

"So stupid," Sarah said. "So stupid."

"It's very stupid," Becky said, knowing Sarah wasn't talking about herself. "Life is stupid."

Sarah drew away from Becky and stood on her own, her body shaking. Her face was the picture of anguish, her lips pulled back, her teeth bared. Tears still coursed down her splotchy cheeks. "How could this happen?"

"I don't know."

"I don't believe in God anymore."

"Shhh, shhh, shhh. Don't you feel it?"

"What? What am I supposed to feel?"

"Marsh." The words came out of Becky, as if someone talked through her. "He's an angel now. He's your angel."

Sarah lifted her hand, curled it in a fist. "Stop! Don't say that. I don't want a damn angel. I want my husband." Letting go, she socked Becky's shoulder.

"Ouch." Becky put her hand on her shoulder and stumbled back.

"Oh God." Sarah sank to her knees on the kitchen floor. "I didn't mean that."

Becky's shoulder still hurt as she knelt beside Sarah. "I know."

Life was messy. So was grief. Becky held her sobbing sister while Trey got a glass of water, took the baggy from her hand, then gave the water and the sleeping pill to Sarah.

Sarah took the water from him and then the pill. She swallowed both. Becky tried to pull Sarah to her feet but she wouldn't get up. Sarah didn't fight her, but she was inert. Still sobbing.

Becky didn't know there could be that many tears in a person, though she remembered crying half the night after her mother died. She'd cried alone in her room until she'd gotten up and walked numbly to Sarah's bedroom around three in the morning. She'd been comforted by her little sister's sleeping presence.

Trey knelt down next to Sarah. "Let's get you to your feet."

Sarah looked at him blankly. He slid his left arm under her thighs, his right around her back, and got to his feet, making an 'umph' sound.

"Her bedroom?" he asked Becky.

"This way." She led the way up the steps to the second floor, looking back a couple times to make sure Trey was okay. Sarah was taller than her. Normally slim, she'd gained pregnancy pounds. But there was no strain on his face, just the same grimness Becky had seen earlier. The same grimness that lodged inside her chest.

But he kept going up. One step after another. And with every step he claimed another tiny piece of her heart.

TWENTY-FOUR

Twenty minutes later, Sarah was breathing softly and evenly. Her sobs ended.

"Are you awake?" Becky whispered. She waited a moment, then rolled out of the large bed where she'd been lying next to Sarah.

The bed squeaked. On her feet, Becky went still. But Sarah continued to breathe evenly.

Careful not to make any noise, Becky tiptoed out of the bedroom. The hall light was on, and she looked back at Sarah. Streaks of tears shone on her sister's cheeks, not yet dried.

Becky glanced around the room. It *felt* as if Marsh were there. She almost expected to see sparkles. The air felt...electrified. But she saw nothing.

She didn't know why the sparkles appeared, what they meant, and why she was the only one who saw them. And right now, she didn't much care.

She turned away. Her trip down the stairs was slow. It wasn't eleven yet, but her tiredness came from her soul – from unbearable desolation...and a question that couldn't be answered. The same question Sarah had asked. The same question anyone asked when someone healthy and fairly young died.

Why? Why Marsh?

And an old question she hadn't ever let go.

Why my mother?

After all, Becky knew many people she wouldn't miss if they died. Many that no one would miss. She didn't actively want them to die... But why hadn't it been one of them? Especially when their only contributions to life seemed to be making other people miserable.

Marsh had been a great guy. A great husband. A great father. Maybe his occupation didn't pay a lot – not yet, anyway – but he loved being a picker. He loved his family. For God's sake, he loved his dog.

It didn't make sense that he'd been taken.

Seeing his ghost had made it better for her. And there was a comfort knowing his soul wasn't dead. After all, she'd *seen* him. The ghostly image was seared into her brain.

And if *his* soul lived after he died, then her mother's must be alive, too.

She reached the bottom of the stairs and tears welled in her eyes. Because even with the relief, even though it had been twenty-three years since her mom died, Becky still hurt. She still missed her mom. She still had a hole in her heart.

It didn't matter that now she had proof there was an afterlife. And that had to mean there was a God, too. Or at least a higher power. But right this second, none of that clarity took away the grief.

Dead was dead. Cody would be devastated. Sarah already was devastated.

She would tell Sarah about her experience at the accident site later. Right now it wasn't his ghostly self that Sarah wanted. It was his solid self. His blood beating through his veins. His warm arms holding her tightly. His voice telling her it was all a bad dream.

Becky blinked away her tears. The downstairs lights blazed. Trey must've left them on in case she came back downstairs. She turned off the kitchen light, then headed to the puppy room, wondering why he'd left that on, too.

Peering in, she saw Trey sitting on the easy chair that someone – Trey probably – had dragged into the dining room in case anyone wanted a puppy cuddle. Trey sat there now, his legs spread out in front of him. The black puppy slept on his lap. Trey's head rested against the back of the chair, his eyelids closed.

Gratitude bloomed inside her and soothed some of the hurt.

"Trey?" she murmured.

His eyes opened and his head came up. He cupped the small puppy in his big hands and stood. The puppy squeaked a sleepy protest. Walking quietly for a big man, he took the five steps to Goldie and the other puppies, all tumbled together and sleeping. As he plopped the puppy between two gold-colored bodies, one animal rose to a sitting position. Not a puppy but the kitten. Awake but wary, watching them. Content to view them from a distance.

The kitten was aptly named Lucky – the lone survivor of a bagful of kittens thrown out of a window of a moving car on the highway just outside of the village. Unlike the puppies, Lucky hadn't fully accepted Becky. Considering the kitten's past, Becky didn't blame it.

"Sarah's asleep?" Trey stepped over the wooden barrier into the hall.

Becky nodded. "I'm glad Joy popped in with the sleeping pill."

"She's going to have a rough time. Marsh was a good man."

"The best. Thanks for helping out...and staying. I didn't expect that."

"I wanted to make sure you were all right before I left."

"I'm okay." Her attempt at a smile was an epic failure. Instead she pushed her hair back from her face. She must look like a mess. Her hair flat from lying on it. Probably the mascara on her eyelashes was smeared, too. "Most guys wouldn't have stayed. I really appreciate it."

He shrugged and shifted his feet. Easy to see he was made uncomfortable with her second round of thanks. He was the kind of guy who did the right thing because it was the right thing to do.

Gratitude surged up inside her.

And lust. More than a surge. Like lava boiling in the pit of the volcano. Unexpected and overwhelming.

Marsh was dead. There was nothing she could do to change that. But *they* were still alive. She wanted, no, *needed* to celebrate life. She needed to wallow in it.

Most of all, she needed to do the most alive thing there was – create another life.

She crossed her arms. That wasn't going to happen. None of it was. He was going to leave, and she was going to try to sleep. More likely, she'd stay awake and wish Joy had given her a sleeping pill, too.

"Anything else I can do before I leave?" he asked.

She opened her mouth, intending to thank him and walk him to the door, but her arms uncrossed and words spilled out of her mouth. "You can make love with me."

He stood motionless. Staring into her eyes as if trying to see into her soul.

If it worked, he was looking at her soul on fire. Her body on fire.

Her breath shuddered out of her throat and she swallowed. "Come into the bedroom with me." A statement, not a question.

This was the second guy in two days.

And the most inappropriate time ever.

She was officially a slut.

And she didn't care. She did not give a flying finger for what anyone might think. Her new friend and brother-in-law, her sister's lover and husband, and a great father to his son...was dead. Her body abhorred the vacuum and the loss. So did she.

She held out her hand and it trembled. He looked down and didn't take it.

Maybe he didn't want her?

The thought was a pain in her heart.

A denial came fiercely. She didn't believe it.

There'd been something between them way back in high school. A different kind of electricity from what she'd felt earlier. A charge between them. She'd felt the danger that came along with that, and had turned from it.

She wasn't denying it this time.

But he might.

The thought scared the hell out of her.

Right now she didn't just want him. She *needed* him.

"I wasn't planning on this," he said.

"Neither was I." Please, she thought. *Please.*

It was hard to keep her mouth shut. Hard to hold back the pleas. She wanted this so badly.

"I don't want to take advantage of you," he said slowly, the old-fashioned words sounding oddly gallant.

She pressed her palms against her belly, her lips together to hold back a cry. Nodding, she backed up. "I understand."

The hurt showed in the thickness of her voice. Putting her hand over her mouth, she turned away.

"I don't want you to be sorry tomorrow," he said.

She snapped around, the pain and sorrow wiped away by a lightning bolt of anger. "I can make my own decisions on whether I'll be sorry or not. I don't need you or any man deciding that for me."

Glaring at him, she embraced her anger. It filled her, keeping the searing grief and other sucky emotions at bay.

"Thank you for supporting me and Sarah." She enunciated the syllables sharply. "And for the dinner. I'm sure you'll want to get home to your bed."

Instead of turning away, he stepped toward her and put his hands on her shoulders. "Yes," he said. "Yes, I do want to make love to you."

TWENTY-FIVE

Her breath sucked in as he said the word 'love' to her, and she realized that she'd used it first. Maybe that's why he'd hesitated. Maybe if she'd said 'have sex' his first answer would've been different.

Because she didn't want love. She just wanted sex. Hard and fast and so heated she wouldn't think of anything else.

Becky opened her mouth to tell him so, but his lips came down on hers and stopped the words from coming out of her throat. His kiss, soft and sweet and slow, stopped her heart for a second, too. And she was ready. She realized she'd been ready since she saw him with the puppy on his lap.

A small noise came out of her throat – pleasure, she thought. Surprise at his gentleness. At her body expressing appreciation.

But she still thought about other things. Like how he was bending to fit her, the size of his penis – contrary to the spam on her email, she didn't want a giant-sized penis. And did he have a condom?

At the last thought, her hands came up and clung to his upper arms, feeling the strong muscles of his bicep as she had two more thoughts.

Don't have a condom. I want a baby.

Maybe his swimmers were stronger than Jim's. Maybe they could find one of her few eggs. After all, she didn't need a lot of eggs to have a baby. Just one fertilized egg.

She wouldn't expect him to be a father.

She just wanted to be a mother.

Pulling away, she held out her hand. "There's a bed in the other room."

He took her hand and she led him down the hall into her temporary bedroom. She switched on the light then closed the door. She started to take off the necklace Sarah had loaned her.

A laugh came from him, and she turned to look at him. "You don't waste time," he said.

Her cheeks heated. She'd been married too long. Foreplay was what she and Jim had done naked, actually. And not much of it. But she didn't want to think about Jim now.

He grinned. "Sorry, I stopped you. Go ahead."

Looking at his grin, a bit of the horror melted inside her. A bit of the desperation, too...but not the need. Right now, in the bedroom with him, the need flamed up, more powerful than before. Became a force that consumed her with its wildfire of desire.

She set the necklace and earrings on the corner desk. Then, holding her arms straight out, she barreled into him. He caught her, and his arms curved around her back. All the need and desire and primal emotions that she didn't even understand swirled up inside her. Standing on her tiptoes, she stretched up, wrapped her hands around the back of his neck and head, then pulled his lips down to meet hers, to crush onto hers.

No more softness, no more dancing around, no more, no more, no more.

Just this. Just him and her and the bed as they shifted closer to it in small sideways steps. Her eyes closed, she felt the edge of the sofa bed that was still in pull-out position.

They tumbled onto it, and she felt like Alice falling down the rabbit hole, only in Becky's case, she was happily falling. Pulling him with her. He twisted to his side to let her land on top of him. His erection pushed against her belly. Hardness against softness. Yin and yang. Male and female.

She started rocking, a knee on each side of his thighs, even as he shifted his legs up. His shoes still on. Hers still on.

She should have taken hers off right away.

And why hadn't she worn a skirt or dress instead of pants?

She wasn't ready to leave him yet. To take time to undress. Too maddened. Too busy riding him. Still completely dressed.

Their mouths locked together. Sloppy wet kisses. Coming from her, not him. And she didn't care. Her mouth mimicking the wetness below her waist and between her legs.

He broke away and held her apart from him.

No! No, no, no! She choked back the words and only a moan escaped.

His breaths were harsh and loud. "If we don't take our clothes off," he said, his voice guttural, coming from deep in his belly, "I'm going to come in my pants."

She rolled off him so fast that she came down on her knees on the carpet. He didn't notice, pulling his shirt over his head. By the time he got it off, she was busy taking off her top, frantic to get rid of her clothes, wishing she'd taken them off earlier.

No buttons popped but her hands seemed clumsy and she found out kicking off her shoes and unzipping her pants at the same time didn't work well. Her teeth ground together but her frustration didn't lessen her need. Instead it increased. The need grew louder and more imperative until it became a thrumming in her blood.

Then she was naked and she turned and he was naked, too. His arms held out to her. His muscles defined, his legs long. And his penis...

She froze for a minute. Her skin chilled as she stared at the condom-covered penis.

All she could think of was that there would be no baby.

Then he sat up and reached for her. She let him draw her down to the mattress. Let him position her on the bed. Let him kneel over her. Let him lay on her. Let him touch her.

The need slammed back at her and she was wholly aroused again, wrapping her legs around him. Keening in a high, small voice. He made noises, too. A moan as they came together. Foreplay short, not needed. Both of them on fire.

The first orgasm hit her. Shivers of delight. She curved her back up and put her mouth against his shoulder to muffle her cry. The shivers went on and on. Then they stopped abruptly, and she slumped back onto the bed.

And then another one.

And another.

And another.

Sometime after the tenth orgasm, she stopped counting. She was shivering when his body jerked, and he cried out, a hoarse shout of release.

He held her tight as small shudders went through him. Like the aftereffects of an earthquake. His skin was damp, though the house had cooled with the night. His breaths came out on gulps that lessened in magnitude with each inhale and exhale. Finally his breaths were shallow and he lifted his upper body, the separation of their sweaty chests making a sucking sound.

"Wow," he said.

She laughed, and was a bit surprised that she could laugh after all that had happened tonight. "Yes, wow."

"I can't remember the last time it was so..."

"Intense," she said.

He nodded. She reached her hand up. "It's a first for me," she said.

She didn't say so, but she supposed Marsh's death had made her feel more alive. Made it matter more. Turned sex into an affirmation of life.

He leaned down and kissed her, their lips closed. Then he slid out of her and rolled out of bed...

And something leaked out between her legs.

She sat up, all her senses that had been lulled a second ago snapping to wakefulness. "Either something tore inside me or your condom has sprung a leak."

He looked down at his shrinking condom-wrapped penis. "Where's the bathroom?"

Directing him across the hall, she got out of bed and ascertained the stuff leaking down her thighs was definitely semen.

She was not surprised. Nothing inside her hurt. In fact, her insides felt pretty good.

"A baby," she whispered, and put her hands over her belly.

The possibility was tiny. So tiny she shouldn't even be thinking about it. But, oh, if she could have a baby it would be...

A miracle.

TWENTY-SIX

A soft cry woke Becky. Half asleep and lost in a fuzzy dream, she thought it was a baby's cry, a baby just waking up. A cry that said, 'I'm lost. Help me.'

Opening her eyes, she looked straight into Sarah's face. Her sister's mouth was twisted with anguish.

"I felt someone in bed with me," Sarah whispered hoarsely. "I thought it was Marsh and this whole thing was a bad dream."

Becky propped herself up on her elbow. After Trey left, she came up and crawled into bed with Sarah. She had the feeling it would help in the morning. "I didn't want you to wake up alone. Sorry."

"No, no, no." Tears dampened Sarah's eyes. "I would've felt worse. Thank you for being here."

Becky reached out to her, but Sarah rolled to face the wall. "I'm going to be okay. I just want to be by myself for a bit."

"Of course." Becky drew her arm back and scooted out of the bed. "Do you want breakfast?"

Sarah's head shook. "I'll get up before Cody comes back. I have to be strong for him." She gave a half sob, half laugh. "It's going to sound crazy, but it felt as if Marsh were with me last night. I couldn't see or hear or touch him. But I sensed him. Almost as if I'd turn around and there he'd be."

Becky stood still, not leaving. In her mind, she saw Marsh's ghost again. His open face, bewildered and surprised and sad. But there had been something more...

"When I did turn...he wasn't there." This time Sarah sobbed aloud for a few seconds before she shuddered to a stop. "I was...bereft all over again. As if someone stabbed me in the heart."

"There's something I didn't tell you last night." The scene of the accident still strong in her mind, Becky leaned forward and lowered her voice. "I didn't think you were ready."

Sarah rolled over and pushed up on her elbows. "Ready for what?"

"Trey and I had gone to Tomahawk for dinner at the Thai place." Becky paused. Sarah nodded, two vertical frown lines between her eyebrows. Becky squared her shoulders and continued. "We came upon the accident just after the emergency people got there. Minutes after it happened."

Sarah sucked her breath in audibly, and Becky winced. She hurried to get on with the rest of her story.

"I tried to get to his truck, but a fireman blocked me. And suddenly, I saw..." She stopped. Awe and grief and horror and happiness swelled inside her brain.

It was too much emotion. A huge overload.

"What?" Sarah swung her legs over the side of the bed and pushed off. She stood two steps in front of Becky. Her face looked ravaged. Her eyes red and dull. Her complexion ashy. Her cheekbones hollow. As if she weren't far from death herself.

"I saw his..." Becky paused again, and the lines between Sarah's eyebrows deepened. The words rushed out of Becky's mouth. "His ethereal body."

Sarah's forehead scrunched. "What?"

Becky grimaced. "That didn't come out too well. I was trying not to say this, but I saw his ghost."

"Don't." Sarah brought up her hands, warding Becky away from her. "Don't do this to me."

She stepped back, and Becky reached out and grabbed Sarah's wrists. "No, listen, Sarah. I *saw* him. I *heard* him." She heard her voice change. Breathless from awe. "He told me to take care of you and Cody and the baby."

"No," Sarah whispered, shaking her head.

"Yes." Becky kept hold of Sarah's wrists. "Yes, yes, yes."

"Why you?" Sarah's voice rose, her mouth and jaw twisted. "Why didn't he come to *me*?"

"I was there. He was rising out of the truck. He didn't hang around and have a conversation. It was all about you."

Sarah wrenched her wrists from Becky's grip and snapped around, her back bent, her shoulders hunched forward, her head bowed. "Just one touch. Just one last touch."

Becky looked at Sarah's stooped back. "Remember when I said he was your angel?"

Sarah shook her head, her blond hair flopping.

"When I was rubbing your back?"

"That's right, I hit you. I'm sorry."

"I'm sure I deserved it from another time."

A laugh came out of Sarah's mouth. Then she lifted her hand to her face. Becky couldn't see her face, but she pictured Sarah putting the back of her hand in her mouth, the way she used to when she was a toddler.

"I was singing *Angel* by Sarah McLachlan," Becky said, "and this feeling came over me that he was your angel."

Sarah slowly turned. Her hand came down. Her head rose. Her eyes glared. "You're one of *those* people now? The *woo-woo* people?"

Becky backed up. She hadn't expected Sarah to believe her right off. It still hurt, but she reminded herself that Sarah was hurting a lot more than Becky. "I'm sorry. I'll leave you alone."

"You do that."

Sarah faced the wall again and crossed her arms. Becky thought if she were an artist, she would remember Sarah's hunched back, sorrow in every line, and try to catch it in whatever medium she used. To create a portrait of grief.

But she was just Sarah's sister and didn't have any special skills besides seeing ghosts and sparkles. And recently she realized she had a skill for appreciating lovemaking.

That was a marketable skill, though not one she was likely to use that way.

So Becky left the bedroom to go downstairs to take care of the dog and the puppies and the kitten. Soon the calls would come, and she would need to answer them.

A bolt of anger shook her. What happened to the miracle that the words on the car windows had promised? She wanted to see Marsh walk into the house, healed and better than ever, with or without the ugly pirate tattoo on his left bicep. It didn't matter. She just wanted to see his grinning face and his laughing eyes as he said, "I fooled you, didn't I? I fooled 'em all."

If Jesus could come back from the dead, why not Marsh? After all, Marsh had a family. Fathers...the good ones...shouldn't be taken from their children.

She reached the first floor and turned toward the puppy room. Moved one foot in front of the other.

But if Marsh weren't the miracle...

She put her hand over her stomach – over her womb – stopped and looked at the ceiling. "Please," she said. "Please."

And then the animals called her, making squeaks, high-pitched barks and meows, and she went to take care of them.

Life went on, even after it seemed to stop.

As she let Goldie outside a moment later, the phone rang. She hurried over to it, looked at the caller's name and backed away. It rang again, and she answered it this time because if she didn't, it would disturb Sarah.

TWENTY-SEVEN

"How's Sarah?" her father demanded, his voice gruff as if he were talking to an employee, letting her know he hadn't forgiven her for defying him. Today she didn't care.

She breathed in, her chest expanded. Not caring empowered her. "She's in bed."

"You need to get her up to take care of her son. That's what I did—"

"Cody's at a sleepover at a neighbor's. We thought it better to leave him there overnight. Sarah will tell him later this morning. If you don't mind, I have things to do."

She hung up because she realized she was getting angry in spite of the not caring thing. Maybe she was having delusions...seeing sparkles and ghosts. But he seemed to have forgotten that when her mother died, he'd left her to tell Sarah while he talked to everyone else but them.

Her hands shook and she took deep breaths. She didn't want this drama today. Didn't want the extra tension. If her father were a decent human, he'd stay away from her and Sarah.

After all, he'd stayed away emotionally most of their lives. Why ruin that record now?

She turned away. Whatever happened, she and Sarah would handle it when it came up. No need to invent catastrophes where there weren't any. Nothing could be worse for Sarah than Marsh's death.

Unless something happened to Cody.

But Cody was fine. Sarah still had her boy. And in four months, she would have another child.

The phone rang again. This time the name on the display was a neighbor's. Becky wished she could leave it go to voice mail, but once again, she picked it up to avoid waking Sarah. She talked for a few moments, told the neighbor no arrangements were made yet, that Sarah was asleep. When she hung up, she barely took two steps from the phone before it rang again. And again and again and again.

The sixth call was from Linda Wegner. After that, there was one more concerned caller before the phone stopped ringing. No miracle there. For the first time, Becky appreciated Linda's big mouth. Linda must have gotten the word out that Sarah wasn't ready to talk.

Finally Becky had time to feed Goldie and the puppies. The puppies were being weaned, though they weren't self-sufficient yet. Becky fed the kitten in the kitchen. The kitten was a few weeks older than the newborn puppies, and they had to keep her food from the puppies or they might eat it and get sick.

These animals were work.

After that, she was about to clean in the puppy room, but the black puppy nudged her ankle, letting her know it wanted to be cuddled.

"I'm spoiling you, aren't I?" Ready for a break, Becky picked up the puppy and sat in the dining room chair, settling the puppy on her lap. She wanted to name it, but if she did that she'd end up keeping it. The only way that could happen would be if a miracle happened.

But if she could wish for a miracle...

She bent her back and kissed the puppy's smooth head. "If there could be a miracle right now, this second, I'd wish Marsh would be here. Alive and well. Saying it was some kind of macabre joke. And if that won't happen, I wish you could be changed into a human baby."

The puppy licked her hand then wiggled, ready to go back to his playmates. Happy to be alive. Happy to be a puppy.

Becky laughed softly. For the moment fully relaxed, fully alive. Still sitting in the chair, she leaned forward and set him on the floor. Sitting back, she watched him run to the other puppies.

"I don't blame you for not wanting to be human. I'd much rather be a puppy, too. I'd play, eat, drink, pee and poop all day. Lie in the sun and take walks. Then pee and poop again...and take another nap."

The black dog was wrestling with one of his brothers. Another puppy was rolling on its back, all four paws dancing in the air. Two others were sleeping.

The kitten was on top of the dining room table. Already nimble. It would probably start leaping over the barrier soon.

A puppy started heaving. She grimaced. Any moment...

The other puppies all stopped what they were doing to watch. *Reality Puppy TV*.

Yep, there it came, out of the puppy's mouth and onto the blanket. The dining room filling up with the sour scent.

She grimaced. "Another puppy bonus. You can throw up and someone else will clean up after you. In fact, you never have to clean anything." Like Jim and her father, she thought, but didn't want to dwell on that – though she wondered fleetingly who was cleaning up after Jim now. "Never have to pay bills. Or clean toilets. Or do taxes."

"Or shave legs," Sarah said from the hall. "I hate shaving my legs."

"Then don't." Becky stood. "I didn't hear you come down."

"The dog was probably getting ready to puke then. Something about that pre-puking sound takes all our attention."

"It's because we know we have to clean it up." Becky walked to the barrier and climbed over it.

"I'll clean." Sarah put her hand on Becky's shoulder. "I'm okay now. As soon as I'm done, I'll call Joy and tell her to bring Cody over."

Becky took a good look at Sarah. Except for the reddened eyes and the bags beneath them, she looked almost normal. But her spark was gone. Her zest. As if she lost a chunk of her soul.

Or the love of her life.

"You call Joy," Becky said. "I'll clean."

Sarah peered past her, at the puppies, her eyes unfocused, her mind far away. Then she gave a sad smile. "Neither of us needs to pick up the puppy puke. It's taken care of."

"Huh?" Becky whipped her head around and saw the puke was gone. "How did—"

"Goldie. Don't look so disgusted." Sarah climbed over the barrier into the puppy room, not clumsy despite her burgeoning tummy. "That's what dogs do. I'm sorry your date was ruined last night."

"Don't apologize." Becky held up her hand to stop the stubbornness that was making Sarah's jaw stick out like their father's. "Just don't."

Sarah gave a shaky laugh, her jawline now her own. A puppy barreled into her ankle and she leaned down, scooped it up then held it against her breast. The puppy craned its head up and licked her chin. She smiled down at the puppy before looking at Becky. "I was hoping you'd get lucky and now it didn't happen."

Becky put her head down and turned to the kitchen. "There should be something I can do. Just tell me."

"No, there's nothing— Ouch!"

Becky turned back and saw Sarah set the puppy back on the floor. Sarah straightened, a red mark on her chin – probably from the puppy's teeth – but a smile dawning on her face. "You did it, didn't you?"

TWENTY-EIGHT

The question stunned Becky. She couldn't talk about *this*. It was tacky enough she'd done it with Trey only hours after Marsh's death. But to confide the details to Sarah... She made a face and shook her head.

"You don't want to talk about what Trey and I did."

Sarah's face tightened. Anguish seeped the color from her face, and she looked sick with desolation. "Don't tiptoe around me. Just don't."

"Sarah, there's just no way you're ready for this now."

"Don't tell me what I'm ready for." Sarah's voice rose with the last word. The atmosphere in the hall between the kitchen and the dining room thickened.

"Honey, I just know that if I were you—"

"You'd what? Suddenly become Mother Teresa? Become untouchable? Sit atop a mountain and pray?"

"No, I don't know what I'd want to do."

"Then let me tell you," Sarah said, her voice harsh and sharp at the same time. "I want to crawl into a grave with Marsh and hold his dead body. Is that what you want to hear?"

Becky kept herself from showing her revulsion, but couldn't stop from pulling back.

On Sarah's face, she saw the flash of anger. "Don't expect me to be *that* person." Sarah spoke low, through her teeth.

"What person?" Becky held out her hands. She didn't want to make this worse for Sarah, but obviously that's what she was doing. All her years as the counselor to her almost ex-husband's parishioners were failing her now when it mattered most.

"The kind who goes into a nun's silence. I don't have the luxury to shut down. I have a kid. I'm not going to be like Dad and ignore him."

"Oh God, no." Becky rocked forward on her toes then back on her heels.

"When Mom died..." Sarah stopped sniffing as tears coursed down her cheeks. "You kept going. You didn't crawl into a closet and lock yourself in."

Becky tried to talk but couldn't. Tears got in her way. She swallowed them, but some escaped. In fact, a flood of them traveled down her cheeks, her chin, her throat, into the V-neckline of her top.

"You're my hero," Sarah said.

Becky's tears dripped faster. She hurried into the kitchen, toward the box of tissues next to the microwave. She grabbed a couple, blew her nose hard, then reached to grab another one. Her fingers collided with Sarah's and she had to wait for Sarah to pull one away before taking another.

They both blew their noses gustily at the same time.

"I had to be there for you," Becky said. "I cried myself to sleep at night for a long, long time."

Sarah nodded. Not saying she'd do the same for Marsh. Not needing to say it.

"I still mourn Mom," Becky continued, her voice rough. "I don't think I ever got over it."

"Because you didn't mourn? Because you couldn't?"

Becky frowned. "I missed her because I loved her." Her voice broke. "I still do."

"I don't think I'll ever get over Marsh." Sarah stared down at her hand with the thin gold wedding band. "I'll be ninety years old and miss him."

"Yeah." Becky frowned at Sarah's hand, too. And wished there was something she could do. Something that would help Sarah...

But Sarah had only asked one thing. She wanted to know what she and Trey did last night. And Becky had said 'no.' Thinking she knew everything. Just as her dad and Jim had thought when they told Becky how to live her life.

"Yes," she said, lifting her gaze. "Yes, we did it."

Sarah's head tilted up at Becky, two lines between her eyebrows as if she didn't know what Becky was talking about.

Becky took three steps to the table and sat down. She needed something solid beneath her butt when she said this. "You asked if Trey and I did it. Yes, we did do it. We had sex."

Sarah's jaw dropped, her eyes widened. Trading sad for stunned. As if Becky had broken a water balloon on her head.

"I feel guilty about it," Becky continued, "but it was after you went to bed with the sleeping pill."

Sarah blinked. Her lips pressed together. Becky cringed inside. How to handle this was not in the chapter on counseling she'd read. Not that it said 'Don't talk about your sex life to a bereaved person' in any of the books. It was just assumed that the counselor had more sense.

"I *knew* I shouldn't have told you." Becky started to get up.

A hand clapped onto her shoulder and pushed her back down. Sarah sat across from her. "I want to hear about it. All about it."

"I'm not good at talking about sex."

"Just answer me. He's better than Jim, right?"

"Like I said before, Jim really liked getting blow jobs." Becky made a face. "I'm thinking of sending Diana a thank you email."

Sarah laughed outright. The kind of laugh where, if she had coffee in her mouth, it would've spewed out. "You should. I'd love to see it."

"And maybe I should Cc the church members."

Sarah gave a shriek of laughter, but it had an edge of hysteria. As if tears weren't far away. "Jim is a selfish asshole. Let the whole world know."

"I see that now." Becky swallowed a lump in her throat. This conversation was bringing to life the hollow place inside her. But if it helped Sarah get through the day... "I don't know why I stayed with him so long. They say the wife has to *know* all along, but I didn't have a clue. I didn't think he was that...well, passionate. I just knew there was something missing..."

"Decency?" Sarah suggested.

Becky shrugged. "On the surface Jim seems perfect. But it's all just surface. Underneath that surface, he's..."

"Rotten?" Sarah suggested.

"Inauthentic. I felt like an actor in a show he'd made up. Like I was living in a sitcom, pretending to be this perfect minister's wife – only I wasn't as good an actor as he was. That's why so many of the congregation didn't rally around me."

"Fuck them."

"They don't want the truth. They want to believe in a *Leave It to Beaver* world that Jim and Dad represent. Even though there never was a real world like that. But I lived it with him." She looked up at Sarah, astonished that Sarah was comforting her when it should've been the other way around. "I was purposefully blind. I didn't want to see what he was."

"You were indoctrinated to serve." The sadness streamed back into Sarah's face. The grief. "Daddy did that to you."

Becky nodded, an ache clogging her throat. And her heart. But she knew her ache was tiny compared to the one in Sarah's heart right now. Then Becky said out loud what she suspected Sarah had already thought. "I wish it were Jim instead of Marsh."

Sarah's face crumbled. "Or Daddy. I shouldn't say that. I'm an awful daughter. I'm an awful person. I'm a bitch. A selfish bitch."

"No!"

"Yes." Sarah got to her feet and turned.

Becky surged up. Sarah was moving toward the hall. Becky stepped after her. In an attempt to distract Sarah, words Becky had never in her life thought she'd say blurted out of her mouth.

"Trey's condom tore."

Sarah snapped around, her eyes bright. "Really? Do you think..."

"No. Yes." Becky's hands covered her abdomen. "It's too early to tell anything. And it's unlikely." She wouldn't get her hopes up. She wouldn't do that to herself.

But her hands still remained over her belly. Protecting whatever might be cooking inside.

"You never told me the problem," Sarah said. "I heard it was you, but was it really Jim? Is he too busy getting blow jobs to procreate?"

Becky laughed. Funny how it had hurt so much a short time ago. Now leaving him was the best thing that happened to her in a long time.

"No, it's me." For once it didn't hurt to talk about it. Maybe because what Sarah was going through was so much more horrible. "We had fertility tests done."

Maybe because now she had hope.

"You're sure? He could've been fudging the test. Jim's ego is as big as...well, Dad's."

Becky grimaced. "They're two of a kind. But I read his report. His sperm are healthy and swimming just fine. I just don't have a lot of eggs."

"It only takes one."

"The one we needed didn't show up. I wanted to adopt, but Jim wanted to wait."

"I bet he's sorry now. He doesn't have that hold on you. Jim won't remain single forever. When he hooks up with someone else, Dad won't stick with him."

This wasn't about Jim. "I don't care." Becky turned her head away, because she was a liar. Sometimes she didn't care that her father turned on her. Other times she felt grief like a knife twisting in her chest.

Even now, though she could see what her father was and how he'd taken advantage of her, the strings were still there, tugging at her heart. Wanting his approval and his love.

A car door slammed on the street. The phone rang. Sarah looked out the front window. "In a minute you can tell Dad to his face."

TWENTY-NINE

Her father wasn't alone. While Sarah answered the phone, Becky stood on the front porch and crossed her arms. She felt like a knight guarding the castle from marauding intruders.

"Hello, Dad." Becky nodded at Jim. She would show him chilly politeness. Nothing more. She brought her gaze back to Carl. "Why are you here?"

"To talk to your sister." Carl stepped up, but Becky didn't move aside for her father even though he stood inches from her. So close she could see the pores in his skin. The lines on his face. The fading in his narrowed blue eyes. The pinched nostrils. The pressed-together lips.

A man unhappy with the person he was staring at.

The unhappiness was mutual.

"She doesn't want to talk to you."

"I'm her father. She has to talk to me."

"You're too late, Dad. Too late for both of us." She raked her gaze over him and then at Jim behind him. "I hear there's a strip bar in Wausau. Why don't you two *boys* head over there? It's a bit early, but you might get lucky."

"Becky!" both men exclaimed at once.

Choked laughter came from the open door behind Becky. "It's okay," Sarah said. "Let them in."

Twisting her upper body, Becky gave Sarah her 'what now?' look, narrowing her eyes to see Sarah through the tiny crisscrosses of the screen.

"That was Joy on the phone," Sarah said.

Becky nodded, getting the message. Joy must've seen Carl and Jim drive up to the curb. If she could see them, so could Cody. Sarah wanted to get this party out of sight.

Becky backed up to let the two men step inside. Sarah led them into the living room. When the men sat, Sarah remained standing in front of the window. Becky stood beside her. Two against two.

It was horrible to feel that their father was against them. Their family wasn't just fractured, it was broken into tiny pieces that would take an army of therapists to glue back together – and they would still end up with holes and extra pieces that didn't fit anywhere.

Carl got to his feet again, and then Jim did, too. Monkey see, monkey do, Becky thought. Then she realized that at that moment she was mimicking Sarah in her defiant, the-hell-with-you attitude, and she held back a laugh. Yes, she was a monkey, too.

Looking at Jim right now, she was very happy she'd been up to her own monkeyshines. With *two* men. Though not at the same time.

The thought gave her a secret pleasure.

Then it hit her that he must've thought the same thing about his 'women' while looking at her every morning as she served him eggs over easy, the way he liked his eggs, even as she spread his favorite blueberry jam on his toast.

Inside her belly, she felt a twist like a corkscrew turning.

She'd been a fool.

"No matter what happened between us, we're family," her father said.

Sarah touched the back of Becky's hand, stopping her from shooting back a sarcastic remark. Becky glanced at Sarah, but Sarah was staring at her father...not saying anything. Her mouth

165

closed. Her eyes were open but with a faraway gaze, as if she looked right through him.

"Jim isn't family," Becky said.

"Though your sister left Jim," her father said to Sarah, ignoring Becky, "he's a part of our family. He has been since he was a child. His father was like my brother. The church has been part of our lives, too. Your mother and I were married there. You and Becky were christened there. Your mother's buried in the church graveyard."

"So, what's the point?" Becky asked.

Her father's face reddened but he still kept his gaze on Sarah. "I came with Jim to make the funeral arrangements. You don't have to worry about the expenses. I'll take care of it."

Sarah frowned. "The church hasn't been a part of my family's life for more than eight years. And neither have you."

"I'm sorry for the separation, but you need me now and I'm here for you. I'm your father. The one you can count on to take care of you and your children."

Becky stepped forward. Though his gaze remained on Sarah, Becky spotted a nervous twitch in his right cheek. Good, he's not as confident as he sounds, she thought furiously. His whole body should twitch.

"I'll take care of myself," Sarah said. "And my children."

"And the person who took care of Sarah before she married Marsh is right here." Becky jabbed her index finger at her breastbone. "And I'm ready to do it again."

Finally her father looked at her, his expression annoyed. "Don't act as if I was absent while she was growing up. I was there, too."

"When it was convenient for you." Becky heard the wobble in her voice, the seesaw of anger and hurt.

"When you were home, you were always telling me what I was doing wrong," Sarah said, stepping up to Becky's side. "I used to be glad when you left."

"You were a difficult child." He planted his black leather shoes apart, his chest puffed out. "You have a son. What are you going to do when he gets out of hand? Tell him what a great kid he is?"

"I'll still love him."

"I loved you."

"You turned your back on me. You think throwing a few dollars at me now will make me forget that?"

"I admitted I was wrong." He looked from Sarah to Becky. "I wasn't a perfect father or a perfect husband. I'm trying to make up for that now."

Becky stared at him stonily. She didn't look at Sarah, but she *felt* Sarah giving him the same death stare.

His cheek twitched again. "Maybe I was too harsh on you."

"It's too late," Sarah said. "I've gone on living my life without you in it."

"Honey, you need me."

"You're wrong. You think because Marsh is gone, I'll crawl back to you and ask you to take care of the poor widow and her son?" Her voice thickened. "It's not going to happen. No way."

Glancing at Sarah, Becky saw the splotchy redness on her face that always bloomed before she started to cry. She'd been like that when she was a chubby baby and now she was a full grown woman, and that hadn't changed.

Becky faced her father. "That's enough. You're upsetting Sarah, and I want you to go. Both of you." The look she gave Jim should have seared a two-inch part through his perfect hair. "I don't even know why you're here."

"To offer your sister comfort." Jim couldn't quite look her in the eyes, and she knew the real reason he was here – because her father had insisted.

"The only comfort you can offer either of us is to take him out of here." She jerked her chin toward her father.

167

"Becky, I hurt you, too. I should've been...more understanding." Carl frowned, as if apologizing gave him a pain in his belly. Then he put out his hands in a pleading manner that made Becky's skin itch like red army ants were crawling along the inside layer. "But we can all change. I'm changing. Jim is changing."

"Stop!" Sarah's voice filled with tears. "I can't handle this right now. Becky's right. Just go."

Becky stepped closer to Sarah, touching her arm, letting her sister know she wasn't alone.

"You'll need money." Carl took out his wallet. "I'll give you money."

"No." Sarah put her hands behind her back.

"If she needs money, she can have mine," Becky said. In the second of silence following that remark, as a muscle in her father's cheek twitched again, she heard a car pulling up to the curb outside.

"How long do you think that will last?" Carl's voice was harsh, no more pleading. "Who's going to pay for all of this? What about the mortgage? I heard the other driver didn't have insurance. You won't get anything there."

"That's none of your business." Sarah stared between Carl and Jim, her face blank.

A car door closed, and Becky twisted to gaze out the window behind her. Walking up the sidewalk, she saw Elsa, sunlight tangled in her white-blond hair.

Becky's tense muscles relaxed. She had the feeling everything was going to be all right.

"For the sake of the community, let me do his service." Jim focused his blue eyes on Sarah, and Becky could feel him amping up the force of his personality. Compelling her to listen to him.

When he did this, he shone like a star. Channeling his father, who had done the same thing, though his dad had done it without conscious effort. "Marsh had friends in Miracle. People cared about him. They're mourning him today. A service isn't just for the family. It's for Marsh's extended family. You owe it to his friends to do this."

Becky squeezed Sarah's arm, feeling the stiffness under her fingers. As if Sarah were holding herself together through willpower alone.

Becky switched her gaze to the man with the real power: her father. Jim and her father were like a politician and his special interest group. The front man and the moneyman. And the moneyman in this instance was the one that pulled the strings.

"Then it's a good thing that yours isn't the only church in Miracle," Becky said.

Jim made an incoherent sound but her father's face turned the color of a pimple about to burst.

Before either of them said anything more, the doorbell rang.

Great timing, Becky thought. "Now I'm going to ask you to leave – again."

She was wasting her voice. Her father looked out the large living room window and though he couldn't see Elsa, he saw her Mustang Convertible.

His face turned from red to purplish red and he stomped to the front door.

THIRTY

Becky hurried after her father. He was already out the door, and the screen door clanged behind him. In the puppy room, Goldie barked and puppies squeaked, upset by all the commotion. Becky's heart thundered in her chest.

The fury she'd seen in her father's eyes had brought back a memory she'd forgotten. It was after her mother's diagnosis. Carl's home office was in an addition he'd built onto the house. It was his place, and she rarely went into it. She rarely heard noise coming from it, either. But that night she had. Furniture breaking and someone shouting at her father to stop.

She remembered she ran to the office, calling 'Daddy, Daddy!' She'd thrown the door open and seen the room was wrecked. Papers and folders were scattered over the floor, his office chair overturned and a leg broken. A mounted fish her mother had always disliked lay on the floor along with a picture of the family that was ripped jaggedly, the frame cracked. And cowering in the corner was a man she recognized as their bookkeeper, holding his arm in a funny position and sobbing, begging Carl not to hurt him.

Reaching the door now, she peered through the screen. Carl and Elsa faced each other, their sides to Becky. At least six inches taller and sixty pounds heavier, Carl glared at Elsa and his complexion blanched. From demon red to vampire pale in less than a minute.

It reminded Becky of that night.

"You," he said, his voice low. *"You."*

The fine hairs on Becky's nape rose.

"Hello, Carl." Elsa sounded amused, as if she didn't realize she was in danger. "There was a time when you were much happier to see me."

"I'm not letting you tear my family apart." His fury shook Becky. She held her knuckles against her lips to hold back a cry.

All those years ago, the bookkeeper had scrambled to his feet upon her entry and fled the office. Later, she'd heard that he'd moved his family to Madison. Since then Becky had never seen her father like this – teetering on the edge of a fury that could drive him to madness.

She didn't know what had come over him that night. She didn't know why Elsa caused the same reaction.

What was between the two of them? What caused her father's hatred?

"Let me out," Jim said, next to her.

Startled, she glanced up. His face had its pained 'someone is behaving badly in public' look. Not that Jim didn't behave badly; he just preferred to behave badly in private.

Her feet heavy, Becky shifted to the side, glad to let Jim take control of this. As if her father were a dangerous animal Jim would keep from springing at Elsa.

Elsa shook her head, still smiling, still calm, still missing the signs of jeopardy. "From what I hear you've already torn the family unit apart. Alienating both of your daughters isn't very well done of you."

"Don't you—"

"Yes, me." Though the smile never left her face, steel edged her voice. "No one has more right to be here than me."

Becky frowned. Something was going on between her father and Elsa, but right now she was more concerned about Sarah than finding out what it was.

Jim stepped onto the porch the same instant that Carl leaned closer to Elsa. Jim clasped Carl's shoulder.

"Don't let her goad you," Jim said, his words putting the blame on Elsa.

Slowly, Carl turned to look at him. Jim's head blocked the view of her father's eyes, but Becky felt the air crackle. As if a bad electrical storm were going to explode around them any second.

"Pastor Jim," Elsa said, the steel in her voice gone. She sounded pleased to see Jim. "It's too bad we're meeting on such a sad day." She peered over his shoulder to Becky. "Hello, Becky. May I come in?"

Though Becky couldn't see Carl's eyes, he twisted from Jim to Elsa, and his big body tensed, as if ready to spring. Becky jerked the screen door open, and Jim shifted out of the way. With a smooth move, Elsa nodded at the two men then strolled inside while Becky held her breath.

For a moment, hatred flashed across her father's face. Becky feared he would chase after Elsa.

The screen door clanged shut. Becky grabbed the wooden front door that looked thick enough to hold off a band of marauding Vikings. She shoved it shut. Her arms straight, her palms flat on the door, fingers splayed, she slanted against it with all her weight. As if the Vikings were on the other side, about to slam a giant tree trunk against it and batter the door down. She turned the deadbolt.

Fingertips brushed against her upper back. She jerked, then whipped around.

"It's okay," Elsa murmured. "You can relax. You don't have to save the world."

Becky stared at her. "You don't know."

Elsa put her hand to the side of Becky's face. A strange but familiar gesture from someone she hardly knew. But it didn't feel strange...

Elsa's palm was cool and calming against Becky's heated skin. Then her hand slid off and she stepped back. "I know more than you think."

She walked to the living room, as if she'd been in this house many times before. As if she knew she'd be welcome.

Becky almost expected to see sparkles as she kept her gaze glued on Elsa's straight back. There did seem to be a glow about her, but Becky marked it up to her powerful personality. Super charisma, as if rays of light and sun sought her out.

What did Elsa know? And how? And why did her father hate Elsa so much?

THIRTY-ONE

Elsa acted as if she'd forgotten Carl. As if he bothered her less than a mosquito bite. Instead of dwelling on the scene that just happened on the doorstep, she helped Sarah and Becky make phone calls and funeral arrangements. Not taking over and pushing them out of the way. Just there to do whatever needed to be done.

Sarah was happy to let her take over some of it, as was Becky. Becky had helped parishioners through this, but it had never been easy for her. The questions and considerations brought back memories of her mother's funeral. And with every newly surfaced memory it seemed as if death stalked her.

Elsa left twenty minutes later, the bleakness of the day a bit brighter...the toxic pall left behind by her father dissipated.

Sarah's expression was strained when she went across the street to get Cody. She told Becky that she needed to go alone.

When they came back, Sarah's attention was on Cody. He took the news badly. He'd been getting too old to cuddle, or so he'd said, but he reverted. Sarah and Becky took turns sitting with him. Only a few more phone calls trickled in. Becky thought people were either respecting their privacy or they were fearful of offending Carl by offering his daughter sympathy.

Though Sarah's house was on a fairly secluded dead end, Becky had no doubt that news of her father's unsuccessful visit was keeping the phones buzzing. If Homeland Security were half as diligent as the citizens of Miracle, there would be no need for body cavity searches at airports.

In the afternoon, Cody fell asleep in the puppy room and their Uncle Sam came over. Tall and lanky, he wore his black-streaked white hair pulled back in a rubber band. In his late sixties, he was still good looking with a bony face that was sculptured by age. The deep, vertical lines on the sides of his face came from grinning. He was a man who enjoyed life. According to the gossip, he'd enjoyed it a little too well.

Becky's mother had adored her stepbrother. Her father, on the other hand, often said he thought Sam didn't live up to his capabilities. But Becky suspected her father was jealous of Sam's contentment.

Like her dad, Sam could've been the guy in the western that everyone looked up to, but not because he was the rich rancher who acted like John Wayne. Sam would've been the maverick. The loner who came in to save the day, make love to the senorita and then leave to do it again at the next town.

Right now Sam was saving the day for them, sitting at Sarah's kitchen table, telling her he'd taken care of Marsh's truck. He even offered to talk to Elsa about paying for the funeral arrangements. But Sarah held her head high and said taking care of the truck was enough and she'd take care of the arrangements.

"Guess I'll get going then." He stood. "Don't worry about the rent for the storage buildings. It's not like I'm growing anything there anyway." He winked.

"You hardly charge us anything as it is."

Becky noticed the way Sarah said *us*. She had to look away from Sarah's sad face, suspecting it would be a while before she would say *I*.

But Sarah still had Cody. She was still part of an 'us.' And she had Becky, too – for as long as Sarah needed her.

"Don't make anything big out of it," Sam said. "I don't need the extra money."

"Uncle Sam, you—"

"Not a word." He held up his hand. "You need anything, you just call."

He headed toward the back door, but a whining noise made him shift to face the hall. It took Sarah and Becky a half second longer to turn. They all saw Cody in the hall, barefoot and carrying the black puppy.

"You been listening?" Sam strode toward him, looking down.

Cody nodded.

Sam nodded, too. "Good. Sometimes you gotta listen to know what's going on."

"He's got a name." Cody looked down at the puppy, then up at Sam. "You wanna know what it is?"

"'Course."

"Sam. I named him after you."

"That's a real honor." Sam put his hand on the puppy's head and rubbed behind its left ear. "But what if he's outside playing and I'm over on the other side of the trees, looking at my plants, and at the same time you and your mama call out 'Sam?' What if we both come running?"

Cody laughed. Though he stopped right away, his eyes remained bright. "I'll call him Sammy then."

Sam straightened. "Good name. No one calls me Sammy. I don't have to worry about anyone mistaking me for the dog."

"As long as you don't grow a tail." Cody gave a choked giggle.

"How do you know I don't have one?" Sam winked, ruffled Cody's hair, gave the puppy's ear a soft pull, nodded at Sarah and Becky then strode out the back door.

The door closed after him, and Becky and Sarah breathed a sigh at the same time. Becky turned to Sarah. "I wonder why he never married," Becky said.

"He was married!" Cody said. "That's why he's got Katie."

Becky and Sarah shared a glance, then Sarah swiveled to Cody and told him to take the puppy back into the puppy room. A good way to get around the subject of a couple never marrying but having a baby. A good way to avoid talking about their cousin Katie's addict mother.

As soon as he was gone, Becky said, "I think Uncle Sam was in love with Mom."

"No!"

"It would've been legal. They're steps, not real brother and sister. Not even halves."

"I know, but..." Sarah stopped, her mouth closed but her eyes still big.

Becky nodded. Knowing what Sarah was thinking. That they could've been Sam's daughters instead of their dad's. "She was two years older than him, but she was pretty." She thought of Derek and their age difference. "Besides, two years is nothing."

"She wasn't pretty," Sarah said. "She was *beautiful*."

Becky frowned and pictured her mom in her mind as she'd looked in the last year of her life. Bald, with a face rounded from the steroids she took for the pain. Sarah obviously remembered her mostly from the photos hung around their house when their mother was young and healthy...when she shone brightly like a star.

"She was...special," Becky said, and the ache inside her started again. The whole time her mother was sick, she always smiled to see Becky and Sarah. Even when she was in the deepest pain. Even as she lay dying.

Her mom had been sick for so long, but every once in a while Becky still missed her so much it felt like a boulder had grown inside her chest and would never go away. "Sam enlisted just before she and Dad married. He was seventeen, but he'd graduated from high school and his father signed his papers."

"I wonder what happened to turn him to—" Sarah shrugged and lifted her hands in a 'you know' gesture.

"War happened." Becky shrugged, too. If Sam grew a few medicinal plants in his field, she didn't see the harm in that. Neither did anyone else in the village, including their constable. From what Becky heard, Jerry's brother, Rob, home from Afghanistan after a medical discharge, was a big user of their uncle's plants.

"Death happened." Sarah's whisper cut through Becky's thoughts. Sarah stood slowly, her spine a sad curve. "He saw men die. He learned what counted."

Becky stared at her. Not knowing what to say as sorrow for Sarah pulsed through her blood.

"I'm going into the puppy room with Cody. He was napping with the puppies before." Sarah shrugged one shoulder. "Maybe I'll sleep with him there, too. At least for tonight."

The phone rang, and they froze for a moment. Becky stood to get it, but Sarah shook her head and moved toward the counter. "I can't be babied all the time. I have to—" She stopped, looked at the phone, and her back straightened.

Seeing the sudden change, Becky stepped to her side and saw the name on the Caller ID.

"I think that's for you." Sarah looked at her with a sly smile. "It's Boy Number One."

THIRTY-TWO

"How is Sarah?" Derek spoke in the hushed voice people used in a hospice when the dying person was in the same room. As the minister's wife, Becky had been in too many of these situations.

Now she had a personal stake. It was never easy, but being on this end was a million times worse.

"She's fine," Becky said, hearing the deadness in her own voice.

"You're sure? You don't sound the same."

I've been through a horrible experience. Last night my brother-in-law was killed. I saw the truck after the accident, I knew he was inside. I knew he was probably dead. What do you think I should sound like?

"It's been a rough time."

"Of course." He cleared his voice, a sound that made her think of Elaine. Becky liked Derek's mother, but Elaine always cleared her throat during Jim's sermon. Elaine blamed it on her MS, but Becky had done an online search and didn't find that throat clearing was a symptom of the disease.

She liked Elaine. She really did. But she had to admit Elaine enjoyed being the center of attention, with people feeling sorry for her.

"I wish I could come over and help," he said, "but I have to take Mom to the doctor's."

"Oh? Is she worse?"

"As soon as she heard the news about Marsh, she got very agitated. Because of her condition, she's sensitive to these things." He sounded like he was quoting words he'd memorized. "Especially when it happens to someone she knows."

"Really? That's too...too...bad." Even more than Elaine's cough, Becky disliked the way Elaine always had to be worse than anyone else.

"I really wanted to be with you," Derek said. "We should be home in an hour or two, depending on how long we have to wait. Dr. G is squeezing her in."

She leaned forward, her elbows on the counter. She was becoming cynical and bitter. And feeling like a bit of a fool for having sex with him when he was turning out to be a huge mama's boy.

Not that she faulted him for taking Elaine to the doctor's. She admired him for taking such good care of his mother. She admired him for still wanting to come over and take care of her this afternoon.

But she would admire him more if once in a while, he said no to Elaine.

"You need me to do anything," he said, "I'm your man."

"I'm sure." But right now she didn't really want her own man. Right now she'd prefer a baby. And Derek wasn't a candidate.

A whine came from the puppy room.

Or a really cute black puppy.

"My mom has to go now. She said to give you and Sarah her condolences."

"Tell her thank you. I hope she's better soon. Bye."

"I'll be thinking about you."

But you've chosen to be with her. She put the phone down then hung her head over the table, squeezing her eyelids tight.

She had to stop this silent angst and sarcasm. Before this she'd been too nice. Now she was too bitchy – in her thoughts, at least. If she weren't careful, she'd turn into someone she didn't like very much.

In the end, it wasn't what other people said that mattered: it was how she felt about herself.

Her cell phone rang, and she picked it up. This time she saw Trey's name, and she put it to her ear with a smile. Not thinking any sarcastic thoughts. Not after last night. Not with her body still humming a sweet song.

"Hey," he said.

She stood, took a step to the counter and leaned back against it, crossing her legs. "Hey yourself. Where are you?"

"Michigan. I overslept this morning."

One corner of her mouth kicked up, and she felt warm and fuzzy inside. "Had a late night, did you?"

"A full night."

His voice was wry, and she was hit by the memory of his grim expression when he realized what happened to his condom. She uncrossed her legs and stood straight, not feeling the warmth and fuzziness anymore. The hum of her body silenced.

"Before I left," he continued, "I tried to take care of Marsh's truck, but your uncle was there before me."

"He's a good man." Her mind had shut down but her minister's wife and cheesemaker's daughter's manners kicked in. She suspected she could make polite talk in her sleep. "So are you. Thanks for being there last night."

"I wouldn't have done anything different."

That she didn't believe. She knew one thing he'd have done differently.

"I want you to know..." Trey paused and she cringed because he wasn't the kind of person who paused. She knew he was going to talk about what happened. And she knew she didn't want to hear it.

"It's okay," she said. "If anything happens from last night, I'll take care of everything myself."

"Bullshit. Whatever happens, if anything does happen, I'll be a part of it."

"Fine, fine," she said, her voice thick, emotion engulfing her, drowning her, so she was gasping, clutching the phone tightly. "I have to go."

"Just one moment," he said, and his voice was different than she'd heard it before. Low and emotional. "I missed the first sixteen years of my son Scott's life. I don't want it to happen again."

"I wouldn't do that to you."

"I can't be there for Scott all the time. Not as much as I'd like. But when I am, I'm a good dad."

She sucked in a deep, shaking breath, a thought creeping into her mind. A tiny light bulb turning on. "Do you *want* a baby?"

"I'm a selfish bastard. I'd make a lousy husband. And not the best dad. Not because I don't want to be, but I wouldn't be there all the time. And I know the best dads show up. But I'm good at what I do, and I like doing it. I'm not going to change."

That sounded like a 'no' to her, but she wasn't devastated. Not even disappointed. This wasn't about him or any other man. It was about her.

"I'm not asking you to change. When I find out what's happening, I'll let you know." She hung up because she didn't know what to say to him. She realized then that she didn't know him, not really. Her life was changing by the day. Sometimes by the hour, and he couldn't know her, either.

It hadn't even been a month since she caught her husband with another woman. In the short time since then, she'd filed for divorce and had sex with two men. She'd seen sparkles and her brother-in-law's ghost. Her world and her sister's had been turned upside down.

And there was a tiny possibility that she might be pregnant. Not even a possibility, really. Just a hope.

She put her hand on her belly. *Please. Please, please, please.*

Sarah stuck her head in the kitchen. "Cody and I are going to play with the pinball machines in the third shed. You want to come?"

Becky thought of a list of things she should be doing to help Sarah. If they were planning to have people over to the house after the service, she should start cleaning and baking.

"I've never played a pinball machine."

Cody stepped out from behind his mom. "Then you gotta do it, Aunt Becky."

"Who am I to argue with a six-year-old boy?" She walked along with them, and as they neared the sheds, the aluminum reflected the sun. Not sparkles but flashes of light that lifted the ache in her and warmed her heart. In that instant, she felt more like a part of a family than she had done since before her mother's death.

Except this wasn't her family. It was Sarah's.

She stopped. Putting her hand to her upper stomach, she made a face. "My tummy's giving me bad messages. I'd better go back. You two go without me."

Sarah gave her a sympathetic look and so did Cody. Tummy aches were one thing everyone understood and no one questioned.

Becky turned back toward the house, her hands still on her stomach, keeping up the pretense of not feeling well, and striding fast. A big ball of sadness swelled in her throat. The only reason she was here instead of looking for a job and an apartment she could afford was because Marsh was dead. His life ended.

She would stay with Sarah as long as she was needed, but this would be a temporary situation, not a permanent one. This was Sarah's life, and she needed to find her own eventually. Whatever that would turn out to be.

THIRTY-THREE

"Marsh Lowtower was the finest man I've known," Becky said. There were gasps from some of the pew sitters who perched like crows on the graceful wooden benches of Elsa's church. These pew sitters had come today not out of respect for Marsh or Sarah, Becky knew. They came because they didn't want to take the chance of missing any delicious morsels of gossip.

Glances flickered to Jim and Carl, who both stared at Becky stonily from their seats in the right front row. The people behind them no doubt wished fervently that they could see the discomfort on their faces. Instead they had to look at the back of their heads and only imagine their disapproval.

The spectators' glances shifted to the left front row, where Marsh's mother, sister and brother-in-law and their ten-year-old daughter sat near the inner aisle, Sarah beside them. Cody, Sam and his daughter Katie sat on Sarah's other side, guarding her from ill wishers. Or from people she didn't want to talk to. People who'd never supported Sarah's marriage. Who never believed in Marsh the way Sarah believed – with all her heart.

Becky took another good look at the audience. Derek and Elaine sat in the second row behind her father. And coming up the aisle was Trey and a young man she guessed was his son. Though it was foggy outside, a gleam of late afternoon light shone in from one of the many windows and lit up Trey and followed him up the aisle.

Trey had called this morning on his drive back from Ontario. He told her he had an eight-hour drive to Miracle and he wasn't sure if he'd make the service. She'd told him not to worry about it.

But here he was. He must've driven without stopping to eat. Not the smartest thing to do, but she couldn't stop her leap of happiness or her quickened heartbeat to see him there.

Someone cleared a throat and she became aware that people were staring at her. Waiting for her to go on. She sucked in a breath, as usual, ready to do what was expected. But this time the words weren't going to be what the majority expected or wanted. They were for two people. Her sister and her nephew.

"I'm honored to have known Marsh." She stopped and looked around. Another throat cleared, and she recognized this as her father's. He was glaring at her now. She knew that look. He wanted her to finish up so he could get out of there.

She looked him straight in the eye. "He was a man of integrity. He loved life." She switched her gaze to Sarah and Cody, because they were the ones who mattered here. "He was a great father and husband." She could hear her voice soften and she spoke more slowly. "He loved his wife and son more than anything else.

"People used to call him the junkman's kid, but it never bothered him. He once told me that he'd had the best father in the world. But I think Cody had the best father in the world and he should be proud to be descended from a great line of men."

A gasp came up from the row on the right, but Becky didn't look. Instead she backed off the podium. She passed Elsa, who patted her on the shoulder.

Like a benediction.

As Becky headed down the steps at the side, she heard small hiccups from Sarah who sat with her hand over her mouth, staring at her lap, her shoulders heaving.

Becky hurried. She had a sinking feeling in her stomach for making Sarah cry. She reached her seat and Sarah looked up. Tears shone on her face, but so did a giant smile.

"Thank you," Sarah whispered, her eyes radiant. "Thank you so much."

At the pulpit, Elsa said a few more words, then the service broke up. Sarah brought Marsh's ashes home in an urn and placed it on the mantel in the puppy room.

Sarah's house soon filled with people coming to pay their respects. At least, that was the idea, Becky thought, as she avoided Linda Wegner and her probing asp's tongue. Some came who genuinely cared for Marsh, Sarah and Cody. Others came because there might be a family drama here and heaven forbid they'd miss anything.

To top that, there was free food. The one thing the people of Miracle liked more than gossip was food. They liked cooking it; they liked smelling it; they liked looking at it. Most of all, they liked eating it.

The table and counters were laden with so much food brought by villagers that Becky was surprised the table legs didn't buckle. The small house was packed. At five, as if an unspoken signal went off, mingling stopped and the villagers lined up in the kitchen like pigs to the trough at Pete Martin's Happy Hog Farm.

Becky had lost her appetite since the night of the accident. Since the flu, actually, but usually she would've regained it by now. She hadn't weighed herself but her dress felt loose. She wasn't about to run out and get new clothes, though. Not after spotting the mini-tiramisus that Rosa and Mike had brought over in shot glasses.

"Aunt Becky, is your tummy hurting again?"

Becky realized her hands were splayed over her stomach again, and she jerked them back to her sides. "I'm fine. Are you hungry?"

"Uh-uh. Two people tried to buy Sammy."

It took Becky a second to remember he'd named the black puppy after her uncle. "Is your mom saving him for you?"

He shook his head, and she felt his grief. "They didn't offer enough money, but Mom says we need the money we're getting for all the puppies."

"I'm sorry, sweetie."

"You could keep Sammy."

She opened her mouth to tell him gently she wouldn't be living here forever, but this wasn't the right time.

Then she looked at his sad face. He'd just lost his father four days ago. If Sammy could help Cody get through this... "I'll talk to your mom later." Becky's shoulders relaxed. Keeping Sammy wasn't practical, but...it felt *right*.

Especially since she was half in love with Sammy already. She would make it work. She'd find a way to fix it.

"Maybe you should do it now?" Cody looked up at her with earnest eyes. "Before someone wants to give her more money."

She didn't answer right away, but...how could she resist those eyes that looked at her as if she were his last hope? "You know, that sounds like a good idea. I'll do it."

His face brightened and his slumped spine straightened. He looked two inches taller. "I'll tell her! Right now." Then he was off, squeezing through the crowd as if he raced to save the puppy's life.

Becky's eyes prickled. At that moment, it came to her that the first thirty-six years of her life were lived by design. Only they'd never been by *her* design. She was going to damn well change that in the next thirty-six-plus years. She would live them by *her* design.

A warmth grew inside her. As if her heart approved.

She turned and walked into a man's wide chest.

Trey. She knew it was him even with her nose buried in his gray shirt. She recognized the feel of his chest and the height and the breadth of him. Recognized the spot where her nose met his chest, right between the first and second buttons. Recognized the feel of the big hands that curled around her upper arms. Recognized the faint spicy scent.

She stepped back and smiled at him. Letting go of her arms, he smiled back.

"Hey," he said. "Fancy you running into me here."

Cody, his face still bright, grabbed a handful of Becky's skirt. "Aunt Becky *lives* here."

A laugh brought Becky's gaze to the young man standing next to Trey. Easy to see he was Trey's son. He looked like Trey, though his eyes were green and his hair a dark auburn, the color of burnt leaves. He was two or three inches shorter than Trey, but she guessed he'd be Trey's height or taller by the time he stopped growing. With the extra years, he'd probably get his dad's muscles, too.

Trey introduced her and Cody to Scott.

"Hi," Cody said. "Aunt Becky's going to keep Sammy." He looked up at Becky. "Mom was talking to someone but you'll tell her later, right?"

Becky smoothed Cody's silky hair with the pad of her thumb. "I'll tell her. Don't worry about it."

Trey's eyebrows rose. "Who's Sammy?"

"The black puppy," Cody said. "I named him."

"I thought I smelled puppies," Scott said.

"Wanna see them?"

"Sure."

The Kershoff girls, hovering nearby and pretending not to notice Scott, stepped forward to express their interest in puppies, too.

Scott and the oldest Kershoff girl exchanged glances, and her cheeks bloomed a pale rose pink.

"You can all see them. Follow me." Cody led the way to the puppy room, the younger Kershoff girl beside him, and the two older teens following behind.

Becky looked up at Trey. "He takes after you."

"His mom, too. We didn't give him an easy road."

"I don't know anyone who got handed an easy road."

He smiled down at her. "Right this second it's looking brighter to me."

She smiled back at him. Out of her peripheral vision, she spotted someone coming toward her. *Derek.*

The sinking feeling returned to her stomach. She shifted her gaze to him. Though the corners of Derek's mouth lifted, his brow was furrowed, his eyebrows puckered together.

She groaned inwardly. She really didn't want to deal with this now.

THIRTY-FOUR

"Sorry I wasn't able to get here sooner," he said. "My mother hasn't been well this week."

"I'm sorry Elaine's been sick." She glanced behind him. Elaine sat on one of chairs, her cane slanted against the wall. Though she was talking to Linda Wegner, she was glaring their way. Becky had thought that Elaine was her friend, but she was scowling at Becky as if she were her worst enemy.

"She said she left a message but you didn't call her back."

"She left one for Sarah."

"Oh. Well, she probably thought Sarah would pass it on to you."

Becky raised her eyebrows. She felt sorry for him and for Elaine, but she wasn't playing their game. "Sarah and I have been busy."

"Oh, of course." He looked miserable but remained standing, shifting from one leg to another. "How is Sarah?"

"She's...okay."

"I'm going for some coffee." Trey gestured at the kitchen area. "Can I get you anything?"

"If there's a mini-tiramisu left..."

"Got it." He nodded, then headed for the food, leaving Becky with Derek.

Derek shoved his right hand in the pocket of his black slacks. "I guess you feel that I let you down?"

She opened her mouth to say no, but instead she lifted her chin and looked him straight in his eyes. "Do *you* think you let me down?"

He looked down and then up. "I didn't *want* to. My mother needed me."

"So much that you couldn't call?" she asked, her voice gentle. She wasn't angry; she was sad. Not for herself. For him. For his wasted life.

His curled hand came up and he hit his knuckles against his right jaw. "I didn't think you'd understand."

She raised her hand and put it on his, curling her fingers around his fist so he couldn't hit himself again. "I think I do understand."

"Hey, Derek," Linda Wegner said, and he jerked his curled hand away from Becky's, as if her touch scorched his skin. He turned to Linda.

"Your mom isn't feeling well. She wants to go home."

He whipped his gaze back to Becky. She forced the corners of her lips up. "It was nice of you and your mom to come. I'll see you at the next board meeting."

His features collapsed, then snapped back to normal so fast that Linda probably missed it, her gaze on the desserts at the end of the table closest to them.

"Let's go," he said. Linda reluctantly turned her gaze from the table and walked back to Elaine with him, as if he were a lost child being returned to his mother.

Becky's heart was sore for him. He knew his mother was ruining his life, and he wasn't stopping her. Becky wanted to think that he could easily say no to Elaine. But Becky was seven years older than him, and it had taken her walking in on a blow job before she left *her* husband.

Too bad Derek wasn't likely to catch Elaine in a sexually compromising position.

Sarah was heading toward her and Becky made herself smile. "I hate this," Sarah said, her voice low. She swept out her hand toward their guests. "All these people... Most of them didn't respect Marsh while he was alive. I feel dirty having them in the house."

"Kick them out."

"I wish I could." She'd lost weight in the last few days and her cheekbones were hollowed out. "I have to think of Cody." She took a quick glance around. "Do you know where he is?"

"Showing off the puppies to a few kids."

"He loves the puppies." Sarah's lips curved, her tensed body relaxing slightly. "For Cody's sake, I'll be sorry when they're gone. A couple of people showed an interest in the black puppy tonight."

"Sammy," Becky said, and smiled. There was something about that dog...

Sarah smiled, too, and Becky saw heads turning to watch them. "Dean Wegner is coming tomorrow to look at him," Sarah said.

"Tell him not to bother. I want to buy him."

"Are you serious?" Sarah's eyes narrowed. "Did Cody put you up to this?"

"You know Sammy's my favorite." Becky glanced over Sarah's shoulder. "Here comes Trey with my tiramisu. Be nice to me and maybe I'll split it with you."

Sarah glanced over just as Trey was stopped by a former English teacher from Tomahawk High School.

From Trey's grin and the way he bent to talk to the much shorter woman, he had fond memories of her. The sight gave Becky a small frisson. She enjoyed reading and wondered if Trey liked to read, too. Wondered if that's what he did at nights in his hotel room while away from home.

"Boy Number Two," Sarah said, nodding toward Trey.

"*Man* Number Two," Becky corrected.

Sarah nodded. "Very much a man. What about Derek?"

Becky pressed her lips together and shrugged. "Very much a boy."

"I see. So it's Man Number Two then?"

"It's neither," Becky said, her tone crisp. "Boy Number One is a mama's boy, and Man Number Two warned me that he's a traveling man."

"In that case, you deserve the puppy as a consolation prize."

"Sammy might be worth more than both men."

"You talking about me?" Trey handed her the plate with the tiramisu.

"Since you brought me dessert, I'll take that back." Becky looked at Sarah. "You want to share?"

"I'm not hungry." Sarah smiled but there was a sorrow in her face that made Becky's heart ache. "I'll see if the puppies need water."

As soon as she left, Trey said, "I have to go to L.A. tomorrow."

"Did you come back just for...the funeral?" She'd been about to say 'me,' but that would be going too fast for him. Too fast for her, too, though so much had happened since she caught Jim with his pants down, it seemed like another lifetime instead of just weeks.

"No, I came back for *you*." He gave her a look that made her wish they were alone. "And my son," he added. "I want to be home as much as possible for him. I should be back next week."

"You're taking more cars?"

He nodded. "And a couple Indian motorcycles. I'm using parts I got from Marsh."

"I'll tell Sarah. She'll be pleased."

"Tell her I want to rent one of her storage buildings."

"I will." She tried to clamp down a spurt of happiness. If he rented the shed, that meant he'd have a reason to come back.

"The weather is great in L.A. Want to come along?" He didn't take his eyes off her face, as if her answer mattered.

She pushed her hair behind her left ear. "Not this time. Sarah will need me."

He nodded. "And you've got a puppy now."

"I imagine I could bribe Cody to take care of it for me..." She smiled at him, and he smiled back.

Then she caught sight of Linda Wegner less than a foot behind Trey, a paper plate of food in her hand, her eyes bright. Linda stared at her and Trey like a bird that spotted a fat, juicy bug to eat. Becky lifted her eyebrows at Linda, who scurried away so fast that chunks of her sandwich fell off the plate.

Linda went straight to Angie Schuster, the second biggest gossip in town.

Trey followed her gaze. "Trouble?"

She smiled and shook her head. "For people like that to hurt you, you have to care. And I don't care."

He lowered his head toward her. "If I stayed," he said, his voice lowered, "I could fall in love with you."

THIRTY-FIVE

Becky felt lucky today. She stepped out of Sarah's house into the sparkling sunlight.

Inside her belly – maybe her womb – it felt like there were other sparkles.

It was the first day warm enough to wear shorts this year. On the front sidewalk, she stopped to breathe in the spring air, her face up to the sun in a worship position, her eyes closed. Getting her daily dose of Vitamin D3 from the source – and maybe even encouraging some color on her pasty white legs.

She opened her eyes. Yesterday while driving home from the hardware store, she'd spotted a couple neighbors on their knees in their gardens. With each passing day, she silently prayed that she and Trey had planted a different kind of seed. As soon as she had time, she planned on driving to Tomahawk to buy a pregnancy test. The Wegner's sold them, but no unmarried women in Miracle would buy one there. Anyone who did that might as well post a sign in their front yard that read: I'm a slut and might be pregnant.

She headed to the second storage building. When she reached the first one, she felt a cramp in her stomach.

Despite the warm air, her skin chilled.

And the feeling of sparkles in her tummy disappeared. Just like that. As fast as a snap of fingers.

No, her mind screamed. *No.*

She kept going, but her smile was gone and she was breathing faster. By the time she reached the last storage building where Sarah was restoring carved angels on a wooden wall sculpture for Elsa's church, the pain was gone.

Becky inhaled deeply. This had to be a one-time glitch. Maybe she'd eaten something that disagreed with her. After all, Bad Fortune had been knocking stones down on her and Sarah, and it was time for some good stuff.

Hearing her enter, Sarah stood and arched her body. Her baby bump was more prominent every week, and she put her hands on the small of her back. It had been two weeks since the get-together at the house. Nearly three since the night Marsh had been killed.

Nearly three since the broken condom incident.

"The baby hurting your back?" Becky asked.

"Bending over the worktable for twenty minutes is hurting my back." She nodded at Becky. "What about you? You're not used to this work. Any backaches yet?"

Becky remembered the stomach cramp, but that was gone already, and it had happened so fast it didn't count. No need to imagine catastrophes. Plenty happened without having to make up crap. Besides, she wasn't even sure that she was pregnant.

"The backs of my thighs are killing—"

A swift pain low in her belly cut off her sentence.

Oh no. Oh God, no.

It was followed by another one. And suddenly she knew for sure that the bloating she'd felt this morning wasn't because she was pregnant.

She put her hand over her stomach. Tried to smile but knew she failed.

"I think I started my period."

"Shit," Sarah said. "Shit."

Becky hurried out of the building, her jaw tight, her mouth set, holding back her tears.

There was no baby.

And the horrible part was that she knew there never would be one.

Next to her mother's and her brother-in-law's deaths, this was the blackest moment of her life.

A car was coming down the road, but she didn't look, not even when it stopped. Right now she couldn't bear to talk to anyone. She feared the only thing that would come out of her mouth would be a long, mournful scream.

THIRTY-SIX

B ecky stayed in the bathroom for about twenty minutes, but Sarah and someone she'd brought with her into the kitchen didn't go away. She heard murmurs and between her sobbing breaths, the refrigerator door opened and the microwave bell dinged. Someone eating or drinking... Going on with life while she worked her way through the first four stages of grief.

A fast process because there was nothing to grieve about. Never had been. She wasn't delusional. The pregnancy had been a tiny possibility, never a certainty.

It started with the message about the miracle in the church parking lot. And then there were the sparkles. As far as she knew, no one else had seen the sparkles. She'd never said she was pregnant aloud – she'd even hushed the thought every time it occurred – but it had seemed that *she* must be the one who would receive a miracle.

A baby.

She'd been wrong. So wrong it was now a joke on her.

She looked at her reddened eyes in the mirror and told herself if Sarah could make it through her great sorrow for Marsh without falling apart too often – at least not in public – she certainly could over this.

She put on her moisturizer again. Nothing she could do about her eyes or her nose that looked as if she could substitute for Rudolf in December, but at least her complexion wasn't splotched with red.

Combing her hair, she thought Trey would be glad when she reported to him that she wasn't pregnant. And now she wouldn't have to drive to Tomahawk for a pregnancy test.

These thoughts brought on another round of tears until her cheeks were blotched along with everything else. She finally sniffed back the tears and splashed cold water on her face.

She was tired of being depressed. Tired of crying in the bathroom and feeling sorry for herself. If she couldn't have a baby, there were other things she could do. Positive things. Perhaps not now with her life in flux. But later.

Breathing deeply, she stood with her spine straight and her chin high. Opened the door. Strode out. *Here I am world. Becky Maria Hoffman Diedrich, soon to be Hoffman again.*

Or another name, she thought, heading into the kitchen.

Maria. Her middle name was Maria after her mother's mother. It was a good name. Using it, she could reinvent herself. She had a home with Sarah now. She had half the money from her savings with Jim – enough to keep her going for a while. She would get half their investments, too. She wasn't penniless. But she realized her most valuable asset was the people who loved her.

Not many people were as lucky as she was.

The sight of Elsa in the other room made her relax her militant, don't-pity-me stance. She even felt a small measure of happiness. Since she'd left Jim, she'd lost people she'd believed were friends. But it was good, because she'd found out who her real friends were. She'd reconnected with her sister and her nephew. She had a dog.

Her best new friend – besides Trey – was Elsa. Every time Elsa smiled, it was like being in the sunlight. In fact, Elsa was smiling right now as she stood and held out her arms to Becky.

Becky went straight into Elsa's arms. They were the same height, and Elsa hugged her tightly, as if she were concentrating on sending love into her.

When Elsa's grip finally loosened, Becky drew back. "My mom used to hug like that."

Elsa blinked, and her smile was wobbly. She put her hand up, her fingertips touching Becky's lips.

Becky gasped, slammed with a sudden sense, a memory. Something she'd thought she'd forgotten. "My mom used to do that. She called it kissing with her fingers."

"My grandmother used to do that, too. She must have taught it to your mother."

"My mother knew your grandmother?" Sarah asked.

"We had the same grandmother." Elsa looked from one to the other. "Your mother and I were cousins."

Sarah's mouth gaped, and Becky was sure hers was doing the same thing. "I'm...delighted." Becky said. "And kind of mystified about the secrecy. I would've loved to have known you as a kid."

"I lived in California."

"California isn't the end of the world," Sarah said.

Becky nodded. "Was it because of Dad? Is that why didn't you tell us earlier?"

"There's a...history in our family." She smiled. "I promised not to tell you."

"But you're telling us now."

"Only part of it. And you're adults now." She looked from Sarah to Becky and her smile straightened. "One of the two people I made the promise to is no longer on this earth. I think now she would want me to tell you that there's a family connection."

"Our mom," Becky said.

"And the other one?" Sarah's voice came out in a whisper.

Elsa looked at her sadly. "The other one may not be acting in your best interests."

"I can guess who that is." Becky frowned. "I don't see how Dad's acting in his own best interests, either. I don't get it."

"He's acting out of fear. Fear is never a good place to be. Not for anyone."

Meeting Sarah's frowning gaze, Becky saw the same confusion she guessed must be in her face. What was it that their father feared?

"You've been crying," Elsa said. "Why don't you tell me what's wrong with you?"

Becky shared another long look with Sarah. Elsa leaned forward and touched her arm lightly. "That's okay. You don't have to tell me."

As if Elsa had turned on a switch, Becky poured out the pathetic tale of her paucity of eggs. All these years she hadn't talked to anyone but Sarah about it – and Sarah only recently. Her father had emphasized that she and Jim must come to the parishioners from a place of strength. Jim had bought into her father's viewpoint, though she privately questioned it, thinking her own troubles would make her more empathetic to the congregation.

But who had she been to argue with these two leaders of the community? Both older than her. Both so secure in who they were.

The only thing Becky had been sure about was that she needed to try her best to deserve their respect. Try to deserve everyone's respect. Even if it felt like she was burying her true self.

Talking about her desire for a baby, and her disappointment now was actually a relief.

Her true self was bursting into life now. She'd told herself she wouldn't cry, but she lied. More tears welled up in her eyes.

Sarah held one of her hands, Elsa the other. Becky sniffed and let go of Sarah's hand to grab a napkin and dab it at her cheeks, blinking back more tears.

Enough tears. Enough self-pity. Enough sadness.

"You'd make a wonderful mother," Elsa said.

"I know." Becky shrugged, as if it didn't matter, as if tears weren't threatening to swim out of her eyes again and dive down her face.

"Do you care if it's not your egg?" Elsa asked.

Sarah gasped and brought up both hands over her breastbone. "I never thought of that. After I have the baby, I can donate eggs to you." Her voice rose with excitement. "On my next check-up, I'll ask about it."

"I had my eggs harvested years ago." Elsa stared into Becky's eyes with a curious intensity. "I never used them for myself, but I couldn't bring myself to let them go."

She paused, and Becky held her breath, her heart thumping in her chest as she waited to see what Elsa would say next.

Waited and while she did, hope began to grow.

THIRTY-SEVEN

"I'd be happy to give you whatever you need," Elsa said.

"I'm her sister," Sarah said. "I should do it."

"And I'm a second cousin." Elsa leaned forward, her gaze intent on Becky, as if she were focused on convincing her. "We share genes. When I was your age, I looked a lot like you." Then she turned to Sarah, her shoulders more relaxed. "Besides, it's pricey and the procedure isn't very comfortable. I'm not sure what the costs for egg harvesting are now, but I believe it's over ten thousand dollars."

Sarah sat back, then forward again, turning to Becky, her chin mulish – mirroring a look she'd gotten from their father. She opened her mouth, and Becky held out her hand, stopping her from arguing.

"Save your money for Cody's college fund."

"He might be a picker."

Becky lowered her hand. "Then you can start him out with a hefty down payment for a new truck."

"You have an answer for everything."

"Of course. I'm your older sister." Becky turned to Elsa and opened her mouth to thank her...

And the room filled with sparkles. So bright, so radiant, it was hard to see anything else. Hundreds, no thousands of sparkles. Tiny twinkling stars filled Sarah's kitchen. Filled it with possibilities. With magic. With *miracles*.

Becky gasped. Awe filled her. Pure awe.

The sparkles blinked out, leaving Becky gawking at a plain kitchen with a white refrigerator covered with pictures of Cody's drawings. But in her mind, Becky still saw the sparkles. And she felt overwhelmed by the sense of magic. Overwhelmed by Elsa's generosity.

She turned her gaze to Elsa's face and saw tears glimmering in her eyes. "I don't want you to thank me," Elsa said, her voice rougher than usual. "It's my honor to do this. I can't guarantee that it will work, but I can tell you that I have a very good feeling about this. *Very* good."

Becky grabbed her hand so tightly that Elsa winced. Becky immediately let go. She leaned forward. "This is the most generous thing anyone has done for me. I *know* this will work." Her breathless voice reflected her inner wonderment. "I know it."

"Are you forgetting that you'll need one more thing?" Sarah asked.

Becky whipped her gaze to her sister. "What?"

"Sperm. You'll need sperm."

Instantly Becky pictured Trey.

"You could contact a sperm bank," Else said.

Becky frowned. Not sure how she felt about that. Her baby would be created from a donated frozen egg and sperm from an anonymous man. It would be...manufactured. Impersonal. Created without any emotion. A robo baby.

Of course the baby would be manufactured any way she did it. It wasn't just that. It was...

She bowed her head. When she'd woken this morning, her first thought was that she might be pregnant with Trey's baby. And she'd been quietly ecstatic.

She wanted that sheer happiness back. She *wanted* her baby to be Trey's baby.

"I could." Lifting her head, Becky gave Elsa a small smile, hiding her thoughts and hopes and uncertainties. "That will be Plan B."

"You have Plan A picked out?" Elsa's left eyebrow arced and her lips curved up.

Remembering Trey's dismayed expression when she told him about the condom problem, Becky grimaced. "I can't count on it. It's a long shot."

"It's a good idea to go after the long shots. You might be surprised at the outcome."

"I'm surprised a lot lately."

Sharp barks and a hiss came from the puppy room. Sarah stood, frowning slightly. But instead of leaving right away, she put her hands on the table and leaned over it, her gaze on Elsa. "Do you mind telling us why you froze your eggs?"

Elsa gave a half shrug and a half smile. "I suppose I should."

Becky touched Elsa's right arm. "Not if you don't want to."

Elsa put her slim fingers over Becky's, her fingertips cool, just for one second. Then she shifted and Becky drew back her hand.

"It's fine now." Elsa spoke in a low voice. "I was married to an artist. He was paralyzed in an accident after we'd been married only a few years. I loved him deeply, but I knew that one day I might want children. Andrew was the one who convinced me to harvest my eggs. In case mine dried up by the time he died."

Sarah breathed in a harsh breath and Becky sucked in her lips, feeling for Elsa and her husband. Though Elsa smiled, Becky was close enough to see the sadness in her shadowed eyes.

"I had to take care of him, so having a baby wasn't possible while he was alive." Elsa gave the same sad smile again. "It was my privilege. I was past fifty when he gave up the fight, and then I traveled. Finally I thought I'd come here to the place my mother lived until she was a teenager." She reached out a hand to Sarah and one to Becky. She looked from one sister to the other as they gripped her hands. The three of them connected. "I've been around the world but something called me here. Now I think it was you two, my extended family. I've wanted to tell you so many times before this..."

Becky's heart opened. Like a page in a book unfolding, she thought. Making room for new words, new pages, new people to love.

Elsa was one of them.

The puppy was another. It had snuck into her heart on first glance. Even before Cody's pleas, she'd wanted him. He just gave her an excuse to do it.

And her heart was open for a baby. Wide open.

Now all she had to do was convince Trey that he should be the lucky father.

THIRTY-EIGHT

The kitchen smelled of cinnamon and garlic and tomatoes and olive oil. Becky hoped that at least one of the smells made a particular man say yes to pretty much anything. Like 'Will you donate your sperm and make a baby with a donated egg?'

It had been a long week and a half since Elsa's generous offer. Becky had seen Trey once when he brought parts and a couple of motorcycles to the storage building. He'd popped in to say 'hi,' but just stayed to tell her he was on his way to someplace else.

Now Trey was back again and said he planned to remain in his Tomahawk condo for a few weeks. As she checked the sweet potato for doneness, she felt his gaze on her ass. A good start to a date night, she thought, despite what Sarah said about her lack of booty.

When she'd talked to Trey on the phone, he'd said he liked Greek food, so she made a moussaka dish with eggplant and feta cheese – using a recipe Jim had never liked. As she prepared it earlier, Sarah had asked, 'Is the moussaka a test?' Becky had said, 'No, it's dinner.'

But perhaps it was a test. Perhaps if he didn't like her food, then he wouldn't like her to have his baby. Even if she swore that she'd never expect money from him. Swore that she'd never expect him to be a father to the baby.

Not that he'd agree to that. Not after what he'd said subsequent to the split condom incident. After all, he'd come back to Wisconsin as soon as he found out about Scott. He turned his life upside down for his son. One reason she admired him so much.

No wonder she wanted his sperm. How would she know if an anonymous sperm donor had those qualities?

"How're Sarah and Cody holding up?" he asked.

"They're...surviving." She put the moussaka on the table, along with the garlic green beans she'd cooked earlier that day and was serving cold with almonds and green onions. She went back for the potatoes.

Everything seemed to be done just right. That was a good sign.

"I hope she didn't feel kicked out of her house because I was coming to dinner." He dished a large rectangle of moussaka onto his plate and made an appreciative hum in his throat.

"You want me to call her and tell her to come home?" she asked.

He chuckled as he reached for the beans. "Nope. Anyway, it's good for her and Cody to get out."

"They're just across the street." There was silence for a few minutes while they dug in and ate. After the first moment without much to say, she got nervous. She should've put on the stereo, but Sarah never used it and Becky wasn't sure if it worked.

"It's quiet," he said.

"I was just thinking the same thing. All the puppies are adopted."

"I noticed it smelled better. I thought it was the food." He scooped up another forkful. "This is great."

She thanked him and grabbed her wine glass. She felt unusually awkward today, knowing what she was going to ask him. She'd make a lousy conman. Or politician.

"Where's Sammy?" he asked. "I thought you were keeping him."

She set the wine glass down and smiled, a real one this time instead of the nervous stretching of her lips that she'd been doing since he came in.

"He's across the street with Cody and Sarah. Cody insisted. Joy said she didn't mind, and to bring Goldie along, too."

"So he commandeered your puppy?"

"Sammy sleeps with Cody." Her smile dropped off, sadness hovering near, ready to envelope her if she let it. "Sammy and the kitten. Sarah keeps thinking she shouldn't allow it, but it's helping Cody get through Marsh's death. To be truthful, I think Goldie is helping Sarah get through it."

"Dogs are great. Maybe someday I'll..." He frowned and took a big bite of moussaka. He chewed a few times and nodded his approval. Giving him an excuse not to talk, Becky thought.

She wondered what he'd been about to say but stopped her thoughts.

She didn't need to know if he secretly yearned for a home and a dog.

She didn't need his love.

She didn't even need his body.

She only needed his sperm.

Breaking the silence, she told him that Lucky the kitten was probably hiding somewhere. Or sulking because he wasn't invited to Joy's. He laughed at that, and she smiled. Not telling him she was serious. The kitten thought of Goldie as his mom and Sammy as his other brother. He didn't seem to hate humans, but he preferred dogs.

Sometimes Becky understood that completely.

Not tonight, she thought, watching Trey eat. For tonight she especially liked one favorite man.

For dessert, they ate German chocolate cake that Sarah had made from a mix, with frosting she'd bought in a can. Becky ate the small piece she'd taken for herself, sipping wine between each bite to moisten her dry throat.

Sarah didn't have a dishwasher, so once they were done eating, Becky put the casserole dish in the fridge and piled the dishes next to the sink. She gave Trey a beer from a Wausau brewery and told him she'd wash up after he left.

He put the beer aside and headed to the sink. "It goes faster with two."

For no reason at all, tears sprang into her eyes. She blinked them away and then followed him to the sink.

She couldn't talk, her throat choked by his easy domesticity. This was something Jim would never have done.

His loss. She found it...uber-sexy.

Trey turned on the water and asked where the detergent was. She found it behind the paper towel roll then grabbed a towel and dried as he told her stories about his first years in California when he was a teen and washed dishes to earn enough money for a truck. After he got the truck, he graduated to waiter and worked at a fancy L.A. restaurant Fridays, Saturdays and Sundays. The other four days he drove out of the city, far out, finding country roads and looking for anything old and valuable – especially anything to do with motorcycles and old cars.

He learned as he went. Made money on great deals, lost money on lousy ones. Spent hours reading reference books and on the Internet. Talked to other pickers. Went to museums. Stuffed his head with knowledge until he was the go-to guy for anything to do with motorcycles.

"You listen too well." He pulled the plug and the soapy water slurped down the drain.

"I feel...kind of in awe." She bent to put the dinner dishes and dessert plates in the lower cupboard.

When she straightened, one side of his mouth was quirked up in a sardonic smile. "You must be kidding me."

"Don't undervalue yourself. You carved a spot of your own in the world. You're independent, doing what you enjoy, following your passion. You're not like me. I did everything safe, everything that was expected of me." Her voice was getting hoarse but she pushed through it. "Everything other people wanted me to do."

"Hey," he murmured, as if he were comforting a child. He put his hand on her shoulder. "Don't beat yourself up."

She wanted to lean her head against his chest. Instead she stepped back. "Your life is authentic. Mine...isn't."

"Baby..." He took a step toward her.

Panic slammed into her, along with a wave of self-disgust. "I can't do this. I just can't." She rubbed her hands together, as if she were rubbing dirt off her palms. Realizing what she was doing, she stopped and put her hands behind her.

His brow furrowed. "What can't you do?"

She tried to smile but her lips trembled and she gave up. For years she'd kept her emotions neat and contained. The same way she kept her house. But now everything was getting messy.

"I was going to try to seduce you into doing something, but I can't do it. You're too...real. Too nice."

"Nice?" His eyebrows contracted and he looked a little disgusted.

Despite feeling as if a ball of barbed wire was stuck in her chest, she smiled. "It's not a dirty word. Nice is...sexy."

"You're probably the only woman in the world who thinks that."

"You're nice and you're a hero and you're real..." She gestured at him. "And just *look* at you. Any woman who doesn't think you're sexy has to be blind or crazy."

He laughed, low in his throat, sending shivers through her.

Her face and neck heated. She may as well just throw herself at him and say, 'Take me. Take me now!'

"Why don't you just tell me what you want?" He smiled, slow and sexy. "Maybe I'll let you seduce me after all."

THIRTY-NINE

S he melted. Like marshmallows on a tiny tree branch held over a fire, she was melting into a gooey mess. "Can't we do the seducing first?"

He laughed and pulled her against him. Then he lowered his sexy head, his open lips slanted against her open lips. A sigh shivered through her melted body and the individual parts came to life, igniting a fire deep down inside her.

She clung to him, even as he pulled his mouth away.

"Don't you know how to bargain?" he asked.

She shook her head. She didn't know. She didn't care.

"You hold out, and when you get what you want, then you give what the other person wants."

"This is what I want." She put a hand on each side of his face. "You. I want *you*."

His mouth came down again, silencing her, and she slid her hands onto his back. She lifted a leg, wound it around the back of his thighs and pulled his length against her. His erection pushed against her belly.

When he pulled away, she wanted to cry out. But she held it back, even as an overwhelming darkness settled in her. A fear that he didn't want her, though she'd felt the evidence that he did just a second ago...

But this...this dance that men and women did...with all its dips and turns and gavottes and secret glances...was ridiculous and insane...and sometimes so wonderful they wanted to do it again and again. That's where she was...at the wanting to do it again.

"Your bedroom?" he asked.

No. The walk to her bedroom was too far. She wanted him now. Right this second. After all, they'd cleared the table. He could take her there. Like in a scene from a movie.

The thought excited her, and she glanced at the table...and winced. It didn't look comfortable. And how would she feel afterward? Eating on it?

Her gaze switched to the floor. No, not there. It had to be even less comfortable than the table. Plus, this floor had had a puppy, a dog, a kitten and shoes that walked about on it. She'd vacuumed before he came, but she hadn't washed it.

How was it that making love on tables and floors looked so sexy in movies?

She stepped toward the hall. "Yes, the bedroom."

Moments later her clothes were on the floor and so were his. She was usually so neat, but today she felt wanton. Unlike herself. She'd shed her clothes with abandon.

She wanted his skin sliding against hers so badly it was an ache in her center. In her womb. For once she didn't care if any of her body parts jiggled. He was looking at her as if he were eating up every jiggle. As if he wanted to taste every inch.

She stretched out on the bed, her arms reaching for him. He didn't come down on her right away. Just stood and looked at her.

Chills whispered up her skin. Except for her center. That heated. Became furnace hot.

Then he was on top of her. He was gentle and slow and made her mad with want. Until they were together, as close as a man and woman could get. Connected more securely than any two pieces of a puzzle.

She didn't see sparkles, but one small quake after another quivered through her. She clung to Trey, holding on tight, small screams coming out of her throat.

She wanted to do this forever.

Then it was his turn to shudder. A long growl roared out of his throat before he dropped onto her, breathing hard, his body shaking. She held him until his quakes stopped.

They lay there for long moments, his spicy scent filling her nostrils.

He was heavier than Jim, who prided himself on only gaining twenty pounds since college, but Trey's weight came from muscle – probably from lifting parts in and out of the truck. He was a man's man. And she could testify he was a woman's as well.

She smiled at the white ceiling and thought she must look like a blissed-out porn queen. Certainly making love with Jim had never left her feeling so satisfied. So...complete. A word she hated to use in this context. As if without a man something inside her was missing. But just this one time, that's how she felt. She had been missing out on this joy.

He rolled off and she held her breath, but this time there was no leakage between her legs.

She hadn't expected it, and really, it was a relief, despite the tiny pang she felt in the one small part in her where hope still bloomed. But she'd been down this hopeful road so often, and it was a route that always ended in disappointment. She didn't want to go there anymore. It just led to her getting a slap on her head and a kick in her heart.

He left to go in the bathroom. Staying in bed, she watched his glutes contract as he walked. They looked magnificent. Probably better than hers, but she wasn't about to check her behind in a mirror to make sure. Some things were better off not knowing.

Once, after watching an *Oprah* show years ago, she'd sat naked on her bedroom carpet in front of the door mirror, opened her legs and looked at her vagina. Wasn't that enough?

He came back into the bedroom without the condom and with his penis smaller than before, but still a nice size. Not that size counted...though early in their marriage Jim had her measure his erection, so she was certain it counted to some men.

"Now that you've seduced me..." He grabbed his black briefs and lifted his knee. "What did you want to seduce from me?"

FORTY

The silly grin she knew was pasted on her face like a 'Great Sex' badge slid off. Followed by a sinking feeling in her stomach. Not the kind of sinking from a few small holes in a rowboat. This was the Titanic-meeting-iceberg kind.

Becky slid out of bed and stood. She should have practiced this. Wrote a script and memorized it. She should have followed the original plan. Made him so wild for her body that he would say yes to anything she asked.

Even as she thought it, a yucky feeling rose up inside her. She didn't want his sperm *that* way.

Besides, he wasn't that kind of a man. If he were, she wouldn't want him to father her child.

"Your sperm," she said.

His head whipped up, and his foot, about to go into his briefs, came slowly down to the floor. His gaze never left her face as he sat on the edge of the bed and studied her with a seriousness that didn't look one iota less grave because he was naked and holding his briefs.

Her words dried in her throat. She'd dutifully listened to CDs about self-empowerment and positive thinking during her years with Jim, but looking at the creases between Trey's eyebrows and his set mouth, negativity whooshed through her.

She inhaled deeply. Getting oxygen into her chest and belly and, more important, to her brain. Aware of her nudity, she kept her arms at her side. If he could do this nude, so could she.

His gaze remained on her face. Didn't dip below her chin.

"I always wanted children," she said, forcing the words out. She started this; she would damn well finish it. "I've been having a hell of a time getting pregnant. Apparently I don't have a lot of eggs. My doctor says it could be a genetic defect, but to my knowledge, I can't trace it to either of my parents' sides."

"Doctors aren't always right."

"I had a second opinion, and the conclusion was the same." Tears burned her eyes but she kept her gaze on his. "Neither doctor said it *wouldn't* happen. Just that the odds were against me. And when the condom broke last time..." She swept out her hand in a wide arc that ended with her hand over her heart.

And when she spoke, her voice lowered. "I hoped. I thought if I did get pregnant, that would be the miracle that was prophesied."

His eyebrows contracted. *"Prophesied?"*

"At church a few Sundays ago. You didn't hear about it?"

"Like in a bible?" he asked.

"No, like on car windows in the church parking lot." She shrugged. "I forgot that you live in the big city of Tomahawk."

He grinned, and she felt relief that he could still smile at her. That he didn't hate her as she poured her heart out to him.

"Laugh if you will, but I'm used to everyone in Miracle knowing everyone else's business." She frowned, because Jim had hidden his infidelity fairly well. As her father had done before Jim. *"Almost* everyone's business. It's gotten so that if I see a line of birds perched on a telephone line, chirping away, I suspect they're talking about the second bird to their right and what bugs it ate the day before."

He laughed. "You think they know about us?"

"I don't care if they know about us."

He nodded at her, and at this sign of approval she breathed easier, her chest opening like an accordion stretched wide.

Quickly she explained the letters on the cars. With the words flying out of her mouth like space trash, she thought about telling him about the sparkles and Marsh's ghost. But when she told him about the letters his eyebrows lowered in a frown again, and her words faltered and slowed. And her chest, so open and wide, closed up a little.

"You believe a miracle is really coming?" He looked at her as if she were a small child who believed in the fairy godmother.

She supposed she did, because she kind of had found one in Elsa. But Elsa was flesh and blood, and much, much better than a fairy.

"I believe anything is possible." She pushed her hand through her hair. "The miracle didn't quite happen. Not a big one. But..." She shook her head and looked at him. One of his eyebrows was arched in cynicism. *Not a good sign.*

"A small miracle then?" he asked.

"To me, it's a miracle of sorts." She was starting to feel a chill but remained standing, naked. It seemed important to be literally and figuratively naked. No clothes, no barriers, no lies while they talked about this. "A...friend had her eggs harvested and frozen, and she's offered them to me."

"Sarah?"

She shook her head. "Someone else. I accepted, and now all I need is sperm."

He blinked, and gazed down at the bed. Or maybe he was looking at his penis, considering the conversation.

His gaze shifted back to her face. "If I fathered a child, I'd want to be a real one."

She nodded. "I'd be fine with that. Of course, I wouldn't ask for any money."

His frown told her that she shouldn't have mentioned money. She shut her mouth before any more words spilled out. Her hands felt nerveless and her nipples were tightening, and she thought maybe she should've put clothes on after all.

How stupid was she to think that being naked meant something? All it really meant was that she was a little goofy. Maybe a lot goofy.

"Are you considering it?" She clenched her hands.

He looked away from her, at the door. Her hands clenched tighter. She'd read a couple of body language books. Looking at the door meant that mentally he was already one step outside of it.

When he finally turned, she could see the 'no' in his face. It was shut down. Not showing emotion. "I can't do it."

She nodded and even managed a smile. "Of course." Her voice came out thick, but the curve of her lips didn't dip. "I understand. We'd better get dressed."

He got up and finally put on his pants. She quickly grabbed her clothes from the floor, not wanting him to see her butt in a bent-over position. Though she wasn't getting his sperm, she still wanted to date him.

A thought occurred to her and she held her clothes to her chest.

Would he want to see her again?

"What are you going to do now?" he asked.

She turned, still holding her clothes against her. "I'll use a sperm bank."

He nodded, his expression still shut down.

"Are you..." She stopped and shook her head. "Will we see each other again?"

"You mean dating?"

She nodded then waited, hardly breathing.

His gaze dropped from hers and now he pulled on his jeans. "I'm sure we will."

More hot tears prickled on her eyes. She could tell Trey was doing the one thing she hadn't expected.

Lying.

He left without kissing her good-bye.

As soon as he was gone, she turned on the computer. Dry-eyed, she typed two words into the search box: SPERM BANKS.

FORTY-ONE

Laughter rang in Sarah's kitchen. The scents of Chinese takeout hung in the air though the food containers were cleaned off the kitchen table, replaced by three laptops spaced out for the four women. Joy and Elsa had brought their own notebooks. Becky and Sarah shared one, which wasn't working so well as they both tried to type at the same time.

Right now, Becky looked around the table at their faces. Sarah, Joy and Elsa all smiling. But no one's smile was as wide as hers.

A warm, fuzzy feeling grew inside Becky's chest.

Happiness. She had it.

With all that had happened lately, and all that might happen soon, she treasured this moment of pure contentment.

"The sparkling grape juice is good." Sarah lifted her glass, the dark purplish red liquid glowing under the hanging light. "But I'm still eager for the day when I can drink wine again." She glanced sideways at Becky. "You sure you want to do this?"

"I'm sure." Becky put her hand over her stomach. Nothing in her womb now. But soon, she hoped. Soon.

"I thought Dr. Johnson was letting her patients have wine occasionally?" Joy lifted her own glass to her lips. She was on her second already, taking advantage of their girls' night while her husband kid-sat their son and Cody.

"I know, but I..." Sarah shook her head, her smile wavering.

Becky patted her shoulder and knew what her sister was thinking. Life was fragile and Sarah preferred not to take chances.

"I'm just glad you invited me," Elsa said.

"You're absolutely necessary." Becky leaned toward her, and touched her arm. She was becoming touchy-feely tonight, and she'd only had half a glass of wine.

"Me, too?" Joy asked.

"You, too," Becky agreed. In the two weeks since she'd made the decision to look for a sperm donor, she'd gotten to know Joy better. Joy loved to laugh and talk trash. Becky thought since Joy trusted her with the size of her husband's erection – which she shared last week while Kevin was playing baseball with his friends – she could trust Joy to keep it quiet that she was having a 'hunt for a sperm donor' party.

"I like your third choice," Elsa said.

"All seven kind of look the same." Joy squinted at the screen, and Becky suspected she needed reading glasses. "Brown hair, six feet tall, muscular."

"Reminds me of someone," Sarah whispered, and Becky elbowed her in the ribs.

As Sarah squeaked, Becky pointed at the screen. "I happen to like that look, but they're all different otherwise. The first is a linguist. The second is going to school to be a quantum physicist. The third—"

"Is only twenty-two," Sarah said. "A little young, don't you think?"

"It's his sperm I'm using. Not his body."

"Healthy swimmers, too." Joy giggled. "Already there's been one pregnancy."

"Your fifth choice is twenty-seven and he has three children," Elsa said. "He plays the saxophone in a major orchestra. I adore the saxophone."

"Let's see him." Sarah craned her head closer to the screen and clicked on the picture. Up popped a photo of Number 5 donor in all his glorious color – which Becky had paid extra for. Totally worth it, she thought, bringing her head next to Sarah's.

"I like saxophones, too," Sarah said. "And he's pretty yummy."

"He looks familiar," Joy said.

Sarah giggled and Becky hunched down in her chair. Glancing at Elsa, Becky saw she was smiling. Becky put her hands under her thighs to keep from putting them over her face.

Yes, the donor did look a little like Trey. Okay, maybe a lot. But that was nothing to be ashamed about.

At least Trey would never know.

Goldie barked, and so did the puppy. A higher-pitched, less-loud, but more enthusiastic version.

"I hope it's not a coyote." Joy glowered toward the front of the house.

"I heard about the coyote killing your cat a couple months ago," Elsa said to Becky. "That must've been frightening."

Becky shuddered and nodded. Though Lucy had been more Jim's cat than hers, she'd shed tears over Lucy's violent death.

The back doorbell buzzed before she could say anything. As if on cue, Goldie and Sammy rushed into the kitchen, barking. The kitten was close behind them, staying back a little in case he needed to run and hide.

Sarah pushed up from the chair. "Did Derek say he's coming over?"

"He called today, but I told him we were having a girls' night." She hadn't dated him since that one time, but he still called once a week or so. Still hopeful, even though she'd finally told him that it wasn't a good idea.

"It's not him then," Sarah said.

Becky nodded. Just the thought of being alone with four women probably would terrify Derek – way too much estrogen for him.

Sarah headed to the door, her stomach preceding her. Becky felt a quick pain that Marsh wasn't here to go through the pregnancy with her sister.

At least Sarah wouldn't be alone. She and Becky were there for each other now – thicker than ever. And Elsa, too.

A warmth washed over Becky, and sparkles appeared behind Sarah as she reached the back door.

Becky gasped at the sight of them, the sound drowned by Sammy's bark at the door.

Joy and Elsa were watching Sarah, too, both holding their glasses of wine. Neither appeared startled. Neither dropped their glasses or stood and shouted 'holy shit.' Nothing showed that they saw sparkles or anything out of the usual.

Only Becky, who felt a sense of wonder inside her as the sparkles formed a hand that brushed over the back of Sarah's hair.

Becky mouthed a name. *Marsh.*

The sparkles twisted, as if nodding at her, then twirled back to Sarah. They hovered over her. Sarah opened the door and more sparkles shimmered down on her. Sarah's skin glowed.

The next second the glow was gone, along with any stray sparkles – as if the whole thing had been a figment of Becky's imagination.

But she'd never had much of an imagination. She'd always been the worker. It was other people who had the creative vision.

Even now, she couldn't imagine why the sparkles had appeared. Then she thought it had nothing to do with her. They'd appeared for Sarah, though Sarah couldn't see them.

Maybe at some level, though, she knew.

"Hey, Sarah," Trey said from the back door. His deep voice reverberated into Becky's gut like a fast kick.

Sarah stepped back to let him inside. The dogs pushed in front of her, though she protested in a weak tone. Becky knew the only way to shut them up quickly was to open the cupboard where their treats took up half a shelf.

Trey petted both dogs and greeted the kitten who was rubbing the side of his head against Sarah's pants leg. When the dogs' excitement subsided, Trey straightened. Though he said 'hi' to all of them, he gazed straight at Becky.

"I interrupted something?" he asked.

"Ah..." Sarah glanced behind her at Becky, and she shook her head. Sarah faced Trey again while Becky drank him in with her eyes. He looked big and strong and sexy.

And a lot like the photos of her potential sperm donors.

Elsa turned to her laptop, her back to the door. Bending her head, she studied the screen, turned back and smiled. Looked at Trey and nodded, too.

Joy slapped her hand over her mouth, but a giggle escaped. She smirked at Becky. "So that's it," she said softly.

"That's what?" Trey asked.

"Never mind." Joy shot him a grin.

Becky wanted to sink below the table and not come out until he left. Instead she lifted her chin and her eyebrows. Her days of shrinking because of a man were over.

"We're having a girls' night," Sarah said.

"I won't be long then." He shifted his gaze to Sarah. "I just stopped off to pay the rent for the storage buildings. How much?"

"I'm an idiot." Sarah scrunched her face. "I can't remember what we agreed upon."

"You never named a price."

"Oh. Is two hundred a month too much?"

"Two fifty," he said.

Sarah's eyes glittered with instant moisture. The two fifty would be grocery money. Or pay for medical bills. A small drop in a large bucket. Though Becky was helping her out, Sarah was determined to pay her own way.

"Okay, two fifty. Do you want a beer? Or wine?"

"Another time. You take credit cards?"

"I do." Sarah beamed, obviously proud of herself for being part of the twenty-first century. "I'm on PayPal, too."

"PayPal works even better. Can I use your computer?"

"Sure. It's in front of Becky." She gestured toward Becky, and as he crossed to the table, Sarah's eyes rounded and her mouth formed a silent howl of horror, as if she were an actress in one of the *Scream* movies.

Elsa's mouth opened in an *O*, too. Once again, Joy slapped her hand over her mouth and a giggle escaped.

Three steps. Didn't even take him one second and Trey reached Becky's side, moving faster than she could gather her wits.

The laptop was in front of Sarah's chair, and Becky lurched forward, blocking his view, her arm reached out to—

"What's going on?" Trey's hand curved over hers and she froze. "Why is everyone acting like I'm about to discover the real Declaration of Independence?"

"I'm looking at something private." She stared fiercely at him. "Do you mind?"

But his gaze wasn't on her. It was on the laptop screen. He was peering over her shoulder, straight at the face of a guy that could've been him ten years ago.

On top of the page, were two hard-to-miss words: SPERM BANK.

FORTY-TWO

"I'll get PayPal." Becky angled the laptop closer to her and sat down. She was normally a decent typist, though never speedy, but now she kept typing the wrong letters and then had to delete them and type the right ones.

Finally the PayPal page showed. She stood and pushed the chair back. "It's all yours."

He didn't move. "We need to talk."

"Not really." She crossed her arms. She refused to be embarrassed or intimidated. "I told you I was going to do this."

Not budging, like a six-foot pillar of cement, he continued to gaze down at her. "We still need to talk."

"Go ahead." She gave him a stare that said she wasn't budging, either. She'd always been the one to budge since she was a child, but it was time to throw off her childish ways. Lately she was tossing them off like they were dead bugs on her skin.

She tilted her head toward the others, her gaze still locked on his face. "I'm sure everyone would love to hear what you have to say."

"I would!" Joy gave an up-and-down chair hop.

"Me, too." Sarah stood behind Elsa. "But Becky will tell me when you leave anyway, so I can wait."

Becky rolled her eyes while Trey rubbed his forehead. Then he did something she didn't expect.

He grinned.

She gaped at him. A show of independence had never been treated with humor in her father's house. Or Jim's.

As it hit her that she thought of the place where she'd lived for sixteen years as Jim's home and not hers, Trey did something that shocked her.

He chuckled.

She melted like butter left out in the sun. She wanted to purr like the kitten.

Her father would have snapped off an order. Jim would've stiffened or looked at her with sadness...letting her know she was letting him down, not acting like the good wife.

But this man...this man who she wanted every time she saw him...

Her independence *amused* him.

"We can talk in the living room." She walked around him, careful not to brush against him. Her nerves were quivering. Her skin felt exposed, as if a touch from him would electrify her.

She led him into the living room. The dogs were already there, on the floor. Though if someone brought out food in the kitchen, that would change in an instant. The kitten was there, too, crouched on the top of the sofa, ready to jump off and run if they came too close.

Trey stopped in the middle of the room. "I'll do it."

"Do what?"

"Be the father."

Her heart stopped for a beat. Then it started again. Faster and harder. "Because you don't want me to use a donor?"

"I've been in L.A. for the last eight days." He scratched his chin and gazed at the drapes. His eyes narrowed, as if he could see through them all the way to Los Angeles. When he brought his gaze back to Becky, his eyes were hooded. Not telling her anything when she wanted to know everything with just one look. "I spent a lot of time thinking. Not just in L.A., but on the drive there and back."

She nodded, her emotions held back tightly. Desperately afraid to say anything. Desperately afraid that what she was hoping for, what she thought he was going to say, might not be said.

"Scott is almost an adult. I never saw him as a baby, a toddler. Never knew he was alive. Never went to his soccer or football games until this last year. And he's good. He's damn good. But I didn't get to see it. I didn't—"

He stopped, his throat working. He sucked in his breath, then exhaled before he spoke again, his voice rough. "Next fall he'll be off to college. He'll be making new friends. Starting his new life. He doesn't even know what college he'll be accepted into."

A coldness grew in her. Shards of ice lodged in her chest, pointed at her heart.

What was he telling her? That he would be leaving Miracle?

She nodded and felt like one of those dolls with a bobble head. She was reverting back to type, listening and nodding...too numb to do anything else.

"I missed most of his life."

"It wasn't your fault." Her voice was hoarse. Her throat was dry. She needed water. Or wine – a large bottle of wine.

"Doesn't matter. I wasn't there. I...don't want to do that again."

"I see." A sick feeling started in her throat. She'd already decided to do this without him. She'd been okay with it. So why did he drag her in here, letting her think that he might—

"This time I want to be there for my child."

Her knees wanted to buckle. A noise came out of her mouth. *Eeep.* She grabbed his arm to keep from falling. She bit her tongue and closed her mouth to keep words from babbling out. And her gaze locked onto his face, as if afraid he were a genie and if she glanced away, even for an instant, he would disappear in a puff of magic smoke.

"You might find someone else," she whispered. "You might be sorry."

"You might find someone else," he shot back. "You might be sorry."

Never. She shook her head. "I'm doing this with you or without you."

"I can't offer anything more. It wouldn't be fair. I'm a traveling guy. You're a stay-at-home woman."

She frowned. She'd dreamed of traveling. With a baby, it might be tough. But she'd never thought it would be easy. A single mom. Newly divorced. Her father not supporting her. No job yet.

It didn't matter. From the start, none of the obstacles mattered. She had enough money to carry them for a while. She was learning to repurpose old items and was already making money. She planned to start online classes in the fall. They wouldn't starve. Maybe she and her baby wouldn't live in luxury, but they would be okay.

And she had the one thing that mattered most to any child.

Love. Inside her body, she had an ocean of love.

"I don't know if I'll be a stay-at-home mom," she said. "Don't expect that from me. I might work outside the home."

"The only thing I expect of you is to be a great mom."

Her throat thickened with unexpected emotion. So inconvenient. "You'll be a great father."

"It's set then," he said. "No donor."

"Technically, you'll be the donor."

"No." His gaze didn't waver from her face. His expression still grave, but his eyes... They warmed and softened and darkened. And so did his low voice. "Technically, I'll be the dad."

Sunlight burst inside her. Brilliant sparkles of happiness. Like a picture in a cartoon movie, they lit up the room, too. Sparkles shimmered all around them.

She stepped back. This was the happiest she'd been in her whole life.

Then he stepped back, too. He looked around the room, his lips parted, his eyes reflecting the sparkles. Even the air felt electrified. As if tiny lights were coming down, shimmering on her skin.

"You see *that*?" His voice was hushed.

She gaped at him. He couldn't be talking about the sparkles? Impossible. No one saw them but her.

"See what?"

"It's like little twinkling stars are in the room. Swirling around us."

Her breath came out in a quasi laugh. Her hands shook, and she held them against her thighs. "I do see that."

"What is it? Where is it coming from?"

She shook her head. It was still hard for her to believe someone else was finally seeing them. "I've been seeing them for a couple of months, but no one else did."

"This is...crazy." He laughed. "Crazy wonderful."

"Crazy wonderful. Just like life." She reached out to his laughing face, touching his cheekbone with her fingertips. Her hand wasn't shaking anymore, but her voice trembled. "Remember I told you about the message written on the cars in the church parking lot?"

"Something about a miracle coming soon," he said.

She drew back her hand. Nodded. Licked her lips. "That's when I first saw the sparkles. And no one else saw them except me."

"And now me," he said.

"Now you. I think I know what the miracle is."

The stars were disappearing slowly. One by one. As if they'd sent their message and could rest for now.

"The twinkling stars?" he asked.

"The baby." She smiled at him. "Our baby."

He stared at her, the laughter leaving, and the look in his eyes made her hold her breath though her heart was hammering in her chest. Then he leaned down and kissed her. Not with passion, but tenderness. He pulled back and she breathed. And she smiled. And she felt tears well up. Happy tears.

"It's going to be magic," he said.

"A miracle." She wondered if Elsa could see the sparkles, too. After all, she was part of this. Without her egg...

But Trey was smiling at her, his head coming down. And behind him, she saw the sparkles lighting up again, as if someone plugged them in. Or they just liked her and Trey kissing.

She reached up. So did he.

"*Our* miracle," he said, and then he kissed her and her eyes closed. But she still saw sparkles. Hundreds of them. Lighting up her life. And this wasn't the end of a miracle, she thought as their lips met. This was just the beginning...

Miracle Lane

Edie Ramer

She forgot how to hate, and now she's learning how to love...

Brain-damaged Nia Beaudine can't remember her life before The Accident. Someone intentionally ran over her and left her for dead. Now she's living in the 'witch's house' she inherited in the village of Miracle, relearning how to live on her own. Well, almost on her own – the talking cat helping her cope is a bonus. But when a hate-filled family member shows up with a gun, Nia knows she needs *real* help.

Former Army Sergeant and PTSD sufferer Rob Ackerman regularly covers for his identical twin, the village constable, and answers Nia's emergency call. This strange young woman immediately sees he's not his brother. In return, he sees that the only way she can fully live in her new life is to find out why someone in her old life tried to kill her...and might try again.

As they dig up Nia's past, the attraction between them grows. Their brains may be damaged, but their bodies and hearts are working just fine.

Excerpt:

Chapter One

The thin man wearing the tan constable uniform at Nia Beaudine's front door was a liar.

People told Nia she'd been a liar in her old life. Those memories had been lost along with pieces of her skull and brain matter. Her new self couldn't understand why people lied. Truths were hard enough to remember.

Why would this man – *any* man – want to pretend he was a constable in this village of only 629? Most of them odd. A place she should fit right in.

This man...he didn't look odd, but she knew he must be very odd. Not dangerous, though. For one second she considered closing the door on him, but every instinct told her she could trust this man.

Instead, she said, "I think my cat is trying to talk to me."

Her words seemed to hang in the air like bubbles. She studied his face, waiting for his reaction. Ready for anything.

He studied her back. Just watching.

Yesterday Nia had learned the word *cryptic* while doing a crossword puzzle in an exercise to expand her word skills.

Her cat was cryptic. A cryptic, talking cat.

The man blinked. Not talkative like her cat. Perhaps even more cryptic. The silence stretched out between them. Nina heard the birds chatter and small rustles of leaves. Probably a squirrel or animal running across the wooded lawn of the house her mother's aunt had bequeathed to her.

"Why do you think that?" he finally said.

Nia's arms prickled. She was sensitive to sound – as if to compensate her for losing twenty-five years of memories – and his resonating baritone made her skin itch from the inside out.

"Because I understand what she's saying," she said.

He nodded, his expression serious.

Better than she'd expected when the words tumbled out of her mouth. Any other person would frown, a conviction of her insanity stamped on their disbelieving face, and step back, as if fearful that crazy was catching.

She always wanted to tell them it was catching only if someone was trying to run them over in a car.

And to make sure it worked, that someone would back up and run them over again.

But instead of giving her the *loco* look, this man stared at her steadily. His full lips closed and pressed into thinness, his eyes steady on her face. Mournful brown eyes that matched his nut-brown hair.

He made her think of a tree. Solid but not broad. One that would bend but not break. And his face... Like his body, his face was long and lean. Deep lines of pain scored each side of his mouth, though she guessed he wasn't more than thirty. He couldn't be much older. Not with his skin clinging tightly to his bones. His nose was blade-like, half a triangle. His jaw resolute. His eyebrows and hair thick.

He was a man's man, making up for his few words with an excess of testosterone.

Pheromones shot straight at her. She could smell them. They twirled around her like invisible dust motes, capturing and captivating her, putting a magical spell on her, bringing to life senses that had been sleeping since she woke up in the hospital bed, the world fuzzy, her mouth dry, and no thoughts in her mind.

But her mind hadn't been silent, not with a scream shrieking through it that no one could hear but her.

Later, she recognized the scream must have been her own voice. Even later, she realized that must have been the last sound she made as the car ran over her.

She shivered, the memories upsetting, but not as upsetting as the way he made her feel.

This was not the kind of help she'd hoped for when she'd called the constable's number.

Maybe this was the trouble her cat had been warning her about.

If only Bast had been more specific.

This cat and human communication was new to both of them. They'd been living together for only three weeks. She'd just started to understand Bast's yowls and meows and mrows and an entire orchestra of sounds yesterday. Like the first few pieces of a thousand-piece puzzle coming together.

Maybe they would get better with time.

She shifted her feet, the silence pressing down on her. Early on in her recovery, she discovered other people hated silence. The need to fill the wordless void compelled them to speak. To say things they later wished were unsaid. To say the truth.

Apparently he'd reached the same conclusion, since he kept his gaze on her, not moving a muscle. As if the loser would be whoever spoke first.

The silence was like a chewed piece of gum...growing longer and longer and longer...

"What's the prize?" she asked.

"Prize for what?"

"For talking last."

His lips stretched slowly then kicked up at the edges. "You talked first. You tell me what my prize should be."

She glanced down at his shoes. She'd amused him. Maybe

there was a prize for making him smile.

Maybe there were no prizes in life.

"Something's crawling on your shoe."

He glanced down, not twitching. The most unmoving man she could remember. Since her memory went back only eighteen months, she supposed there might have been others.

"Caterpillar," he said. "A monarch."

She peered down at the yellow, black and white stripes on the fuzzy thing. "How do you know?"

"By the colors."

She nodded. That made sense. Every day she found out something new. "I'll look it up on my computer."

"When you called, you said someone was trying to kill you."

Her head came up. "I called the constable, but you're not him."

His stillness became different. More than just holding his breath. As if his blood stopped pulsing through his veins and his heart stopped beating and even his soul closed up, hiding itself.

Then a shudder shivered through him. Like a car that wouldn't start, coming to life. He blinked and his lips parted. "Jerry and I are twins. Identical. How did you know?"

She'd learned about twins. Her therapist had advised her to watch TV to learn about life. And she did learn. One twin could be evil. The other could be good. But by now she knew not everything on TV was true, and she guessed most twins were neither good nor evil, but just people trying to get through life without being killed and not wanting to kill anyone else. People like her.

"You aren't identical. You have deeper lines on your face."

He frowned, as if the thought displeased him. She looked him straight in the eye and didn't take it back. Pretending to be what she wasn't was too complicated. Life – with all its strange scents and flashing colors and loud sounds – was already too complex.

"You're thinner than he is," she said.

His frown didn't smooth. "Anything else?"

"Your voice is deeper."

"No one's said that before."

"My hearing is very sharp."

He looked at her oddly. A look she got often. One that said *what are you?*

If they asked her, she would tell them she was like a book with most of the pages blank, the words wiped off.

"My sense of smell is sharp, too." Smells could be awkward. And unpleasant. Except food. Most of the time, the smell of food cooking was wonderful. If there really were a heaven, she wanted it to smell like an Indian restaurant. Or Italian. Or pumpkin pie baking in an oven.

If it were heaven, the smells could alternate days. Every soul could walk around in its own cloud of scent.

This man's scent wasn't unpleasant. She wanted to lean in and give him a good sniff to identify the smell. To imprint it in her memory. But the thought of getting too close to him made her skin prickle again.

"Is that it?" he asked.

She scratched her head on the left side. The thinking hemisphere, Dr. Whitcomb called it, the reason her thoughts weren't quite normal. As she scratched, she avoided the area where her head indented.

"I think I should wait for your brother to come. He's the real constable."

"My brother's sick today."

His deep voice snapped her gaze back to his face. Though he still looked into her eyes, she could tell he was lying. Maybe because he was staring too hard, watching to see if she believed him.

"If this was a TV show," she said, "he would be with a woman."

The shadows in his eyes lifted and the skin around his eyes crinkled, while the corners of his lips curled up. She warmed inside, an unusual feeling. She tried to figure out what it was so she could explain it to Dr. Whitcomb.

Happy. That's what it was. An ice-cream-melting-on-her-tongue feeling. Only this melting happened inside her chest, warming her heart.

Maybe she wouldn't tell Dr. Whitcomb after all.

She'd tell Bast instead.

Bast didn't say, "Uh-huh, uh-huh," after every sentence, as if she were analyzing her words like they were math problems. Instead, she had a way of saying *mrrow*. Meaning: *That's interesting. Go on.*

"So you came instead," she said.

"You said someone was trying to kill you."

"I didn't actually say that. I said someone had tried to kill me in the past. And someone was on my property last night."

The crinkles around his eyes deepened, as did the creases on the sides of his face. "Did you see anyone?"

"Bast heard whoever it was first. And then I did."

"You didn't call last night. You called this morning."

"I heard them leave last night." She paused. This was when the way he looked at her would change. But she had to say it because it was the truth. "I only called this morning because Bast told me trouble was on the way." His expression didn't change,

239

but Nia didn't allow herself to relax. There was more. "What if it was the person who tried to kill me?"

The sense of lightness coming from him turned suddenly dark. Though no clouds dimmed the sun above them, the air around Nia chilled as she looked at the hardness of his face, as if his outline from the chin up were carved on a sword hilt.

"I'll protect you," he said. "I'll make sure that doesn't happen."

Now Nia relaxed. For this second, she thought she wouldn't want to be the person he caught on her property. For this second, she was fiercely glad he seemed to be on her side.

Second Chances

Leigh Morgan

History professor, Rhiannon Thorson, flees her life in Milwaukee to pursue research in Southern Wales and get a new start in life. Ramsey Macleod, international rock star, is burned out from life in the fast lane and is looking for a new lease on life. When they meet in a small village in Glamorgan, sparks fly, music is made, and they may get a second chance at love, life and happiness.

Excerpt:

Chapter One

There were two of them lounging in his bathtub, immersed in what appeared to be copious amounts of spaghetti. He was going to kill the concierge, or who ever let Bimbo and Bimbet into his suite. The thought that the hotel was going to have a hell of a time getting vats of pasta out of the oversized Jacuzzi assuaged some of his anger, but just some.

Leaning against the door jamb, Ramsey Macleod crossed his arms over his chest and threw both women his trademark grin. He knew it didn't reach his eyes, it rarely did these days. Bimbo and Bimbet didn't seem to notice, if they had they'd be halfway down the hall by now given his reputation for trashing hotel rooms when he was unhappy. A reputation that he'd earned ten years ago and had yet to live down.

Ram hit the button on his pager summoning his head of security, so he didn't need to be the hardass. Stark would take over that role soon enough. He'd learned long ago not to handle any issue himself that Ben Stark could handle for him. Stark was simply better at getting rid of trouble, not to mention more polite.

"I didn't think you were into sharing, Becca. You never were before." Ram raised an eyebrow at the raven haired woman he'd dated far too long.

"I had to do something to get your attention. You haven't been taking my calls." Her affected sultriness grated, making Ram's jaw tighten.

"You've got my attention now. What was it about 'have a good life' you didn't understand? I thought I made myself pretty clear. I expected our last meeting to be our last meeting. Ever."

Becca shook her full mane of ink black hair and shot him a wounded expression he knew from experience was totally false. The woman just didn't do wounded.

"You know you didn't mean that. Besides, I've changed my mind. I think we should get married. I can be faithful, Ram." She batted her thick eyelashes at him and her tone deepened again. "The two of us were good together. Stunning, even. All the tabloids said so."

Ram would have laughed, but he was afraid Becca would take it as an invitation to take this farce to the next level, something he didn't have the stomach or the patience for. Where the hell was Stark?

"This is your idea of being faithful?"

"Of course." Becca smiled and leaned over to give her blond counterpart an open-mouthed kiss. "I didn't touch her, at least not before you got here. We were waiting for you."

Ram just turned and walked away.

Stark let himself in and met Ram's gaze without a word. Ram nodded toward the bathroom and before he knew it Stark was ushering two starched and toweled women from his room. One befuddled. "Don't you like girls Ram?" And one irate. "I'll get you for this Ramsey." Stark handled them both with respect and the quiet authority he was known for.

Five years ago Ram would have been flattered by Becca's impromptu appearance. Hell, ten years ago he would have taken a nose dive into that tub and come up with a blond in one hand and brunette in the other. He had done exactly that after his first U.S. tour. Since he was only twenty at the time he didn't beat himself up about it. That was then. Now he was older and if not wiser, at least he was more discriminating.

Becca had obviously heard about some of his more seedy escapades and tried to recreate a moment he wasn't exactly sorry he'd experienced, but didn't want to experience again. She must have been desperate. She didn't lean toward women in his experience. Plenty of men, but never women.

It was moments like these that had Ram rethinking the path he'd cleared for himself twelve years ago when he'd laid down his first hit. It was a good path then. Now he wanted a real life, with a family that consisted of more than anorexic super models and burned-out roadies.

Ram knew he was whining. He'd gotten everything he thought he'd wanted. Fortune and fame just weren't all they were cracked up to be. He'd trade both for a wife who loved him for the man he was now, not because of his wealth and fame. The Beatles had sure gotten it right. Money couldn't buy him love.

Ramsey pulled out his cell and speed dialed his manager. "Frank, find out whoever is responsible for letting Becca into my suite. I want them gone. If you knew about this, pack your bags. Stark will cut you a severance check. Cancel the rest of the tour, Frank. I'm done."

Ram listened to the sputtering on the other end of the phone with half an ear. He didn't really care if cancelling the next show trashed the band, he was looking to go solo anyway. This little event just gave him an excuse to disappear for awhile.

"You're not hearing me Frank. Tonight was the last show of this tour. I'm outta here." Ram held the cell away from his ear as his manager screamed about contract clauses and 'substantial compliance'.

When Frank was no longer roaring but pleading Ram continued. "No not for a few days. Can whoever knew about this shit, I mean it. If it ever happens again the whole crew is fired and I'll sue your ass. I'll call you in a couple of months." Ram hung up before he threw away his entire career. He knew better than most that in his business you were only as good as your next show. Unfortunately for his crew, the way he was feeling the rest of the tour would tank and no one would make any money.

Frank would issue a press release saying that Ram came down with something and the remaining shows would have to be rescheduled. They were on the last leg of the tour anyway. Their last stop was Milwaukee, a venue Ram usually loved. They'd reschedule in the fall and he'd make sure to give the best show he knew how to give.

It was going to be his farewell show with *Purple Orchid*, although the band didn't know it yet. Ram wanted a second chance at a real life. That was worth jeopardizing his next contract for.

Some days it sucked being a rock star.

***

"William. Are you listening to me?"

When William finally looked at her, Rhia wondered when exactly in the course of their seventeen year marriage he'd learned the fine art of tuning her out completely.

"I heard you Rhia. There are two weeks worth of frozen meals for the kids. Oh, and by the way, you want me to clear out the rest of my stuff before you get back from Wales." William waived the spoon from his cereal bowl in the air. "Yadda, yadda, yadda."

Rhia sat at her kitchen table next to her ex-husband. "We've been divorced six months. Don't you think it's time you stopped sleeping in the guest room?" Rhia asked.

Their children were already gone for the summer at their grandparent's ranch and Rhia finally had the time and the opportunity to do the research she'd wanted to do since grad school.

"William, you know it's time for both of us to move on. I've got the chance to do my research on Celtic goddesses, and you've got a chance to do something other than work sixty hours a week." Rhia was being more open and honest with William than she'd been in years. Funny how finally admitting her marriage was over freed her to see the good in William again. He really was a decent man, for the most part. She just wanted more than a decent man who made time for his family only after work and his golf game.

If she ever contemplated a serious relationship again, which was doubtful, Rhia would pick a man who was capable of using the words 'hot' and 'Rhiannon' in the same sentence. Of course this mythical man would also want only her and not every twenty-two year old intern who worked for him. Rhia shook off the thought. The last thing she needed now was a man in her life...

Rhia pulled her t-shirt away from her neck. There'd be plenty of time for that when she left. It was time for her to make some positive changes in her life, she thought with a smile. It was time for her to explore her inner warrior woman, just like the Celtic goddesses she yearned to write about. Rhia intended to come back to Milwaukee at the end of the summer more independent and experienced, a woman capable of taking on life's challenges on her own, without a man who considered her an after thought.

She didn't want William, or his presence, in her house when she returned. She had no intention of falling into old habits.

William shoved his face closer to his cereal bowl. "My condo's almost done." He muttered.

"You have to leave William. This isn't doing either one of us any good. I don't mind if you stay here awhile, just make sure you're out of here before school starts. I want a fresh start." Rhia finished her coffee wondering why they hadn't shared breakfast together while they were actually married.

William looked into his cereal bowl as if he weren't certain what he was supposed to do with its contents. He'd stopped eating when Rhia said she wanted him out of her house. She studied her ex with the eyes of a woman no longer tainted by hurt and expectation.

With his athlete's body and silver streaked dark hair William was still a fine looking man; better looking at forty than he had been at twenty-two when she married him. Being one of Milwaukee's most successful litigators hadn't hurt his appeal either. Rhia didn't know how many women he'd fallen into bed with over the years, and she no longer cared. She had a second chance at life and she was going to take it, without looking back. Looking at William no longer filled Rhia with regret for what might have been, she was too busy looking forward to her independence.

"I'm comfortable here. I like it. I like you too." William sounded like a little boy who had just been told he couldn't keep an old toy he hadn't played with in years.

"If you wanted to keep the house, you should have bought me out."

"It's not the house." William's pleading brown eyes held hers, Rhia remained unmoved.

Rhia got up and put her coffee cup in the dishwasher. Her bags were packed. She'd kissed Ethan and Hunter good-bye before they went on their annual pilgrimage to their grandparents' ranch just west of Yellowstone. They both had summer jobs lined up when they got back. They wouldn't even know she was gone.

"You can't have a family and be single at the same time William. It doesn't work that way. You made your choice a long time ago. I made the choice to move on. Let's stick with that." Rhia kissed the top of his head and grabbed the keys to her minivan.

"I'm willing to sell you the house if you still want it. If not, I expect to pick up the kids at your condo at the end of the summer."

Rhia left feeling lighter than she had in months.

Sometimes being a history professor on sabbatical really rocked.

Second Chances by Leigh Morgan
www.leighmorganauthor.com

Acknowledgments

I'm blessed to have wonderful friends who are also wonderful writers. Thanks to Dale Mayer, Michelle Diener and Liz Kreger for supporting me on this journey. And to Leigh Morgan and Mary Hughes for our monthly lunches where we share information and laughter.

Many thanks to editor Pat Thomas for her wisdom. And to my fabulous cover designer, Laura Morrigan, for her vision.

About Edie Ramer

Edie Ramer is funnier on the page than in real life. A multiple award-winning writer, she writes stories with heart, attitude and magic. She lives in southeastern Wisconsin with her husband, two dogs, and one important cat as she writes her next Miracle Interrupted story. She loves hearing from readers.

Connect with Edie Online

www.edieramer.com
Twitter
Facebook
Goodreads